HEAVENSHIRE

THE
PROPHECY

LEGENDS *of* HEAVENSHIRE

THE
PROPHECY

Richard C. Lee

Tate Publishing *& Enterprises*

Legends of Heavenshire: The Prophecy
Copyright © 2008 by Richard C. Lee. All rights reserved.

This title is also available as a Tate Out Loud product. Visit www.tatepublishing.com for more information.

No part of this publication may be reproduced, stored in a retrieval system or transmitted in any way by any means, electronic, mechanical, photocopy, recording or otherwise without the prior permission of the author except as provided by USA copyright law.

This novel is a work of fiction. Names, descriptions, entities, and incidents included in the story are products of the author's imagination. Any resemblance to actual persons, events, and entities is entirely coincidental.

The opinions expressed by the author are not necessarily those of Tate Publishing, LLC.

Published by Tate Publishing & Enterprises, LLC
127 E. Trade Center Terrace | Mustang, Oklahoma 73064 USA
1.888.361.9473 | www.tatepublishing.com

Tate Publishing is committed to excellence in the publishing industry. The company reflects the philosophy established by the founders, based on Psalm 68:11,
"The Lord gave the word and great was the company of those who published it."

Book design copyright © 2008 by Tate Publishing, LLC. All rights reserved.
Cover design by Leah LeFlore
Interior design by Isaiah R. McKee

Published in the United States of America

ISBN: 978-1-60462-817-3
1. Fiction: Fantasy: Epic   2. Fiction: General: Romance

08.03.18

DEDICATION

To Robyn: this book would have never come to be without your encouragement and excitement.

ACKNOWLEDGMENTS

I would like to acknowledge Cara, Chris, Chuck, David, Deb, Katie, Krystal, Kathy, RC, and Tracie for their assistance in reviewing, editing, and providing creative suggestions.

CHARACTERS

Mike—Sir Michael; aliases Roland and The Hero of Blackthorn Hearth; part of "the Pair"

Mary—Lady Marilyn; alias Rachel; part of "the Pair

Abigail—Abstidian's first sweetheart

Abstidian—The king of the middle kingdom's wine taster; the first servant of the Dark Lord; alchemist

Alexis—Fairy: one of the five sisters trapped by the curse of the Jeweled Castle

Alicia—Fairy: one of the five sisters trapped by the curse of the Jeweled Castle

Alothen—Guardian of the Tome

Alsharon—Male Elf; teacher of Sir Michael; twin brother to Elsharone

Alexar—Chosen One of the dwarfs; master forger

Arica—Fairy: one of the five sisters trapped by the curse of the Jeweled Castle

Ariel—Fairy: one of the five sisters trapped by the curse of the Jeweled Castle

Arnyea—Elf; King of Elvhome

Arrissa—Fairy: one of the five sisters trapped by the curse of the Jeweled Castle

Bardwind—Wizard; the Watcher; true name revealed before the final Battle

Belzar—Goblin captured at the last battle of Blackthorn Hearth; freed of the shadow but still a bad goblin

Captain Gandy—Honorary Captain of the ill-prepared militia attempting to defend Blackthorn Hearth

Cracktooth—Orc; leader of the White Tear

Dark Lord—Shadow beast; the Evil One

Elsharone—Female Elf; teacher of Lady Marilyn; twin sister of Alsharon

Fobnish—Goblin captured by Mary

Grybon—Evil creature; feeds on elves, very powerful and deceitful

Ilsidora—Elf, Queen of Elvhome

James—One of two skilled warriors from the chamberlain's escort

Kextar—Dwarf; King under the Mountains

Lastiter—Good goblin captured at the same time as Belzar

Lieutenant Norris—Leader of a company of the King's Cavalry

Naroin—Leader of a band of Elven Archers who help defend Blackthorn Hearth

Niatia—Girl Dwarf that killed the beast guarding the way to Silverthorn's Hammer

Ogala—Cracktooth's wife

Orcai—Term to refer to goblins and/or orcs; means outcast in the ancient tongue

Peter—One of two skilled warriors from the chamberlain's escort

Prince Nesoch—Son of the king that Abstidian falsely accuses of poisoning the King

Rathire—Shadow servant of the Dark Lord

Redshank—Evil orcai leader

Rusty—Mary's unfaithful fiancé

Silverthorn—Greatest of the Ancient Metal Smiths; maker of Steel

Sword of the Ancestors—Sword of Elven Kings
Sword of Kings—Steel sword, forged by the hammer of Silverthorn himself
Tammy—Mike's deceased wife
Ursa—The great bear

PLACES:

Heavenshire—The Magical Land
Aster—The place of the throne of the King of Heavenshire
Blackthorn Hearth—Important port city in the South of Heavenshire
Dark Mountain—The place of ultimate evil
Elvhome—Modern home of Elves
Jewel Castle—Constructed of precious gems; ancestral home of the elves
Raimbre—One of four kingdoms of man; has a reputation as a place where evil flourishes
The Haven—Bardwind's home

CHAPTER ONE

The cashier repeated, "Merry Christmas! Thank you for shopping with us. " Mike smiled, took his purchases, and almost ran from the store, the sound and press of too many people feeling like a crushing weight to him. It was only when he reached the front door that he thought to look to see if Mary was still with him. "I can hardly thank you enough for helping me finish my shopping," he said.

The tall, slender, raven-haired woman looked at him with her searching dark brown eyes. "It is my pleasure, sir," she said wryly, then continued with laughter in those eyes. "It was about the only way to get you to stop obsessing about the gifts for your nieces and nephews. You were as nervous as a thief in church. Actually I thought you were going to bolt a couple of times." She laughed and placed her hand on his shoulder, "I guess you really do hate crowds. I always thought you were kidding when you said that. You really would prefer an empty hillside to this." She swept her hand to encompass the holiday shoppers streaming into and out of the store.

Mike replied with force, "Any day! Now, do you think I would lie to my newest, most dear friend in the universe?" He winced as Mary punched him in the side. "I am just simple folk. I don't like feeling that I am going to step on someone if I walk at a normal pace."

It was a conversation they had held many times. Even though Mike had been born and raised in the city, his heart was in the country. It wasn't that he didn't enjoy the excitement; he just preferred to be quieter, laidback. On the other hand, Mary lived at a pace that could only be described as frantic most of the time. She was filled with dreams and plans and was determined to attempt them all. She had her times of quiet reflection, but they were few and far between. This seemed to be the basis of their friendship; each had elements of their lives that the other wished to sample.

Mike placed the packages in the trunk of his Corvette convertible and opened the door for his friend. The car was a contradiction in itself—a candy apple red, high-powered sports car as the only transportation for a country boy. Mary smiled as she brushed past him and slipped into the front seat of the car. She flipped down the mirror and checked her make-up as he walked around to the driver's side. Just as he reached for the door, she slapped the button to lock it. As he fumbled for the key, she unlocked the door and locked it back when he again reached for the door handle. Finally she allowed him to enter and said, "Maybe you'll let me drive sometime?"

Mike laughed. "Maybe I'll just blow my brains out and get it over quicker." He fired up the high performance engine and sped out of the parking lot. In truth, Mike was by far the wilder of the two when it came to driving. He enjoyed pushing the 'Vette to the limits of its handling ability when he had the chance. He was more careful when he had a passenger, but there were times when the passenger did not believe so. They were soon on the back roads that led to his house, and he really opened up the V-8. Mary was making a show of grabbing the edges of her seat when the road just disappeared.

Mike fought for control as the car bounced over an open field. He did not brake, but allowed the car to coast to a safe speed where he could bring it to a stop. He turned to Mary and asked if she were all right, and then just looked out the windshield. There was no sign of the abandoned manufacturing plant they had been speeding by only moments before. Mary gasped, and he noticed that the dashboard seemed to be dissolving before his eyes. He slapped the door lock and pushed open the door as Mary did the same. They both climbed from the car as it shimmered in the waning sunlight. Mary grabbed for her purse as the car disappeared completely. They just stood and looked at each other, trying to comprehend what was happening.

Mary seemed to be in shock as Mike stepped close and wrapped his arms around her. "What is happening?" she stammered, and he could think of no response. She just pressed against him for a long moment. He held her and took note of their surroundings. He was aware of a clammy feeling against his chest and realized that his shirt was gone. He released Mary gently and reached to open his leather jacket, only to find that the steel snaps were also gone. His hand went to his chest to find that the silver cross he wore was still there. This necklace had been a gift from Mary a year after they met and held special significance to Mike. It was then that he noticed looseness around his waist as if his pants were undone. He looked; the buckle to his belt was gone, as was the snap to his khakis. The brass zipper was still there, which was all that kept them up. Glancing at Mary, he saw a startled expression on her face. "My bra strap has snapped, I think. And my sandals are gone." She was wearing a leather coat with a brass zipper, denim jeans, and a sweater. The glass beads from her fashion sandals were scattered around her feet and her long black hair was now unrestrained. Mike's leather boots with silver toecaps were still in place.

The wind was rising, and they were on an exposed hillside. Not far away was a small shed or hut. It appeared to be empty; it was the most promising shelter around. Mike lifted Mary and carried her to the hut. He called out, "anyone home?" There was no answer; they looked at each other. Confusion and fear were evident in her expression, so he boldly approached the door and called again. Placing Mary on the ground, Mike pushed open the door and led her inside. He saw that the hut was empty, so he turned to close the door. When he turned back he was astounded to find they were in a large room with a fireplace, candles, and oil lamp sconces along the walls. Mary gasped and pointed to the fireplace; in a stuffed chair appeared to be a wizened old man.

Long bony fingers took a pipe from a bearded mouth. For a moment the only sound was the popping and crackling of the fire. At last a raspy voice issued from the aged figure. "Welcome to Heavenshire. Your coming has long been expected and is still somewhat a surprise. I know you have many questions, and I will answer most of them, in time. First, Lady Marilyn, we must make you comfortable. I could only keep with you those materials common to this plane of existence. I regret that your undergarments are beyond salvage. If you would but walk behind the screen to my right, Elsharone will assist you with replacement clothing appropriate to this realm. Ah, Sir Michael, you will allow this; she is perfectly safe, here, now." Mike had started to protest, but the words were shut in his throat. He glanced at Mary, and she nodded to him before approaching the old-fashioned dressing screen.

A pleasant voice greeted Mary as she slipped behind the screen. A beautiful blonde woman was waiting for her. It seemed natural for Mary to slip out of her old clothes and into those laid out for her. The woman, Elsharone, helped when Mary was stumped by the archaic garments, but mostly allowed her to dress herself. The outfit, along with antique styled underwear, consisted of a heavy cotton blouse and sturdy pants that Mary thought were Capri style at first. Quickly she realized that they were riding pants and came with sturdy doeskin boots. She was soon dressed and searched for a mirror to see how she looked. It was then that Elsharone spoke. "Be wary of mirrors in this realm, for they are often the eyes of others, or doorways that are best not used. This is my gift to you, Lady Marilyn, a mirror of elven silver. It will also allow you to speak to me, no matter where you are. Speak my name to the image, and I will hear. Use this carefully, because there is evil that can sense its use and will come. Now you must rejoin the men."

After a quick check in the mirror, Mary stepped from behind the screen. Mike was still across the room, but was dressed in heavy leather pants and a silk undershirt. He held a strange sort of tunic in his hands. It glittered in the firelight and seemed to be made entirely of interlocking rings of silver. The old man was replying to a question. "Have you discerned nothing yet? This is a place of magic and if you ignore that fact, you will be destroyed and all of Heavenshire with you! You must say the incantation each time you don your armor, each piece. Think of it as a blessing if you must, but do not forget the word. The magic will be at its greatest strength if you believe in it without question." As Mary crossed the room, Mike slipped into the tunic as he recited a word in a strange language. "Excellent," chimed the old man. "The mail will protect you from all man-made blades and most magically forged ones. Your belief will grow in time. It must!"

The man rose as Mary approached. "You must be much more comfortable now. I do not have armor for you in this place; you will obtain it during your journey. Learn the incantation from Sir Michael and it will protect you. We have little time so you must suspend your disbelief. Listen well to my story." Mary would have interrupted except that a wave of the old man's hand seemed to lock the words in her throat.

Throughout the evening and long into the night, the wizard told of the history of Heavenshire. Of its creation by God and its many creatures: dwarves, fairies, elves, gnomes, goblins, orcs, and men. Most naturally served light or darkness; only men and dwarves were known to serve either freely. There had been a sort of balance in Heavenshire for millennia—the darkness never able to overshadow the light, and the forces of light ever hopeful of converting the darkness. Against this struggle there was an ancient prophecy that a supreme evil would enter Heavenshire and a pair of heroes would rise to do battle with it. They would come from a far away realm and unite the forces of light for a climatic battle with the forces of darkness. The outcome of this battle was not known, but it would either banish evil from Heavenshire or would doom all to live as slaves of darkness. Bardwind also described the current demographical appearance of Heavenshire.

"In days of old, one king ruled all men. This was the intent of the creator, but man, that unpredictable creature, could not follow a single canon of law. Instead, small bands broke off and created their own so-called kingdoms. Some even sought to have no king at all. Most of these experiments failed." The wizard punctuated his remark with a snort.

There were currently four kingdoms controlled by men, a kingdom of dwarves, and the kingdom of elves. The elves kept somewhat separate from the other races and avoided the dwarves as much as possible. Three of the kingdoms of men were closely aligned. They traded freely and kept only token armies. The main purpose of their armies was to keep the trade route safe, although they occasionally battled goblins and orcs. A separate race of creatures known as gnomes knew no boundaries and kept mostly out of sight of men. Goblins and orcs were detestable creatures that would sometimes gather in great hordes and swarm across the land like locusts. They would steal or destroy everything in their path until the armies of men gathered to drive them back to their underground existence.

The kingdoms of men had formal names but usually they were referred to as the northern, southern, or middle kingdoms. The fourth was the small kingdom of Raimbre. This was a sinister place where evil deeds were rumored to have occurred in the past. The middle kingdom was the largest as it claimed land along either side of the great river that ran from the northern regions all the way to the southern sea.

"The most intrepid adventurers loaded their families into ships and sailed the oceans in search of new lands. Few have ever been heard from again, and most believe these foolish ones sailed over the edge of the world into oblivion."

The dwarves lived far to the south in cities carved from the mountains. They mined material such as iron, ore, and coal and produced most of the metal goods in Heavenshire. They traded freely with men and would gladly join in the occasional actions against the hordes of goblin and orc invaders. Quite a few men lived within their border on large farms that produced food for the underground cities. A vast wilderness extended east from the dwarves' kingdom. Many trolls and ogres lived there. These creatures fought fiercely among themselves, and few outsiders dared venture into their domain.

The elves domain was in the center of the vast continent. Technically it was within the borders of the middle kingdom, but no human king would dare attempt to exert sovereignty over that land. Their main population center was in a valley known as Elvhome, where few men and almost no dwarves visited. They were a beautiful and long-lived people who closely followed the affairs of men and dwarves, only occasionally interfering. Even then their purpose was the stewardship of the land and not any political aspiration.

When the wizard finished, Mary and Mike simply stared at each other. Mike finally broke the silence. "Who are you, sir? Did you bring us here?"

"My name you must not know yet. I will answer to the name Bardwind. I did not bring you here; I only waited for you to arrive, as did all my ancestors. We are known as the Watchers and dedicate our lives to study of the ancient ways and to preparing for your arrival. The magic that brought you was set at the foundation of this world. You are the destined ones, the Pair." Bardwind paused to look both of them squarely in the eyes. "This is your destiny. You cannot escape it, and there is no return to your world except through victory."

"How can this be true? I don't know anything about magic, or swords, or armor? I can barely ride a horse, and I don't intend to—" Mary's words were halted by the wizard's upraised hand.

"All that you require is within you. Your journey will be long, and you will learn much. In the end, it will be who you are and what is in your heart that will bring victory, not skill with weapons or magic. The final battle is far in the future, we hope—for all our sakes it must be. You must have time to prepare. The Evil One does not yet know you have arrived, but soon he will, and he will search for you in order to destroy you before you are ready to face him. I can only hide you here for a short span of days. Then you must begin your journey to Aster, the place of the throne."

Mary found her voice and replied with some heat, "Surely you can send us home. If you think that I will abandon my grandmother to flit away on some harebrained quest for adventure then you are not the 'wise old wizard' that you appear to be. I want to go home!" This last held a plaintiff note, and Mike reached out to touch her hand. She withdrew it and spoke tearfully to him. "Make this old man send us home."

"Sir," Mike began, "how can you be sure we are the ones? This prophesy must be about someone else. Mary designs clothing, and I am just a business owner. How can we destroy an evil that is older than your world? Is there no way to send us home?"

The wizened old man sighed and stood up. "Only the chosen ones of the prophesy can enter the portal to this world. It should not be reopened until the ancient evil is banished. I doubt that it is possible, but to do so would open your world to such havoc as you can hardly comprehend. See the result." He gestured and an image appeared in the air between them.

They could see the red corvette speeding along the road they had left only hours before. The doors to the abandoned plant opened and the machines reached out in search of materials to feed themselves. The car itself stopped and the doors flew open as it shook from side to side until two figures were dumped on the pavement. The 'Vette screeched away in a fury of sound and burning rubber as the machines from the plant reached for the couple who were just rising from where they had been ejected. Mike and Mary were on their feet and the image faded as a miniature Mike threw himself between a conveyor line and Mary.

The old man continued, "See what would happen if the magic of this world spilled over into your own. It is doubtful that either world would survive"

The pair could only cling to each other in stunned silence until Mary spoke. "And if we do this, what then?"

"You will be returned to the moment that you left. It will be as if not time has passed in your world, but you will retain all that you learn in this one. You may see yourselves as only a dressmaker and a tinker, but I can see much more to you. Sir Michael, you were a warrior, an Airborne Ranger. I do not know what that means, but a ranger in this world is very skilled indeed. Lady Marilyn, you have an inner strength that has allowed you to gain respect among your peers. You also have untapped gifts that go far beyond what you have attempted. You possess elegance and grace that is far greater than your considerable physical beauty. Both of you can be compared to the budding rose whose real worth can only be gauged when it is in full bloom." Bardwind would answer no more questions, but asked one of his own. "As are most prophecies, this one is indistinct. What sleeping arrangements do you require?"

Mike tried to cover his amusement. "Separate, I think, but close together." He turned to Mary and bowed with a flourish. "Unless milady would prefer for me to sleep at the foot of her bed with drawn sword."

After a moment's disbelief, shocked that Mike could joke under the circumstances, Mary returned, "Oh, Sir Knight, that will not be necessary, somehow I will survive the hours apart from you, counting every second until I can see your face." Her expression hardened. "So that I can tell if you've managed to sleep without a bedtime story and a glass of milk!" She turned and stomped towards Elsharone, who led her through a door and out of the great hall.

"It is well that I gave you armor first, Sir Michael. If the Lady is half as swift with a blade as she is with her tongue, then you are both in good stead and perhaps great danger. Elsharone shall teach the girl as much magic as is possible in so few days, as I will teach you. I will warn you again that both of you must lay aside disbelief, and I see that it will be hardest on Lady Marilyn. To bed with you. I believe the way is clear now. When you wake in the morning, before you leave your room, you must put on the armor and speak the word of the spell I taught you. This you must do every day, every time you put it on."

A tall man with blonde hair was waiting at the door the women had disappeared through. He could have been a twin to Elsharone, but he did not speak until they arrived at the door to a room. "All that you require is within. Sleep well, man, for tomorrow will be a difficult day."

Mike entered the room, puzzled by the man's apparent coldness. There was a pleasant looking bed, a fireplace where a red glow issued from coals, and a screen similar to the one Mary had used to change clothes. He was surprised to find an eagle-claw footed bathtub filled with hot water. Not wishing to waste someone's effort, he stripped out of the armor and slipped into the tub. The water was warm and had a fresh, somehow, forest-like scent. He relaxed and let the tension drain from his muscles. A good while later the water was still warm, but he decided he should leave the tub before he fell asleep and drowned. Towels were in easy reach, and they were warm and soft. Remembering he had seen a wardrobe in the main room, he turned and was stopped by the sight of leather armor neatly arranged by the dressing screen. He had heard no one enter. The armor consisted of a coat that would cover his torso and upper arms, leggings that would protect the front of the thigh and his shins, and a codpiece that would cover his midsection.

The leather had been lacquered in places to make it harder, stiffening it. It was adorned with a pattern of interlocking scrollwork. The lacquer had been tinted with greens and browns that reminded Mike of his Army jungle battle dress uniform. There was a belt with a single weapon that Mike recognized as a crude form of dagger. The weapon had a T-shaped hilt, a simple wooden handle, and an iron blade.

There was no sign that anyone had been in the room, but he propped a chair against the door before he looked into the wardrobe anyway. A nightshirt was in the wardrobe, and Mike reasoned that this was normal sleeping attire in this place, whatever this place was. Before he crawled into bed, he returned to his armor. He removed the dagger from the belt and placed it under a pillow on the bed.

He looked around the room for a mirror and realized that he didn't have a toothbrush or comb. He rummaged around for a while and found a small stiff brush. It did not smell bad, so he tried dipping it in water and running it over his teeth. The taste wasn't too bad and it did remove the worst of the film from his teeth. He found a straight razor and shuddered at the thought of shaving with it. He returned to the bed and collapsed into it. The events of the day crashed in on him, starting with the Christmas crowds and ending in an antique bed in a fairytale land. Exhaustion encompassed him and his dreams were filled with re-telling of the stories he had heard that evening.

CHAPTER TWO

Mary followed Elsharone through the door and tried to understand her anger. It wasn't just the joke that Mike had made. They both often made jokes about sleeping arrangements although they had never slept together. Their friends would not believe this, remarking that two people who knew each other as intimately as Mike and Mary did must have a great love life. They did know each other better than some of their married friends, but they had agreed that physical intimacy would wait. At first it was because they wanted the pain of failed relationships to heal; later they feared it would change their relationship in a way they could not predict. Neither was foolish enough to deny their affections for each other, but both were strangely reluctant to call it love, as if the act of defining it would prevent their love from flourishing.

She realized that her anger stemmed from the fact that none of this could be explained logically. The talk of elves and gnomes and goblins was pure fantasy to her, yet she could not explain what she saw. The fact that Mike seemed to accept it without question added to her ire. He would be one to charge off into the sunset to slay giants and dragons; an excitement to the thought of sharing that kind of adventure with him caused her heart to beat wildly in her breast. She knew him to be a good and kind man, and she knew him to be physically strong and well built; probably true hero material. There was also some unease at that thought.

Could she lose him to some fair maiden or a damsel in distress? She did not realize that Elsharone was speaking to her until the woman repeated her name.

"Lady Marilyn, everything you require should be within. If you find that you have need of anything else, just speak my name into the mirror that I gave you earlier. The man will be in the room across the hall and down one door. Sleep well." Elsharone opened the door and allowed Mary to enter. When she turned Mary saw her ears for the first time; the tops seemed to curve backward to make a point. Mary stared in disbelief for a long moment, and then realized that Elsharone was indeed an Elf.

The room contained a luxurious bed, a wardrobe, and several brass braziers. Mary found them to be almost hot and decided that they were there to heat the suite. At the far end of the room was a dressing screen, and she was delighted to find a lion-claw footed bathtub behind it. She returned to the wardrobe and found a sleeping gown and a dressing robe. She undressed, carefully hanging her borrowed clothes on the dressing screen and slipped into the tub. She took a long time in the scented water, as if she could scrub the unreality of the place from her body. The water had a soothing effect on her bruised and scratched feet and she was loath to leave it. Leave it she did and returned to the bedroom to find the bed turned down and a bed warmer inserted to heat the region around her feet. She used the long handle to remove it and set it by the door.

She had not heard anyone enter so she examined the door and found that it had a sliding bolt. She slid it into place and then thought better of it. She slipped out across the hall and down one door to where Elsharone had said Mike would be sleeping. She tried the door and the knob turned easily, but the door only opened a fraction. Placing her eye against the crack, she could see another luxurious room like hers. She could just see the bed. While she watched Mike rolled and mumbled something. Mary was strangely satisfied that he was not as comfortable as he had seemed. Returning to her room, she bolted the door and slid into bed, relishing the feel of the new and distinct fabrics against her skin.

Sleep came more quickly than she thought it would, but it was filled with strange and wonderful dreams of spinning cars and men and women doing impossible and fantastic deeds. Just before she awoke, her dreams changed. She saw a man in battered and bloody armor—a knight—standing on top of a small hill in the midst of a great battle with a slightly smaller but no less battered and bloodied armored figure. The smaller of the two had no helmet and as it turned, Mary saw her own face, lined with fatigue and pain, but somehow calm and serene.

The knight plunged his sword into the earth and turned to her, drawing her close to him. A hauntingly familiar voice issued from the battered helm, "Milady, we have come so far and you have never faltered, never doubted me. Now I think I have led you to your doom. The army of evil waits just beyond that hill, and I have nothing left with which to fight, except one thing I have carried in my heart all these years since I met you. The first time I saw you, I did not just see a woman, but a beautiful goddess. My ears were filled with fantastic music, and my heart nearly burst with a longing for your touch. My shame is that I have walled that feeling deep into my heart and denied its depth, even its existence. I have loved you hopelessly and completely from that minute. Only now, when all is lost, have I the courage to tell you, to show you, that I love you."

Suddenly Mary was looking into the face of the knight, seeing eyes that she almost knew, eyes as hauntingly familiar as the voice. She reached up with gloved hand and loosened the catch to the helm. Then with both hands she lifted it and before his face was revealed, she heard knocking and a voice calling her name. She woke with a start and a longing to see the face that belonged to those eyes and that voice. The dream was gone but she knew that someday the knight's face would be revealed.

Elsharone's voice called from beyond the door. "Milady, it is time for instruction, please rise and come to the hall when you are dressed." Mary flung back the covers and reached for the dressing robe. She returned to the dressing screen to her borrowed clothing. She ran her tongue across her teeth and grimaced, her breath must smell horrible. She turned to the basin and found a small jar of white powder. It smelled like baking soda, so she lightly licked the tip of a finger and touched it to the powder and tasted it. The scent and taste were refreshing, so she used a small amount on her finger to clean her teeth. She was able to brush her long black hair with a crude hairbrush before returning to her clothing.

All was as she had left it, but there was an additional tunic that seemed formed to her upper body. The fabric felt like silk and fit her like a second skin. After she had donned it and the archaic brassiere, she noticed another addition—chain mail, much like Mike's, but made to fit the curves of her breasts and well down onto her hips. As she started to slip it on, she remembered the word Mike had used and repeated it as the mail settled into place. The rest of her clothes were the same and she dressed quickly, many questions running through her head, and her dream all but forgotten. As she was slipping her feet into her boots, there was a commotion in the hall. She heard a voice shouting and for a moment she thought it was from her dream, then she recognized it as Mike's. She quickly finished dressing.

The hallway was empty except for a small girl standing in the doorway down the hall when Mary left her room. She smiled as she approached the child and spoke to her. The next she knew, Mary was flung against the wall and a knife was pressed to her throat. "Do not accept things as they appear, especially if they would otherwise be out of place," whispered a woman's voice into her ear. "These are not normal times and you must be cautious!" The knife was removed and Elsharone stepped in front of her. "Doorways often contain magic and can be portals to other places if you know how to use them. I used the door to bring the image of a little girl from the village; you were intent on her and did not see me in the next doorway. Were I an Assassin, you would be dead and the quest failed from the start. I chose this drama to impress upon you the seriousness of what I have to teach you." Elsharone frowned and cocked her head to look at Mary; she whispered a strange word and Mary felt a faint pressure on her chain mail. The elvish woman smiled. "Very good, you have set your defense. Who taught you that?"

Mary was caught off guard and stuttered slightly as she answered, "I heard what Bardwind told Mike, uh, Sir

Michael, and I thought it would work for me too." Mary tried to straighten her garments to hide her nervousness as the elf watched her for a moment before speaking.

"Lady Marilyn, you do not have to hide anything here, in fact, you cannot. Be honest with your emotions because they tend to suppress magic in those just learning. You need not be embarrassed by lack of knowledge; it is ignorance that will most likely kill you and ignorance can easily be dispelled. I am impressed that you remembered the armor spell. If you learn others as quickly, it will bode well for your quest."

The remainder of the morning was spent teaching Mary spells to detect trouble while remaining undetected herself. Elsharone explained, "One well tuned to magic 'hears' the magic around him. Oh, all creatures have it. It is like many voices in a crowded room. Most blend together unless someone begins to shout. Use more magic than you need and your 'voice' rises above the others. Be heard too often and you will be tracked. Only in places like this are you safe to practice without inhibition. Once you leave you must be careful. And, it would seem, you must remind the man of this. His 'voice' is strong and carries far. He must restrain it. Oh, I will teach you how to muffle the worst of it; it would ever seem to be the woman's lot, looking out after their men. Ah, how can Bardwind allow such noise?" Mary had heard what seemed to be a shout in her mind; the *sound* was very familiar to her.

"Yeah, right, I'll be cleaning up after him in a whole new world!" Mary had started to rise but stopped when she noticed Elsharone staring at her.

"Did you '*hear*' that?" When Mary, too startled to speak, nodded assent, Elsharone's eyes widened in amazement. "It took years of training for me to 'hear' the magic, and you have learned to do so in less than a day. Lady Marilyn, you have a wonderful gift, and I must consult Bardwind. While I am gone, practice finding the traces of the spells we have cast this morning." As the elf rushed away, Mary pondered her words as she listened to Mike's magic voice echo in her mind.

Mike awoke feeling refreshed and energized. He returned to the dressing screen and found that the tub was not where he remembered seeing it. The water was hot so he bathed again in the scented water. He dressed in the armor and took care to say the magic word that was the spell with each piece he put on. He was surprised to find the tub gone when he finished and spent a fair amount of time searching for a hidden door to the room. Giving up on his search, he stroked his chin and the stubble of beard growing there. He remembered the straight razor and carefully scraped the beard from his face. He was surprised that he did not cut himself since the only mirror he had was the polished bronze surface of the basin stand. When he finally finished his preparations and left the room, he saw the blonde man waiting down the hall.

Mike raised his hand in greeting. The man straightened and hurled a spear straight at the center of his chest. Mike's training in the martial arts took over; he deflected the spear and turned enough to avoid it. He spun back to face his opponent and an arrow impacted his stomach. The shaft of the arrow broke, but the head barely dented the leather armor across his belly. Mike felt the impact slightly and a feeling of pressure spread from the point of impact outwards around his body and faded away. The man was upon him with a drawn sword, slicing downward across Mike's body. Mike angled his arm to catch the flat of the blade and swept it out away from him. He spun inside the blow and grabbed the man's wrist and the sword pommel, ripping it from his grasp. An elbow to his opponent's midsection took the man's breath and Mike whirled to face the man, aiming a kick to the center of the man's chest.

The man flew over backwards and amazingly landed on his feet as Mike felt several impacts on his back. He turned as several wooden darts fell from his armor and then back to his opponent. The man was smiling and bowed to him. "Well done, man knight, you know a style of combat unknown to us. This was supposed to be a simple demonstration of the magical protection of your armor, but you have taught your teacher. I am Alsharon, of the Elves of Highers Glade." Mike returned his bow but was interrupted by a single pair of hands applauding. He turned to see Bardwind at the entrance to the Hall.

"Well done indeed, Sir Michael. Please come to the hall and we shall speak," the old man said. Alsharon trotted by, slapped him on the arm, and smiled.

Mike stared at the retreating back and shouted, "I prefer Mike!" before following, muttering under his breath, "And not as much as a donut for breakfast." His protest died on his lips as he entered the hall. It had been transformed into a training arena; he paused, prepared for another attack. He was not disappointed when a large, ugly creature swung a huge club at him. Mike easily dodged the blow and struck the creature under the back of its shoulder, numbing the arm and causing the creature to lose its grip on the club. As it returned the blow, it did not realize it no longer had a weapon; Mike evaded the flailing arm and punched it squarely on the jaw, and followed with a knockout blow to the same area. The creature blinked twice and staggered a bit. Then it roared and swung both massive fists overhand at Mike's head as though it intended to drive him into the ground. Mike danced away from the blows and tensed for a flying kick when the word "enough" seemed to freeze him for a moment. The creature disappeared in a flash of light, and Mike turned back to the center of the hall. Bardwind stood with his staff raised. "I see that our carefully prepared demonstrations of your armor have failed. You come well prepared to fight, but I think we will leave the troll for another day. Come, sit for a moment."

Mike sat and was treated to a demonstration of arrows, darts, and spears piercing leather armor such as he wore. Bardwind then put the spell on the armor and the demonstrations were repeated. Only this time the weapons bounced off, leaving only dents in the leather where they struck. Alsharon slashed at the armor with his sword and could not slice it. "Remember, the spell is only as strong as your belief. It will only protect you from a magical blade if your belief is unquestionable. Behold."

Alsharon had approached the armor again, this time with a whip. He struck at the codpiece and split it into two pieces. Mike looked to Bardwind in alarm. The old man replied, "Never be complacent about your protection. There are some weapons that it cannot defend against. We must move on to magic, others will teach you strength of arms; I must begin to instruct you in magic. It will be the greatest threat for now. If the Evil One detects you too soon, and you must face him unprepared, then all is lost."

The remainder of the morning was spent learning spells to detect magic and to shield him from magical eyes. Often Bardwind would say, "You need not shout. You have sufficient magic without shouting." Mike was whispering when the woman who had left with Mary entered the hall. He was sweating, trying to conceal a campfire from sight when Bardwind's hand on his shoulder restrained him. "Lad, did you ever swat a fly with a sledgehammer? That is how you are wielding the magic. Do not try so hard, just allow the magic to work, and use finesse. We will pause for the midday meal and give you and the Lady some time alone. Then Elsharone will continue your training." Mike bowed to the master and followed the others to the far end of the hall.

Trestle tables were set up and servants brought food. Alsharon sat with Elsharone and Mike had little question, but asked anyway. "Twins, actually. Still you might confuse us with any of our kind; men do not easily discern the differences in elves."

Mike nearly choked. "Elves. I had no idea." At that moment Mary approached the table and Mike quickly stood. "Mary, you look, well you look positively radiant. This place is good for you. Please sit here, I will get you a drink and some food." He nearly had to pry the plate from a servant's hand but he soon returned. "There are plenty more, or different dishes. These people are very gracious and generous. Oh, meet Alsharon, and his twin sister, I guess you already know his sister. I'm talking too much, aren't I?"

"Never," Mary laughed. "Thank you for serving me, kind sir. You look quite impressive in the armor, but it must be hot. Do you want to take it off while we eat?" Mary had notice a flush in his face that she did not think was entirely from the heat. He was truly excited about this place. His face was different somehow; she realized that there was no hint of sadness behind those blue eyes. The barely hidden pain that had been there so long was gone. His eyes were different, but familiar. The realization was sudden; she had seen those eyes in her dream, in a knight's helm! Words rushed to her lips, but she held back. Too long she had guarded against saying them, reserving them for light-hearted times when he would not guess how deeply she loved him. Too often they had been said in parting, or over the phone. And now she could not lower her guard because of a dream; she could not risk that he still loved the memory of his first wife more than he loved her. She noticed the twins looking at her, a strange expression on their faces. "I hear that you are having an interesting time," she said to cover her distress.

Mike had been removing his outer armor and had not noticed her moment of discomfort. "I guess, if getting shot by archers and beat upon is interesting. Hey, what Bardwind said about the magic, it does protect the armor, believe me it does." Mary smiled and they talked and ate. The twins were a great source of information about the present time in Heavenshire. They knew which regions were fallen to the Dark Lord and which were safe for Mary and Mike to travel through. Elsharone explained how Mike sounded as he performed magic and tried to explain how he could produce the desired results with the least noise. The servants had cleared away everything except for the table where they sat when Alsharon rose and showed them to a garden and left the pair there to talk alone.

They found an alcove and lay on the grass looking at

the flowers, insects, and birds, telling each other of their adventure so far. Mary felt the sense of foreboding fade as Mike excitedly compared the unexplained incidents. He could always do that for others—make their cares a distant memory. He had done it for her often. On the other hand, no one had seemed able to erase the sadness from his eyes or to ease the pain of his wife's murder. She rolled over onto an elbow to look into his face. She had not been mistaken; there was no hint of sadness, no secret pain in those eyes. He was talking about the tub, theorizing that it walked though the wall to empty and refill itself. As she watched his lips, the thought came to her that she need only to move her head a few inches and her lips would meet his. She would know from his kiss if he were free of the memory. Before she could decide to act, a gong rang and they both knew it was calling them back to practice. As they walked back she rolled up her blouse enough to show the chain mail. He smiled as she told him she had remembered the spell. "Watch out for elves shooting arrows at you now," he said. "They love their demonstrations around here."

The remainders of their days in the Haven, as they came to call it, were filled with instruction, leaving little time for interaction. Mike learned to answer to Sir Michael and to keep his magical voice quiet. Mary absorbed magical knowledge like a sponge, even drawing ungrudging praise from Bardwind. Too soon they were sent to a new destination where they were to learn the art of weaponry.

CHAPTER THREE

In a cave deep in the bowels of the Dark Mountain of Heavenshire a fire burned. In the shadows stood a chair hewn from the stone of the mountain. The occupant of the chair was difficult to discern from the shadows. If one were to look closely, one would see the stone through its body. For one brief moment the fire ceased to flicker and burned with a steady, pure light. The shadow figure stiffened as if in pain and then all returned to normal. "Rathire," the sound that issued from the figure was more a serpent's hiss than a voice. "An ancient spell has been triggered. Go and find out what has occurred." A shadow detached from the wall and formed into something resembling a bat, then flew from the chamber through the cave and into the twilight.

Long into the night it flew, over darkened fields and silent villages shut against the threat of winter. It soared over the walls of a mighty city and landed silently in a window of the great castle. It was a towering fortress that looked over the city and the valley beyond, almost to the foot of the Dark Mountain beyond its borders. Inside a man mixed herbs and chemicals into a vile-looking potion. "Enter, little one, I will trim the lamp." As soon as the room was dim, the bat dissolved into shadow and flowed into the room. "Yes, I felt it also, a great work of magic, but I could not see where it occurred. I know only that it is far to the North. Take word to your master when you return—the King is dying, poisoned by his own trusted wine taster. The heir has no kin and all will be ready when the King dies." The shadow made a chittering noise. "A darkness spell? How intriguing, yes, I have a spell, but it will last only three days. After that you will again only be free in the dark hours." The spell was cast and the shadow transformed into a nighthawk.

Far from the castle the nighthawk landed high in a tree. The creature was still not at ease in the sunlight, and it was early in the morning on the third day of the spell. Something in the grass had reflected the sun and the bird was curious. It peered hard against the sunlight and flew down to the object. The grass around it was scuffed and there were footprints that seemed to come from nowhere. Trampled and half-buried in the dirt were brightly colored glass beads. The nighthawk sniffed the dirt and the beads and then picked up three of them in its beak and swallowed. The bird began to follow the footprints but the sunlight seemed to grow brighter. The nighthawk's feathers were beginning to smoke, so it frantically reversed course and half flew, half-scurried towards the trees as the protective spell failed. It transformed into a rat and burrowed under a rock in the shadows and waited. It would take days to recover from this brush with sunlight.

In the cavern, the shadow creature felt the burn of the light as well. It could sense that its servant had discovered something, but could not determine what it was. It had a more solid form now as new believers and slaves were added to those under its curse. It had waited eons; it could wait a few more days. It spent the time as it always had, examining its plans for flaws and mercilessly correcting them. If a certain pawn began to show ambition, it was snuffed out and another raised to take its place. Empires had risen and fallen under its machinations, kings and kingdoms were raised and brought low; the plans of men were nothing to it, and only the quest for power and a thirst to rule all of Heavenshire mattered to the beast.

The little shadow hid under the rock for three days. Once it heard magic from a distance but it was ordinary, just men playing their games. On the night of the third day, it crawled from under the rock and again transformed into a bat. It had to retain a form or risk losing the glass beads it had found. It followed the footprints to a farmer's hut. Unable to get through the door, it again changed into a rat and entered through a hole in the back wall. All it found were pitchforks, scythes, and other farm implements. Unable to follow the trail, it began its long return to the shadow beast.

A week later the bat again perched on the windowsill of the wine taster. The man once again dimmed the lights and welcomed the bat inside. "What is this? You have faced the direct sun with only my spell? What a brave little one you are. Now show me what you have found." The bat dissolved into darkness and retreated to the deepest shadow in the room, leaving the glass beads behind on the ledge where it perched. "Exquisite," he exclaimed. "I have seen no finer work. These came from a wealthy girl, where did you get them?" The darkness twittered in reply and the man frowned. "It is unlikely for a wealthy girl to be so far from any town. Yes, perhaps this is it, but it may be a coincidence. Stay here and regain your strength until tomorrow night. Then take these to our master and tell him I will travel to check on this. I will be gone at least a fortnight, and tell the Dark One not to worry about the King. He will live until I return, but not long after, I'd say. Rest now, and then go to the Dark One, my little friend."

Abstidian, the King's wine taster, prepared quickly and left the palace, leaving word with the chamberlain that he sought a cure to the King's illness. He did not take his usual escort, knowing he could not explain his destination in another kingdom. He traveled on foot to beyond the near border where he purchased a horse and saddle. He traveled swiftly, sleeping in roadhouses and small country inns when he could be anonymous. As he traveled he read the magic of the land, avoiding wards set against the shadow beast and its followers. He also avoided places that were closely aligned to the forces of light, places that might reveal him for who he was.

Sir Michael tightened the straps on the pack of the pony that carried the last of their gear. He stopped for a moment to appreciate the view. Lady Marilyn was already mounted. She was far happier than he could ever remember and much calmer. Their lives seemed to be running at a breakneck pace, but Mary had spent much time in the gardens and the woods near the Haven. He remembered the words of Bardwind from the night before. *"Sir Michael, if you learn the art of weaponry as quickly as the lady has learned the art of magic, then you will be a formidable team. There is one thing you must remember; neither of you can go it alone. You have different gifts that complement each other, but you must serve as equals. Neither of you can afford to ignore the counsel of the other. Ever."* Mike's heart was filled with an emotion he had kept suppressed for the years he had known Mary, and he continued to push it back. They might have no future, and love was not something he could afford at the moment. She noticed him watching and smiled. His heart ached even more as he returned the smile. He quickly mounted his steed and waved goodbye to those assembled. Their farewells said, the Pair rode from the Haven to begin their journey to fulfill their destiny.

They were wary as they rode; Bardwind had warned them that spies of the Evil One might be watching the way. They practiced using their new names, Rachel and Roland, not sure why it was so important, just accepting that it was. They camped out whenever they could; the spells to conceal their activity second nature by now. Mike did not question Mary when she warned of danger, and he taught her what he could of karate at each stop. Alsharon had been so very impressed with the art that he had learned as much of it as he could and insisted that Mike teach Mary. Nearly a week after leaving the Haven, they decided to spend the night at a roadhouse. To avoid suspicion they took only one room. After a lengthy argument, they agreed that Mike would sleep on the floor, but he had to agree that the places would be reversed at the next place they stayed indoors. Their room was upstairs but they took their evening meal in the common room down stairs.

As they entered, Mary laid her hand on Mike's shoulder. "We should speak to the gnome." Mike noticed the creature sitting near the bar covering most of the end of the room. It was unusual for the creatures to show up in the establishments of men, but not unheard of. They approached; it stood and walked directly towards them.

"You should join the group at the common table. The enemy is near, but you would do well not to hide." The creature passed them and took a place at a table in the darkest corner of the room. The large table was nearly empty as they sat and ordered their meal. The table filled quickly as the evening progressed and was soon full. It seemed that there were no strangers at that table, and they joined in the laughter and joking. Everyone assumed them to be mercenaries on their way to join the army of the King. There had been an incursion by an invading force of goblins and orcs. The intrusions were not serious but becoming more numerous; the King was raising an army to purge them from the realm. When the meal was finished, most of the men turned to drinking mead. Mike and Mary, or Roland and Rachel, ordered herbal tea instead.

The jeers of the table were silenced as one by one they contested with Mike in arm wrestling and lost. When the last man at the table had fallen, Mary challenged Mike and beat him using a trick Mike had taught her. Mike was always aware of those who arrived and departed, but he could not detect any dark magic in the room. He could feel it outside, but that was not beyond normal. He noticed a man sitting alone watching him. The man returned his glance by raising his cup and Mike did likewise. When the man looked away, Mike turned to Mary and whispered, "Did you?" Her curt nod cut him off, and he knew that Mary was searching the man. Her hand soon found his knee under the table and squeezed, a signal that she felt they should leave. Before they could, the barmaid arrived with drinks from the man who was seated alone. They whispered for a moment and Mike repeated the gnome's advice. Mary assented; they bid those at the table farewell and joined the man. Before they reached the table, the gnome brushed by them. Mike felt as though he were wrapped in a warm blanket on a cold winter's day. It felt very comfortable and safe, and he knew that the gnome had used some sort of protective spell on them.

Abstidian sat in the common room of a nondescript roadhouse one evening before retiring for the night. His attention was drawn to a pair of travelers seated at a table near the fireplace, where its light danced across their faces. The woman was very noticeable; she was as beautiful as an elf, but had dark black hair. Her skin was pale but had much more color than any elf and her eyes were dark. He saw that they were brown as they reflected the light from the fire. Her nose was wonderfully proportioned to her oval shaped face and seemed to invite his eyes to rest on her rich, full smile. Her chin provided excellent definition between her face and her slender neck. She turned slightly to take in the rest of the room and her gaze fell directly on Abstidian.

The wine taster felt instantly transported through time

and space to another common room; he could see another face, very similar but very different also. This face was filled with innocence as well as a great sadness. Her skin was darker but her beauty was no less. He heard again the words that caused sadness to overflow in that face, and he again felt a shadow of the anguish he had felt long ago as he said, "I must go, Abigail. When I have discovered my destiny, I shall return." He could not have known that he would become a tool of the shadow, and that he would never return to such a sweet servant of light. The image was gone as quickly as it came, leaving the memory of the long ago pain to linger in his gut.

A feeling of great power in the room interrupted Abstidian's moment of reflection. As he examined the magic of the room, he found that it was well concealed. The pair he watched wore magically enhanced chain mail, as did about half the patrons of the roadhouse. Finally he located the source of the power in a forest gnome who sat in the corner of the room eating his evening meal. Still the woman continued to hold at least part of his attention.

He looked again to the pair's table and this time he examined the woman's companion. The man was big, taller than any of the King's guards, and well muscled. He seemed big enough to take on a troll and win. The fellow was boisterous and seemed to be gaining many friends around the large table where they sat. His eyes were constantly alert, and Abstidian could tell that the man had noticed him and was searching for his magic. The taster smiled and lifted his cup to acknowledge the man's gaze and turned his head. The big man's eyes were blue, in contrast to the woman's. He had a full head of light-colored hair and was clean shaven. Abstidian motioned to the barmaid and whispered in her ear as she came close. He watched her return to the bar and then as she made her way to the pair's table. As she set drinks before the pair, she nodded toward the wine taster's table. The man leaned over to his companion and they held a whispered conversation. It was not hard to follow; the woman was reluctant, but the man, who was beginning to appear to be a likable oaf, prevailed. They raised their cups to him and said their farewells to those at the table.

He watched as they approached; they were consummately aware of their surroundings, obviously mercenaries. The man wore no sword, only a small dagger on his belt, the woman also wore a dagger on her hip and a whip coiled round like a belt. He rose and welcomed them to sit, and they made introductions. He was not surprised that they gave assumed names; he had as well. He was aware of a word of magic being issued in the room but could not tell who in the crowd had spoken. He glanced towards the gnome only to find that it was no longer there. He returned his attention to Roland and Rachel, as they called themselves. He soon dismissed them as of no real importance; he could see an attachment between them that they both denied. They were a pair of starry-eyed adventurers who failed to see that the greatest adventure of all, that of true love, was within their grasp. Still they were enjoyable company even though they drank herbal tea instead of mead.

They sat for a while with the man and made small talk. The encounter had been unnerving to Mike; he could feel when the conversation was turning dangerous and knew just how to turn it to safe waters. In part of his mind he was amazed at the gnome's magic until he realized that it was Mary who protected them. He relaxed, confident in her ability. Soon the man had lost interest in them, and they excused themselves to go to their room. Once the bolt had slid closed and the protective words were said, Mike drew Mary into an embrace. "You are amazing. I believe we have passed our first test, thanks to you."

Mary closed her eyes and just laid her face against his neck. "Yes, we did. You were wonderful, and you were right. There is darkness in that man. Great evil has touched him. If we had acted any differently than we did, we would have been discovered. He is searching for us, but he does not know who we are. The gnome was probably sent by Bardwind to guide us. Oh, thank you for holding me, I am so scared!"

Mike continued to hold her, "I could not see the darkness," he said quietly. "If not for you—" The sentence was left unfinished as they both felt a shout of a magic word that chilled them. The room seemed to reverberate with its echo, but it soon faded. Long moments later he realized that he was still holding Mary and her face was buried in his shoulder. He gently kissed her ear and whispered, "It is all right. Whatever it was is gone. Should we go as well?"

Mary smiled at the touch of his lips to her ear; it was a soothing feeling after the terror of the word. She felt around them for evil magic. "No, it has left a watcher. It will not be able to follow us in the daylight. I believe that he has dismissed us as what we appear to be—a pair of mercenaries."

It was late when Abstidian returned to his room. A shadow detached from the wall and he greeted it. "Hello, little one. I see you have brought me a gift, instructions from the Master, perhaps?" The shadow chittered, and the man frowned. "Tell the Master that I go immediately." He picked up the object from the table where the shadow had left it; he held it up to his face with both hands and breathed a word of magic on it. It dissolved into a mist that he breathed in. His body was wracked with a spasm of pain and then he stood still. He walked to the door of his room and placed a hand on each post. He spoke the word that had just been given him and stepped into the door and out onto a dark street. Behind him was a small house that had the taint of the Dark Lord about it. The sounds from within left no question as to its purpose, and he quickly walked away and into the night.

Abstidian traveled for about an hour before he reached the hut that was his destination. The mark of good magic was strong, and he felt physical pain as he touched the doorjambs. He spoke the word that would open any normal portal and tried to step forward, but was pushed back by a flash of light and a wave of pain. The portal was guarded and would not open to him. He stepped back, hurt and shaken at the strength of the spell guarding the door. Then he saw a small glass bead in the dirt in front of the door. He must have uncovered it as he staggered backward. He stooped to pick it up and paused. He took a clean linen square from inside his cloak and carefully picked up the bead. He could not follow those who had traveled here, but he had found something to report to his master, something worth the risk of opening a new door portal. He hurried back to the village and reached the door just as the dawn began to lighten the sky. He hurried to speak the word and was back in his room at the roadhouse. He was near exhaustion and collapsed on the bed after removing his cloak.

A few hours later he was riding hard towards the town, which held a door that connected to a place near his homeland. He arrived and sold his horse and saddle at the livery stable and then hurried to the next portal. As he strode past a little cottage, he stopped as he felt a long forgotten presence. He stared at it for a moment; there was a low picket fence and a gate. Windows with flower boxes framed the door to the cottage. The flowers had long since been killed by frost and winter's chill, but he could see that they were her favorites. He could see that the yard was dotted with flowerbeds, just as Abigail had described what their house would look like. The phantom pain he had felt the night before returned full force and he found himself drawn to the gate. As his hand touched the latch, he was interrupted by a voice from the neighboring cottage. "You'll not be finding the old maid at home. She goes to tend her dear mother in the winter. Do you wish to go there?" The creature that spoke was a garden gnome, a man-like creature about three-feet tall.

"No, I do not know who lived here, it just seemed familiar. Thanks to you, sir gnome, you need not remember me to her." The word of magic was skillfully woven into the conversation and the gnome never knew that a memory had been stolen. Abstidian hurried on his way, pushing aside the pain to concentrate on his journey. Soon he had passed through several portals and stood before the mouth of a cave. No one save a servant of the Dark master could see the cave and Abstidian entered with ease. He was accompanied by shadows as he made the long trek to the bowels of the mountain. His cloak and outer garments were left behind as the heat increased. Finally, nearly naked and sweating, he reached the chamber. Falling to his knees he crawled into the presence of the shadow beast. A voice boomed, "Give it to me! We shall see if you have failed me!" Terror gripped Abstidian as he handed the linen square containing the bead to the beast. The last time he had been in its presence it had no physical form. Now it was solid and had the face of evil. Scaly hands with gruesome talons ripped open the package and withdrew the glass bead.

A powerful word of magic caused a picture to shimmer into being in air in the center of the chamber. It was of a couple, a man and a woman, seen from behind. The man carried a woman toward a simple farmer's shed. He placed her on the ground for a moment as he opened the door. Their clothing was of an unfamiliar style, and the woman was bare footed. The man carried the woman into the shed and the door closed. The image froze at another word and the beast looked at Abstidian. "You have done well. It is no failing of yours that the portal is blocked. I now know where it leads, to the haven of one who calls himself by many names, which is the watcher. Bardwind has opposed me for a long time, but his time will soon fade. The prophesied Pair has arrived, and we must shape events as we have planned. Return to the King and fulfill your purpose. Make sure that his heir is sent away in disgrace, prepare the false witnesses against him, and perhaps the people will do our deed for us.

"It will be so, Master," Abstidian crawled from the chamber and started for the surface. He was hurried on his way by the peals of evil laughter that chilled him to the bone in spite of the heat. When he reached the place where he had left his cloak, he lay down and slept, too exhausted to continue. His slumber was guarded by shadows and troubled by nightmares. The most troubling was of Abigail, not as she was, but decades older, as was he. She was still beautiful although the mark of sadness was heavy upon her. She called to him in his dream, but as he went to her, she dissolved into the face of the beast. He woke, sweating and panting as though he had run for miles.

Mary lay down on the bed and Mike spread a bedroll near the door. Sleep was elusive with the dark servant so near, and they were nowhere near rested when they were wakened by the return of the dark force. Mike had seen the dark man leave before sunup, riding in the direction they must take. They were extra alert and cautious as they traveled. Their destination was what seemed to be a deserted manor house. Dead leaves were everywhere and the porches had not been swept in a long time. As they approached the stable, hoping to find fodder for their horses, an elf stepped through the open door. "This way, quickly. The Dark One's attention is diverted." At first Mike thought that Alsharon was greeting them, but then he realized that this was a different elf.

Mike dismounted and bowed. "We thank you." The elf cut him off and motioned them to enter. Mike led his horse as Mary rode forward leading the pony. The stable door was a portal; they found themselves in a forested valley after they passed through it.

CHAPTER FOUR

The wind rushed past the stone fence that marked the farthest boundary of a small farm near the citadel where the King lay ill. It swept past a man who had just finished pulling a lamb from a ewe and the farmer who watched with a worried eye. "Yes, a difficult birth. She is ill timed and you will have to keep both ewe and lamb inside, sheltered against the winter. Still it is a healthy lamb and should do well." Nesoch stood and cleaned his arms in the cold water that had been steaming hot when the farmer had brought it from his kitchen. "I shall return and check on her in a week or two," he waved aside the farmer's protests. "I was passing this place at the proper time, and I will see this task through." He slipped back into his fine coat and cloak and mounted the finely bred horse the farmer's daughter held. "Be sure to keep them both sheltered from the cold."

The farmer called to him as he rode away, "May God bless ya, Prince Nesoch. It is said the hands o' a King are healing hands. Live long, Prince Nesoch, our prayers are wit yer Father. May the King live long and prosper."

The prince continued his ride and returned to the castle near sundown. The chamberlain greeted him with grave news, the King was worse than ever. The chamberlain urged the prince to speak to his father about abdicating his power. Nesoch flatly refused. "The King rules at the will of God. Only He can decide when the power is to be passed." Later in his chambers he received word that the King wished to see him. He dressed and hurried to the Royal Chambers where a chaotic scene met him. Guards were everywhere and the Chief Magistrate was present, as was Abstidian, the wine taster.

Silence fell as Prince Nesoch was announced, silence that was replaced by a low murmuring as whispers passed back and forth between those present. He glanced at the chamberlain who lowered his eyes rather than look in his face. "Nesoch," the King's voice rang out. "How could you betray me?"

Nesoch was speechless and could only spread his hands and say, "What, what do you mean, Father? I serve you, and I serve the people as you instruct." The murmured whisper became shouts of "Liar" and "Traitor." Nesoch looked around the room and only the chamberlain did not join in the accusations. Nesoch could only stare at his father through all the confusion.

Abstidian, the wine taster and alchemist, stood and the tumult ceased. He spoke and his words wove a story of treachery and betrayal. Even Nesoch was almost convinced of his guilt as witness after witness stood forth to accuse him. His head bowed in shame as he listened to what he knew were lies that seemed so much like the truth. With his head bowed, the web of magic contained in Abstidian's words was broken and he realized that this was the fulfillment of his destiny—the prophecy spoken about him would be fulfilled this night. He remembered words his mother had spoken to him before her death, things he had not understood before now. He was filled with calmness and he heard a voice, his true Father's voice. "You are my Son, and I am pleased with you. Soon all will be clear and you will be with Me for a time."

The voice of the King rang out, "Have you no defense?" Nesoch raised his head and squared his shoulders.

"These words are not true. Look into your heart, and you will see that it is so." The proceedings had continued through the entire night and the sunrise was visible through the eastern windows of the throne room. The crowd was thirsting for blood and cried out, demanding judgment; the Chief Magistrate looked at the King and declared the verdict, "Guilty!"

The King began to speak, "You are my son, and I am loath to order your death." At this point he was interrupted by a whisper from the wine taster. The Kings eyes grew hard and his face became set in wrath. "In truth, you are not my son. You were born of the Queen, but not conceived of my loins. I was away when the Queen begat you, and I have held her secret beyond her death. Take him, carry him to the north wall, and do as you will with him in view of the people. When he is dead, carry his body to the east wall, and cast it upon the rubbish heap for the birds to feast upon and the maggots to consume. Let this serve as a warning to any who would commit treason to the throne."

The soldiers grabbed Nesoch roughly. They slapped and punched him until he was facing the door. Then they prodded him with swords and pikes to guide him to his doom. As Nesoch passed through the door, he saw that the chamberlain's eyes were filled with tears. The news of the trial had already spread through the town as Abstidian's spies repeated the story he had so carefully prepared. A sizable crowd gathered at the north wall when Nesoch was shoved brutally onto the walkway. His hands were tied to a ring set in a post on the wall, a place where thieves were flogged. There the soldiers whipped and beat him until he could no longer raise his head. They stopped and allowed Abstidian to approach. He bent low to whisper into Nesoch's ear, "What now, oh King to be? Your Kingdom will fall to ashes and its people will serve the Dark Lord. Behold the victory of the beast!"

He spoke a word, but the vision that appeared to Nesoch was not of Heavenshire's doom, but of two warriors, training with wooden swords. They sparred with each other because no others could match their prowess. They were majestic in their power, yet full of humility. The vision faded and Nesoch spoke his final words, "Thank you, Father, and forgive these who fulfill your decree." Only Abstidian heard those words, and he merely sneered

Nesoch's head fell and his body slumped against his bonds. In that instant the air was split with a gigantic bolt of lightening. It was larger than any other ever seen in Heavenshire. The ground heaved in a mighty earthquake, but not a single structure was damaged. In the Palace called Aster, in the hall of the Patriarch, the Sword of Kings fell from its place of honor where it had rested for centuries and shattered against the stone of the floor. The king's chamberlain, weeping almost uncontrollably, gathered the pieces and later hid them far from the castle. On the throne, the King's blood ran cold, and he whispered, "His mother must have told the truth; even the sky mourns his death." On a cold hillside not very far away, a farmer paused to stare into the sky as he gathered a newborn lamb and its mother into his own home for shelter against the sudden storm.

On the north wall, a frantic Abstidian screamed at the guards, "Beat him, break his bones, make sure he is dead." No one was willing to approach the prince and the taster himself grabbed a sword and plunged it into Nesoch's side.

The blood started to settle and both red and clear fluids emerged. The captain of the guard removed his own cloak and had his men lay the body in it. The men were filled with a great shame as they carried the body to the east wall as the King had commanded. From there they threw it from the heights onto the rubbish heap below. A cold rain began to fall from what had been a cloudless sky and extinguished the fires burning among the trash. Soon silence gripped the castle and the city. The hall of the Patriarch was silent as Abstidian entered with the bloody sword and spoke, "The traitor has paid his price." The King looked at him with grief-stricken eyes and waved him away. This was the last appearance of the King before his death three days later.

Two weeks after the death of Nesoch, the farmer guided his new lamb through the field where it had been born. It followed him everywhere, and he had become accustomed to its presence. It brought him great joy even as it reminded him of what was lost the day of its birth. He stopped and sat for a while as its mother searched for a few blades of dried grass. He was startled as the lamb leapt up and ran towards a stranger. The cloaked and hooded figure knelt and placed his hands on the lamb, examining it. Then the stranger rose and spoke, "A fine lamb, Farmer. Keep and care for it tenderly and she will produce a great flock for you. When I return, you will see." He turned and left the farmer wondering who this was that traveled on the day the King was to be buried. He felt he should know him, but he could not be sure.

CHAPTER FIVE

In the forested valley the elf who had ushered the Pair through the portal returned Mike's bow. "Follow me, Sir and Lady. Your way is prepared." Mike remounted and had to urge his steed to a full gallop to keep pace with the running elf. He saw that Mary was as amazed as he was. They rode for at least a half-hour before the elf stopped in front of a fantastic villa. The Pair dismounted as one and then young elves led the horses away. The beauty of the place was overwhelming; Mike took Mary's hand as they walked forward. The doors to the villa were open and seemed to invite them in. Cloaks and hats were given to hands that were almost unseen to the Pair. At the end of a long ornate hallway was another set of doors.

Mary was amazed at the ornate furnishing of the hallway and gripped Mike's hand tightly to reassure herself that this was no dream. The doors in front of them seem to be fashioned from solid gold, inset with rubies and emeralds. Those doors swung open into the most fantastic room she had ever seen. She heard Mike's intake of breath and knew that he was as enchanted as she was. That thought galvanized her into action, and she whispered several words of protection. The words seemed to flow into a symphony of magic, reassuring her that they were safe.

Mike had glanced over at her as she spoke and he was smiling. "Do you know that I love you?"

Mary blinked and when she looked up she saw that

Mike was looking at the hall as if he had never spoken. "Yes," she whispered, but he did not answer. They stepped into the room and tier upon tier of seated elves rose to their feet, their robes whispering as they fell into place. Mary felt the magic tug at her heart, and she squeezed Mike's hand.

This time she knew he turned and spoke. "This is incredible. Even I can feel the power of this place. I am so glad to share this with you, I—" he would have said more, but they had reached the bottom step of a dais where two elves were seated in ornate chairs. The occupants of those chairs rose, and Mike and Mary both fell to one knee.

"You do us great honor, but you need not bow to us. Rise and approach us." Mike did not know which of the elves had spoken, but he rose and inclined his head to Mary.

When she looked puzzled he whispered, "You won the first battle, please don't argue this once. You know I love you but I will kick you up these steps if I have to." Mary smiled inwardly because it was an old threat, but she took the first step, Mike followed a step behind. They climbed six steps to the platform and the elves sitting there rose and embraced them. They stepped back and the male spoke.

"This is Ilsidora, Queen of Elvhome. I am Arnyea, the King. Welcome, Heroes. You may not realize the importance of your encounter at the roadhouse. You were faced with the Dark One's most trusted servant, and you eluded him. You cannot know how much hope this fosters in a time of grave danger. Do not be mistaken, you have much farther to go than you can know. For now, be welcomed to our land. You will train here for the next three years, or as long as we have. You must become masters of several arts, and you will partake of several hazardous journeys to retrieve that which you shall require for the final battle. You will have to visit those allied against the darkness to give them Hope, as you have given us. Only then will you lead the forces of light against the Evil One and destroy him forever!" At these words a cheer rose from those assembled and a crescendo of sound washed over them.

"We have prepared rooms for you, and there will be a celebration this evening where you will be honored guests. In the morning your training will begin." Queen Ilsidora smiled as she took Mary's hand and walked down the steps and out of the hall. Mike and King Arnyea followed, and the quartet was met by Elsharone and Alsharon, who took charge of Mike and Mary and led them to a suite of rooms in the interior of the villa.

"You will note that there are separate sleeping quarters off this common room. This is expedient because much of your training will be conducted here. You must learn the customs and protocols of all the kingdoms if you are to travel undetected. You will not be able to use the mercenary disguise because it will not take Abstidian long to realize that he was deceived. You will be able to maintain modesty and whatever agreement there is between you. You may relax now and prepare for the celebration." The twins left after a brief time of reunion, and Mike and Mary just looked at each other for a while.

At long last Mary spoke. "Do you know how great the power of the Dark One is? If what we felt at the roadhouse is only his servant, how can we stand against him?"

"I do not have the answer. I only know that I never imagined that I could do what I have already learned to do. We are still like babies in this world. Maybe, just maybe when we have learned all they have to teach us, we will be strong enough." He walked over to her and embraced her.

"We have each other, Mary. You know you are my closest friend in this world or any other. I will do all that I can to protect you, even as you have already protected me. Let's hold to that and to the friendship that we have. If we survive this and return home, well, let's first concentrate on surviving." He released her and said, "I hope they have the same sort of baths as the Haven."

He was both disappointed and surprised to find that the bath had plumbing. There was a vial next to the fixture, and Mike could smell the same herbal scents from the Haven. He turned the red handle and soon steaming hot water poured into the bath. It was not long before he was relaxing in the scented water and the grime from the journey was washed away. He found clean clothing in the wardrobe and returned to the common room. Mary was still in her chambers, so he browsed the books on the shelves that covered three walls of the room. He was somewhat surprised that he could read the titles, just as he had been able to understand the language of everyone he encountered.

After browsing for some time, he selected a thick tome that was titled *Heavenshire: A Historical Perspective*. He reclined across a couch and began reading, "In the Beginning…" He was distracted some time later by Mary's hand on his shoulder.

"I did not know you could speed read," she said. Mike looked at her in amazement, then down at the book in his hands. He was nearly three-quarters finished.

"I don't understand, actually I do understand. I know most of the history of this place; it is fantastic. I just started to read while you finished dressing, and I remember everything. Look, you pick a book and start to read."

Mary resisted; she had never been much of a reader,

and she did not want to appear foolish in front of Mike. He finally convinced her to pick up a thin book titled *The Proper Care of Unicorns*. She sat down and began to read. Soon she was finished with the book and looked up to see Mike staring in amazement. "So, tell me about Unicorns."

Mary looked at him and started, "If you must know, they are very different from horses even if they share many equine characteristics." She stopped and raised her hand to her mouth. "I do know about unicorns." They spent the rest of the afternoon looking through and reading books until Mary found *Etiquette and Customs Among Elves*. They each read the book and marveled at what they did not know.

Later, the twins arrived to help them prepare for the celebration and were themselves astounded to see the Pair already in formal dress and greeting them in the Elven tongue. The twins actually laughed when they discovered that Mike and Mary had stumbled onto the enchantment of the books. Alsharon became serious. "I cannot begin to describe the compliment that you pay us by learning our customs. Most sons and daughters of Men do not care that we are a people with long and proud traditions. Learning this will give you even greater honor among our people. Sir Michael, Lady Marilyn, I will ever be your friend. You may call my name when you are in most dire need, and I will come if at all possible." Elsharone repeated the pledge and the four left for the celebration.

They were seated at the head table, and King Arnyea opened with the traditional blessing and the Queen added hers. It was time for the guests to present a toast and the King looked to Alsharon but his eyes widened as Mike rose and lifted the silver goblet. He said in the Elven tongue, "Most gracious King and Queen. May the streams ever flow clear and the birds sing your glory. May the first dew of morning be your crown, and the stars light your way at night." He held his gaze on the King and was relieved when the King smiled and rose to his feet with his own goblet held high. The sound of the entire assembly rising rose in the background.

Then Mary stood and addressed the Queen. "May your children ever serve those around them, and ever tend to the forests and the glades. May they ever be friend to all animals and to all of God's creation." The Queen rose and sipped from her goblet, as did everyone.

Once everyone was seated, the King and Queen again rose to their feet. King Arnyea turned to the Pair and motioned for them to rise. "As our guests have honored us, let us honor them. Let the celebration begin!" Music began and food was served. Much later the tables were cleared away and a different music began to play. Mike recognized the beat as a waltz and led Mary to an open area where they began to dance. They were able to adapt to the Elven style, which was very formal and almost distant—only one hand touching for most of the dance. There was one more surprise for the evening. The King and Queen approached, and the King bowed to Mike as he took Mary's hand.

Mike frantically searched his memory as he took the Queen's offered hand. He realized that this only happened at the wedding of a prince, or to bestow the highest honor on someone. He blushed and whispered to the Queen, "Your Grace does me too great an honor," as he tried to maintain his balance and rhythm.

"Nonsense, young man. You and your friend are the most exceptional guests we have ever had. The honor is well deserved. Not only do you bring hope, but also you validate our ways. You can give us no greater gift. When the time comes the Elven army will stand with you." The King was guiding Mary back towards them, and they exchanged partners.

The music changed and Mike was able to draw Mary closer. She smiled and said to him, "We are not alone in this fight."

"I know," Mike said. "I know."

The dancing ended around midnight and Mary and Mike returned to their suite. "Parting be such sweet sorrow,"[1] he began, but he could not remember the rest of the quote or even the name of the play or playwright.

Mary returned, "But it is already tomorrow, so get your butt in bed." She playfully shoved him towards the door as she headed for hers.

Morning came too soon for Mike. He shared a light breakfast with Mary and was soon learning the basics of fighting with swords, staffs, and all manner of weaponry. The days were long and filled with hard work. A few days after their arrival a great lightning bolt split the air and then the earth itself shook. Nothing was damaged, and everyone marveled at the strange portents. A messenger arrived later with grim news; the heir to the largest of the kingdoms of Man had been executed on his father's orders. Days later another messenger arrived with the news that the same king had died. The King and Queen of Elvhome prepared to leave and pay their respects, for the two Kingdoms were old allies, even if men preferred to forget.

Their return brought even more grave news; the King of the Middle Kingdom's most trusted friend was also the highest servant of the Dark One. Though the chamberlain ruled in place of the King, there was no hope that a true heir would be found. According to ancient law, in three years the crown would pass to a distant relative. All were sure that the kingdom would surely fall to the Dark Lord. The days passed and the Pair trained almost every day, resting only once a week. Even on their rest day, they spent time reading the books in their suite. Their skills soon equaled their teachers, and they began to spar with each other as the only suitable challenge left. While Mary could not match Mike's strength, her speed and agility were enough to make her a challenge for him. Where she excelled in magic, he became a master of strategy. Each of their strengths complimented the other as Bardwind had predicted.

A day came, over a year after they arrived in Elvhome, that they were called to an audience with the King. They had been sparring with wooden swords. Most of the elves refused to spar with them, having learned long before that they could not compete. As they sparred they danced up the trunks of trees, along the strong boughs and the faces of rock outcroppings. Often they laughed as they displayed their lessons. The twins were present to add their encouragement and criticisms. They had been running through the trees, above the ground, when the messenger arrived. They quickly left the field and hurried to the Royal quarters where the King and Queen waited for them.

"My friends," King Arnyea began, for they had long ago dropped formal titles. "There is little more you can learn from us, or the instructors we can bring here. It is time for you to leave on a quest. You must travel to Blackthorn Hearth and from there contact the Dwarf King. He will forge armor for you that is strong and yet so light it would seem you are wearing none. We have supplied Elven silver and you, Mary, must say the proper words as the metal is forged. Sir Michael, you will have to retrieve Silverthorn's hammer from the Dark One's mountain before the dwarves can begin." He looked them both in the eye. "This is no easy task, and your lives will be in danger. The servants of the Dark One have not ceased in their search for you. They have been to our very gates more than once. When you leave through the portal, we will perform a great spell that will end all travel though doorway portals. This will prevent the Evil One from using them to trap you."

Mike and Mary listened carefully; they had long expected this day, and they knew their tasks. But they did not expect the parting gifts that King Arnyea presented them. To Mary he presented a bow and quiver of arrows. "You have the skill to use these, and they are enchanted to never be lost to you." To Mike he presented a sword. "This is the sword of Elven Kings, it is named the Sword of the Ancestors. It was forged in a time long ago. I expect that you will return it to my hand in the appointed hour." Soon Mike and Mary were at the gate they had entered more than a year earlier. Their mounts were sleek and well proportioned, and they had a packhorse most riders would envy. They turned and waved farewell, for the valley was filled with elves. Then they spun and ran their mounts through the gate and into the empty manor grounds. The sun was bright, so they had no fear of the shadow's servants; still they needed to put as much distance between them and the manor as they could. An hour later there was a great shout of magic and something seemed to flow away from the land, leaving it somehow incomplete. The shadow would now know they were abroad, and they would have to use all that they had been taught to avoid detection.

CHAPTER SIX

They traveled for days and avoided all contact with men or other creatures that could be questioned. They crossed borders like thieves and made good progress toward Blackthorn Hearth, the major trading center for metal goods. It was also the main entry point to the Dwarf Kingdom. It would allow them to contact the dwarves without raising suspicions. They would have to be careful; those who served the Dark One would be watching. It was the result, or perhaps the price, of prosperity that Blackthorn Hearth also was a center of man's less honorable activities.

They left their horses at a farm that Bardwind himself had recommended on one of his many visits to Elvhome. The final leg of their journey was on a riverboat as paying passengers. The Pair kept mostly to their cabin pretending to be seasick. The captain had often transported rangers, who he assumed Mike and Mary to be. They dressed the part in forest green cloaks and pointed caps and kept mostly to themselves.

Late one afternoon the Captain called Mike up on deck and pointed to a thin column of smoke down river. "That looks to be our way stop. There have been problems with goblins here lately. I wish to put ye and yer lady ashore to scout. We do not need to sail into an ambush." It was agreed, and soon Mike and Mary were moving silently through the brush towards the stop. The sight that greeted them was sickening. The master of the house and his son had been no match for whatever had attacked them, and Mike had little doubt as to who or what those attackers were. Noises sounded in the brush beyond the burning buildings, so they continued their silent advance. Mike slipped into place and saw eight goblins tormenting a woman as she clutched the remaining rags of her dress around her. As the leader slapped her and grabbed at the last rag of the dress an arrow seemed to materialize in his throat. Mike leapt forward as a second goblin fell to Mary's arrows. His sword cut the remaining goblins down before they could even scream. He averted his eyes and spoke to the woman. "Please, Milady, were there any others?"

The woman spat and cursed. "That way, two more, and they had mah gurl. Please bring back their heads." Mike nodded and began to follow. He signaled to Mary that there were two targets; she nodded and moved parallel to him. He followed them a short distance to a small clearing. What he saw them doing filled him with such rage that he did not even draw his sword. He broke the first creature's neck so savagely that he nearly tore the misshapen head from the scrawny body; the second he grabbed by the throat and lifted it in the air. Then he dashed it over his knee and broke its back. He looked in disgust at the creature in his hands. Its skin was grayish colored as though the flesh were dead. Its feet were large in proportion to the skinny legs, and the toes curled under with nails that were almost claws. The hands were also too large for the arms and looked gnarled as though with arthritis. The head was the worst—the jaw protruded and the teeth were crooked and yellow. Long greasy hair covered the head and grew thickly on the body. It wore some kind of armor that was like sticks bound together but backed by animal hide. He recognized it as a goblin from the description from the Elves' books. An orc would be larger, with a more developed musculature, barrel-chested, and with a larger head.

He turned to see Mary bending over the mangled body of the child. She straightened the broken arms and legs and wrapped the little girl in her own cloak. They returned to the woman and Mary carried the dead child to her. "I am so sorry. We were too late."

The woman replied, "No, lass, my girl was dead when they dragged her off. God bless you that I have sommat to bury." To Mike she said, "Throw them cursed things in the fire, cleanse their stench from muh land!" Mike did as she asked and put all the bodies on the fire after he signaled the boat. The crew helped to bury the bodies of the woman's husband and children and provided clothing for her. After a whispered conference with Mary, Mike informed the Captain that they would proceed on foot. There was one more stop, a trading post, before Blackthorn Hearth. The Pair would be there before the boat. They would hang a piece of yellow cloth on a branch of a tree overhanging the last turn before the post if all was well. They left the crew and struck out in a straight line towards the post.

Once they were well away from the site, Mary spoke. "There was something wrong back there."

"Yes, there was. Goblins move in groups of at least twenty."

"Do you expect to find the rest at the trading post?"

"I expect to catch them before they attack," Mike replied. His voice had a cold deadly quality to it.

"Me too," Mary said. "But this time, use the sword."

Mike smiled grimly. "Oh, I will." They ran silently as the elves had taught them, faster than horses and with less effort than riding. The trading post was about ten miles from the way stop over land, some fifty miles by river. The Pair stopped at sundown; they ate travel bread and drank some water as they waited for the moon to rise. They did not speak and when the moonlight was bright enough for them to see, they began to run again. They caught up with the goblins about a mile from the trading post. Most of their anger had been consumed by the run, so they just stepped from the shadows onto the road in front of the band. "Return to your land and no one will die tonight." Mike's voice still held the deathly chill it had when they left the way stop.

The goblins muttered to themselves; they had the advantage. They could see in the darkness where men could not. They decided to fight. This time Mike and Mary stood side by side and faced the goblin charge head on. It was almost with regret that Mike ran his sword through the heart of the last goblin. Three times that number would not have stood a chance against the Pair that night. They gathered the bodies and Mary concealed the flame as Mike stoked a magical fire that consumed all of the remains. They hung the signal and bypassed the trading post, making their way to Blackthorn Hearth. They did not encounter more trouble, but there were signs of distress everywhere.

CHAPTER SEVEN

Blackthorn Hearth was normally a busy port city. As Mike and Mary looked down from the heights above the city, it resembled a disturbed anthill. They had met the riverboat a few miles upstream of the city and retrieved two of their bags. Mary tried to smooth the wrinkles from her travel outfit while Mike rolled his eyes and observed that it should look like they had traveled a long distance. Mike finally spotted a large group traveling together; they hurried to time their arrival with the group's so that they would not appear to be traveling alone. It seemed that everyone had their own affairs on their mind and there was an almost frantic undercurrent of conversation about some event. When they finally chose an Inn, they found more patrons checking out than checking in. Sitting in the common room, they soon learned that a large force of goblins and orcs was approaching from the west. A militia had been hurriedly formed and was marching to face them. Pleas for aid had been sent to the King as well as the Dwarf Kingdom, but the town would be on their own for at least two weeks.

In the Dark Lord's chamber, a man quaked in fear as the Evil One spoke. "How have you failed to retain your position? How is it that this man, the chamberlain, risks trusting mere servants? Did you give him reason to suspect you? No, no I think that you did not. I have no use for you in the middle kingdom. You have served me faithfully; perhaps there is another task suitable for your talents."

Abstidian received his instructions, rose, and left the chamber. His route was through underground ways known only to the orcai. When he encountered goblins or orcs, he shared water and food with them. He reminded them of the old stories of life on the Overworld. At each of these meetings, he did not leave until he had touched each of the orcai. A small splinter of darkness spread from his hand to the goblin or orc and began its insidious work of quelling their natural fears and stimulating their aggressiveness.

The story began to precede him, and he would be met by great masses of orcai who already knew the story. They would wait in long lines for him to lay hands on them. As darkness spread through the underworld, new instructions were sent via Rathire, the shadow servant of the Dark One. Abstidian began to raise hordes, or goblin armies. He set the orcai to producing iron weapons and taught them to build siege engines. Most of the supplies for war were cached except what was needed to capture the town of Blackthorn Hearth. This port city of the middle kingdom was very strategic because it was the main conduit for sales of dwarven weapons to the Kingdoms of Men.

Abstidian also collected certain minerals for a surprise to the Man armies. Some were foul smelling, reminiscent of the scent of the Dark One's chamber. Small quantities of the mix could be used to created great flashes of light and smoke that amazed the orcai. The Dark One assured Abstidian that larger quantities would create great explosions that could breach castle walls. The alchemist soon discovered that by wrapping even a small quantity tightly in parchment, he could produce a loud popping noise that delighted orcai children.

The danger of the mix was discovered by accident when an orc brought a torch near the mixing area and a spark fell into the mixed minerals. The chamber was destroyed along with several goblins that had become adept at creating the potion. Abstidian changed his procedure to only produce small quantities and to store the potion in locked chests where curiosity would not destroy his work. The time approached for the invasion, and he concentrated on the Dark One's plan. First, he sent many raiding parties into the kingdom to draw the King's army away from the south, where Blackthorn Hearth was located.

The largest problem that Abstidian had to face was not in recruiting enough raiders; rather he had too many volunteers for his logistics. He prepared two hordes as the Dark Lord instructed. A smaller, fast-moving horde would raid the town and dispose of any resistance that it could field. The second horde would have the war machines and siege engines. They would fortify the town and hold it against the counterattack the King would send when he realized the peril. This victory would signal other hordes to attack other strategic targets along the border and cut off the kingdom from its allies.

The real goal of these initial stages of the war was the kingdom to the east that had the Dark Mountain within its borders. The Kings of Raimbre had always had a tendency toward the dark powers, and it would take very little to convince the current king to ally with the Dark Lord. He would send troops to occupy Blackthorn Hearth and control the river commerce. This would be the beginning of a stranglehold on the kingdoms that were supporters of the light, and the first steps to the total conquest of all of Heavenshire.

Abstidian stayed with the horde as it started its march on Blackthorn Hearth and left to visit the King of Raimbre. He passed through Blackthorn Heart and was encouraged by the lackluster defenses that had been prepared. The militia that he observed would not stand against even the smaller horde. He kept in close contact with the leaders of the horde through the ravens that the Dark Lord used as messengers. Trouble reports started the day after he left Blackthorn Hearth. A small band of the King's Cavalry had stumbled on to the horde and was raiding them, slowing their advance on the city. Abstidian sent word to ignore the cavalry as much as possible and to continue on towards their goal.

Mary looked into Mike's eyes and asked, "Do you think they are prepared to face orcs?"

Mike sighed. "No, I do not think they are. The answer to your next question is we can make a difference. I think a more important question is should we?" The answer he preferred was plain in his eyes, but he waited for Mary to speak. She knew that her heart said to help, to prevent more mothers having to watch their husbands and children die. Yet their quest was of the highest importance. As these thoughts warred in her mind Mike spoke softly. "What kind of Heroes would we be if we abandoned these people in their time of need? We must have the armor, but the goodwill of the people is even more important!" He could feel Mary's relief; she did not need to speak. They quickly made plans and then separated to complete them. Mike paid for a month's lodging, expressing "every confidence" in the militia to the Innkeeper. Mary visited several livery stables, walking, leading the horses, and examining them with a thoughtful eye. She refused the pair the owner of the first stable tried to push on her. After visiting several stables she purchased a horse from each of two different places. In the meantime, Mike hurried to the dock to meet the riverboat and retrieve their baggage. They met at the Inn and quickly donned their leather armor. The Sword of the Ancestors was securely strapped to Mike's back and Mary's bow was secured across hers. When they tried to pick up Mike's mount, an armed man who seemed more thug than soldier confronted them.

The man was big and unkempt and often referred to the Kings' service. Mike's patience was soon exhausted; he stepped in front of the man and took the reins. The man shoved him and started to draw his sword. He stopped when the tip of the Sword of the Ancestors pressed against his throat. Mike said in a low voice, "The King does not take property at the point of a sword. Drop your sword belt and step back." When the man complied, Mike scooped it up and handed it to Mary. "We will return this to this spot in three weeks. Now point the direction the militia took." He quickly saddled the horse and mounted, and the Pair left the man in a cloud of dust. They rode hard until they were out of sight of the town, and then ran on foot, leading the horses. They pushed as hard as they could and two days later, they detected signs of wagons. They remounted their horses. They caught up with the supply train and found it to be undefended. Alarmed, they rode hard to catch the militia. Even more disturbing, they were not challenged as they rode past the marching and mounted men. Mary reached the head of the column first and blocked the leader's way. She began shouting at him and Mike pulled up to the side and watched the men.

Mary struggled to get her anger under control; she had to push aside the thought that he was leading these men to slaughter. The man had no answers and obviously had no military experience. Mary began to ask a series of questions; the man began to realize their predicament and started to shake. Mike rode up next to him and spoke in a quiet voice. "Order your men to return to the supply wagons. We will follow shortly." The man did so and rode quietly between the Pair as they explained what the enemy was capable of and how they must combat it. They agreed that Mike would attempt to prepare the men and Mary would scout the area. They thought the horde was several days distant and that would give them some time. The small group arrived at the supply site and the leader was shocked and enraged by what he saw. Men had dropped where they halted, equipment was strewn about, and many horses were untended to. He rushed through the throng and kicked and slapped the men into some kind of order. He then explained in detail what they could expect if they met the goblins unprepared. Mike stopped him and picked up two staves from beside the nearest wagon. "Watch," he said as he tossed one to Mary.

Mary caught the stave and immediately attacked Mike. He blocked the first blow and countered and the Pair sparred for half an hour, leaving the men slack jawed in amazement. Mike turned to face the men and received a whack across his backside. The blow did not hurt, but it broke the trance that had fallen on the men. He turned his head to see an innocent smile across Mary's face. "What?"

Mike shook his head. "You know what! Men! I will teach you what I can in the little time we have. You will learn, or probably die. Tonight as Captain, uh, Gandy has ordered, you will tend to your mounts and your equipment before yourselves. Then you will eat, sleep, and we will begin training at sunup!" The men did as instructed and Mike spoke briefly with his partner. "Mary, be careful. Try to be unseen, but leave no witnesses."

Mary smiled and replied, "I will be safer than you, love. Accidents happen in training." She reached up and touched his face. "I will be careful. I think we both should scout this area before you go to bed." Mike nodded ascent and they both melted into the forest.

Near midnight Mike paused and decided he should return when he noticed an odor on the foliage. It was the same odor as the goblins they had killed; they had passed through within the hour. He determined the direction of the trail and followed silently. He found a group of three goblins and an orc. They seemed to be searching for the militia. Mike drew his sword and stepped into the open. The orc reacted first, drawing a crooked sword and leaping towards Mike. Its blow was powerful but poorly aimed, and it paid with its life. The goblins soon followed it in death. Mike buried the goblins using their own swords but he slung the orc over his shoulder and returned to a site near the camp where he slept for a few hours. At sunup he approached the camp and was challenged by a sentry. It was sloppy and he could have easily avoided the man, but it was a start. It was not encouraging that many of the men lost their breakfast when they saw the orc's body. He began their training with the corpse in front of them. It seemed to be motivation enough; the men soon mastered the basics of thrust and parry, and he could allow limited sparring. Captain Gandy proved capable of overseeing the practice while Mike buried the corpse and left to scout the area again. He returned before nightfall and had the men pack and march to a new location that could be more easily defended by inexperienced men. He scouted again and found traces of the enemy; he ceased trailing them when he found where they had encountered Mary. There was a scorched area that was large enough to have contained four bodies. He expected there to be three more scouting parties, but they might not encounter all of them. He returned to camp, slept for a few hours, and then began training again.

The next day, Mike chose three men who seemed capable to accompany him on patrol. The racket they made seemed enough to wake the dead until he realized that he had been no better a year before. He ranged a little ahead and discovered a third enemy patrol. He returned to his men and alerted them. This patrol was all orcs, but Mike thought these men were ready. They met the orcs in an open glade. The men held their own, killing three, and Mike dispatched the fourth. After they buried the orcs, Mike sent them back to camp while he quickly searched in other directions. He found the camp buzzing with excitement and the sentries more alert, almost to the point of competence. The encounter had reassured the men, but he feared their newfound confidence would not serve them well.

The first farm Mary encountered on her patrol was empty, as were the next three. At the fifth, she noticed activity as she approached, so she left the horse and continued on foot. The sounds were not normal farm activity, so she crept to the barn silently. As she suspected there were goblins inside, tearing the place apart. She nearly gagged as she watched them eating the husks from the feed bunker, feed intended for the farmer's pigs. She drew her sword, stepped into the open, and called to the creatures. "Hello short, squat, and ugly! Where have you been all of my life, and why didn't you stay there?" The goblins stopped and stared, so Mary continued. "I suppose it would be too much to ask if any of you boys know how to dance."

The goblins knew they were being insulted, but they did not understand. They did understand that a human woman was in easy reach; they reached for their weapons. The closest to Mary died before it could pick up the cudgel it had laid beside the feed bunker. The next two died at almost the same time, and the last managed to raise its twisted sword as it screamed in terror. Mary tucked a loose strand of hair back into place before dealing with the bodies. She exerted more effort disposing of the corpses than she had in creating them. She left her horse in the barn with fresh hay and water. She then traveled several miles before she stopped and rested. She rose at midnight and continued, traveling several more miles before sunrise. She had found the back trail of the patrol she had killed and of four others. She knew that Mike could handle the other patrols, so she pressed on to find the main body of the horde. In the end she smelled it before she saw it; the scent of smoke and stench of unwashed bodies carried well on the wind.

She estimated that there were five hundred orcs and goblins. This was more than five times the number in the small group of villagers she had left with Mike. As she watched, though, there was an outcry from the horde; it began to roil and turn away from her. She saw a small band of cavalry making a quick retreat from the far flank of the horde. She noted their direction and moved to intercept after the horde had ceased its pursuit.

She approached their camp just before sunset and easily evaded the sentries. Her appearance, as though by magic, in the center of the camp caught the attention of the leader. They were Royal Cavalry who had encountered some of the first messengers from Blackthorn Hearth. They had been harassing the horde since, slowing its progress and whittling away at its ranks. They had taken losses as well. They had two badly injured men who they would have to get aid for soon. Mary quickly examined the injured men and sent others to gather certain herbs and plants from the forest. Using a magic word and the herbal cure, she soon had them able to ride. The leader agreed that they should meet the force from the town and continue to harass the horde to buy time for the King to send aid.

Mary left immediately and hurried back towards Mike and the militia. She was near the place where the horde patrols had diverged when she ran into a group of three orcs and a goblin. The battle was brief, but Mary had to chase the goblin and in the end shot him with her bow. She did not pause to bury the bodies; time was too short. She had to track the militia to their new location; she approved of the site. Not wanting to talk to anyone, she slipped through the sentries and found Mike sleeping.

CHAPTER EIGHT

Mary sat for a moment looking at his face; he looked tired even as he slept, and she wondered if her face looked as haggard. She reached out and gently felt the days' old stubble on his jaw. His eyes opened. Again she remembered the eyes of the knight in her dream. A feeling of tenderness, an emotion almost forgotten, flooded her as she spoke, "Rest, we have a little time." She felt pampered as he insisted she lay down in his bedroll and enjoyed its warmth as she drifted immediately to sleep.

It seemed as though she had barely closed her eyes when Mike was gently stroking her arm and offering her a hot drink. "I thought you were going to let me rest?" Mary smiled as she stretched. Most of her fatigue was gone, and she desperately needed a bath, but that was a luxury to be denied her. She had informed Mike of the King's cavalry and that they should find them later that day. They were planning how to best use the two forces when they heard a commotion and both rushed to it. They found Captain Gandy and the three-man patrol returning. One man was bleeding from a deep gash in his arm and was being supported by the others. Captain Gandy's face was ashen.

"There were six, most of them orcs. Two of them escaped. I was just about to send the mounted troop after them." Mike shook his head as Mary examined the wound.

"No, assemble the men. They need to see what will happen if they forget their training. There are also new developments; we will be joined by a detachment of the King's cavalry, but we will have to engage the enemy. We will be greatly outnumbered, but we must delay the horde until help arrives. We are all that stands between your homes and this rabid horde. Each day we buy with our efforts will mean lives saved in the city."

The men's demeanor was greatly changed from the overconfidence of the night before as they watched Mary bandage the man's wounds. Mike left the man in Mary' care and followed the trail back to the site of the engagement. Gandy' patrol had been ambushed, and he could see that their overconfidence was the cause. He swiftly followed the fleeing orcs and caught them in deep brush as they rested. He watched for a while and was soon disgusted as they boasted of what the horde would do to the militia. He stepped from the brush and motioned to them. This time the orcs paid for their overconfidence with their lives.

The drill sessions were more urgent as the men sought to perfect what Mike had tried to teach them. They now understood that their lives depended on their skill and on that of their comrades. They were tending to their equipment when the King's detachment arrived, which consisted of about forty healthy riders and several wounded. After a conference—between the young lieutenant, Norris, who led them, Captain Gandy, Mike, and Mary—a plan was formed. They would rest for a day and then move to meet the horde. They would separate the mounted troops into two detachments that would harass the flanks of the horde.

The foot soldiers would be used for misdirection and to hit at the main force if it left portions exposed. Captain Gandy and Lieutenant Norris would lead the cavalry detachments while Mike and Mary would lead the foot soldiers on hit and run attacks. If they could keep the horde chasing them, then the town would have time to prepare defenses and possibly help would arrive in time.

The next day, as the militia prepared to march, unexpected aid arrived in the form of five elven archers. The men cast sidelong glances at the elves; deep-seated mistrust existed between the races, and even the threat of the horde did not erase it entirely. Mike spoke to the men before they marched. "By now you know that I am an honest Man. My words have been proven true many times. I will not lie to you now. Not all who march today will return to camp tonight. If there be any among you who values his life more than those in the city we seek to protect, let him remain in camp and be gone before this army returns. Let no man speak ill of any who march or stay. This fight will be fierce and only those who commit their lives to it are welcome." He left to speak with the new arrivals.

The Pair welcomed the elves warmly and made plans to use the archers to support the troops. They sent the elves ahead to scout, getting them out of sight of the men. Soon the elves reported contact with the horde; the enemy had made good time while they were not being harassed. The cavalry detachments quickly made contact, attacking from opposite flanks. The horde had made an attempt to ambush the cavalry, but it fell apart when the second detachment attacked. As the horde tried to regroup, the first detachment and the infantry enveloped the ambush force and decimated it. The horde realized there was an unmounted force and began to pursue. The unmounted militia withdrew quickly, and as the goblins pursued they were smashed by a lightening-fast cavalry attack. The unmounted militia returned and helped to wipe out the trapped goblins. The cavalry then covered the militia's retreat as the horde continued to pursue. The remainder of the day was spent in a running battle that drew the main body of the horde many miles away from their desired course. As night fell there were several skirmishes between small groups of goblins and orcs as their leaders argued.

Lieutenant Norris brought a messenger to Mike as he watched the turmoil spread in the hordes' ranks. The man brought news that fifty more men had arrived in the camp, and the old veteran soldier that Mike had left in charge was drilling them. Mike was heartened by the news; goblins and orcs almost never attacked a force larger than their own. He sent the messenger back with instructions on deploying the new men and conferred with Lieutenant Norris about a change in the next day's tactics. He left as Mary arrived few minutes later.

"The goblins want to withdraw a day's march. They are expecting reinforcements. The orcs want to press on and ignore the attacks. Apparently they want first choice at the spoils of the town." Mary sat and rubbed her eyes. "They aren't worried at all about their losses, no matter what the *The Official Horde Defense Stratagems* says. I think if we have the Elven archers pick off the orc leaders, the ranks will panic. Our greatest danger would be in pursuing too deeply into the chaos."

"I agree," Mike said. "If we can drive them back a day's march, that will be two more days we have won for the

King to send aid. Do you have any idea how large the second force is?"

"None. Only that the orcs think it is more than enough to overrun Blackthorn Hearth. Can you think of any way to wipe this horde out entirely?" Mary looked at the enemy camp. "We reduced their forces by about fifteen percent. According to 'Stratagems' they should be close to the breaking point. I quote, 'Any time the Horde's total losses begin to exceed twenty and five hundredths, the resolve of individual goblins and orcs will begin to fail. Once the losses exceed thirty hundredths, the horde will dissolve into a melee of goblins and orcs seeking the nearest underground way.' I don't think we can count on that." Mary spread her hands. "This will be a hard fight. If we had not decided to help, they would have been almost to Blackthorn Hearth by now."

"I don't think they can go against their nature for long. Tomorrow we set ambushes and try to split the goblin and orcs. I hope the goblins will flee, and then we can deal with the orcs," Mike replied.

The next morning brought another addition to the small army that had fallen under Mike's command. A force of fifty dwarves armed with stout battleaxes arrived. They were led by a boisterous dwarf named Alexar. Mike took care to keep them separate from the elves because Bardwind had warned him of possible friction between the two groups. He quickly incorporated them into the day's battle plans. The cavalry was combined into one detachment, which attacked the horde at the highest concentration of orcs. They were easily drawn into a slow-moving battle and into an ambush set by the Elven archers and half of the infantry.

The dwarves spearheaded a drive between the orcs and the goblins, leading the remainder of the infantry.

The goblins were unprepared for the dwarf infantry and took heavy losses immediately. They were at the breaking point when Mike and Mary led the reserve force of infantry into their flank. The horde finally broke, and Mike sent the dwarves after them to insure they did not reform. The Pair led the remaining infantry against the orcs who were being pushed back by the cavalry. The result was much like a hammer striking an anvil, everything in between was crushed.

The Pair seemed to be everywhere at once. Any time the men seemed to lose their resolve, one or the other would show up to reinforce them and drive the enemy back. At last, after losing nearly half of their number, the orcs broke. Mike sent the Royal Cavalry after them to keep them from rejoining the goblins.

The next day was spent escorting the supply train to a new location, gathering orc and goblin bodies to burn, and burying the casualties from the allied forces of Man, Elf, and Dwarf. Just before the remains of the enemy horde were set on fire, Mike had an unexpected visitor. It was Bardwind, riding a powerful white stallion. The old man had a few words of praise for the Pair and an admonition. Mike and Mary were both nursing minor wounds; the wizard reiterated that they had to renew the charm on their armor each day for it to be the most effective. "The power will fade as you get farther from the place where the armor was first enchanted, with use, and with time. You must make time each day to remove it and renew the charm as you put it on. Now let us examine the enemy. There may be much the corpses can tell us."

The wizard poked around the piled bodies, occasionally mumbling a word. He examined weapons and cast off equipment, sometimes talking to himself, sometimes thoughtfully stroking his beard. When he was satisfied he motioned everyone away and raised his hands and staff. Blue fire shot from the top of the staff and ignited the vast funeral pyre. The flames appeared to burn cold; very little heat emanated from the pile. Mary saw the power of the magic that Bardwind wrought and something else. It seemed as though little shadows danced within the wall of flame. They swirled but were banished by the flames.

Bardwind turned to Mary and asked, "Do you see the shadows in the flame? There was a spell laid on this horde to inhibit their natural tendencies to cut and run when opposed. This is very troubling because it means that the Dark One has a powerful servant in this world."

Mary thought about this. "Could this have made them do more atrocious things than they would have normally?"

The wizard replied, "I doubt it. Goblins and orcs are treacherous creatures at best. They seem to resent those who live on the surface, but they are ill suited physically to live here."

"Has anyone ever asked them why?" Mary's question seemed to strike the wizard physically.

"No! I suppose that it has never occurred to one of us. Most in this world accept things as they are. This does lead to extreme prejudicial notions. Dwarves and Elves do not trust each other, and only barely trust Men. It is the same with the other sentient creatures here. Only someone from another world would think to ask why." Bardwind was pensive for a moment. "I suppose if you could catch one that was too scared to fight, or too tired to run anymore, you might get it to answer a question or two."

Mary nodded and left to retrieve her pack and some trail rations, a new mission growing in her mind. She left word for Mike and began to track the fleeing goblins. The trail was littered with bodies at first. The dwarves had given no quarter. For a reason that she could not quite understand, she avoided the dwarves when she caught up to them. They were returning to the camp. It was not much later that she found the point where the dwarves had given up the chase and she pressed on.

CHAPTER NINE

Night was falling when she discovered what at first seemed to be another body. It was much smaller than most she had seen. It groaned when she rolled it over and pleaded through parched lips, "No kill. Leave me die." Mary could tell it could go no further and cradled the filthy head in her arms, pouring a little water through the dry and cracked lips. It lay there then, exhausted and panic stricken, pleading with her to let it live. It did not seem reassured by her promise until she gave it a small crust of the hard travel bread she carried.

It looked at the food suspiciously at first, then tasted a crumb. Still watching Mary warily, it shoved the remainder of the crust into its mouth. Mary offered more water and it accepted. It had finally stopped panting and was able to hold the canteen. Mary allowed it enough water to wash down the bread, but stopped before it took enough to make it sick. She gave it a little more bread and then sat and watched the creature. It was ugly by human standards. Its skin had a grayish tinge, and the round head seemed too large for the body. Its teeth, when Mary could see them, were too large for the mouth. The arms and legs were spindly and the feet looked too large for the skinny legs.

"Not kill? All overworlders want kill the People." It spoke as if reciting facts. "Overworld belong People once. Before elf, before dwarf, before man. They drive People to dark ways. People hate overworlders. Except Fobnish," it indicated itself, "not hate warrior. Warrior save Fobnish, give water and bread. Be friend. Why warrior be friend to Fobnish?"

Mary removed her leather helmet and the goblin gasped as her long hair fell over her shoulders. "I did not kill you because you could not fight me. I wanted to find out why your people were killing children here in the, Overworld did you call it? You could not answer if you were dead." Mary carefully wiped the neck of the canteen and drank. "I think there has been enough killing today."

"No! One more dies today. Woman leads Overworld troops. Must die!" The largest orc that Mary had yet seen was towering over her. Three others stood behind it. Mary rolled away from the strike of the wicked-looking blade and drew her sword. She gained her feet and stopped in amazement. The little goblin had managed to get to its feet and was wrapped around the orcs legs!

"No! Can not kill. Woman give food and water. Law say can not kill!" The orc shook it loose and stared at Mary.

"Woman share food and drink with goblin?" It was a question, and when Mary nodded, the orc continued. "Give us food, drink?" It was no longer shouting and had lowered its sword. Mary cautiously reached into her pack for more bread, which she set with her canteen on the ground between them. The orc broke a piece of the bread off and sniffed it, then ate it. It tossed the rest to the others. Then it raised the canteen.

"There is very little left, you may have all of it." Mary watched as the orc shook a few drops out and handed to the others who did the same. It then produced a water skin and tossed it to Mary. She tried to hide her revulsion and took a sip. The orcs then all squatted in a semi-circle facing her and were joined by the goblin.

"By the law of the People, woman no be harmed from this moon until moon is new in sky. It is law!" They orcs just sat and watched Mary. She sheathed her sword and sat, cross-legged, in front of them.

After a time of silence, Mary spoke. "Fobnish tells me that once the People lived in the Overworld. Why do they live below now? It would seem there is room enough for all."

The lead orc sat in silence for a while, much like Mary had, and then spoke. "I, Cracktooth, tell tale of the People. Once the People lived in over world. God of Overworld tell People, 'Live anywhere except my mountain, in the center of the land.' For many years the People roamed the over world, never touching the sacred mountain. One day Dark Lord comes to the People. He tell them sacred mountain good place for People. They never have to work for food, search for water. At first People tell Dark Lord go away. Then some of the People listen. Soon all of the People gather at sacred mountain. God no say nothing, so People start climb Mountain. After that God come. He put chains of fire on Dark Lord and put him under Dark Mountain. He tell People they now belong Dark Lord. God use whips of fire, drive People underworld. People replaced by other creatures, and God take sacred mountain away."

The orc paused and looked at Mary. "Now, Dark Lord not killed. He come back and lead the People back to Overworld. He send man now to make People ready. He say the People have to push others out and make room for Dark Lord. He say Dark Lord grow strong, can win now against God that forced the People to underworld." Its eyes glowed and its expression was defiant. "We let woman live. Woman tell story, and overworlders maybe not all die."

Mary laughed. "You did not let me live. I chose not to kill you. I will prove it to you." She rose gracefully and walked a short ways into the forest. When she returned she carried five stout staves that she had cut from deadwood with her sword. She tossed them in front of the orcs and said, "Choose."

The orcs muttered and then smiled, showing ugly yellow teeth. They each chose a stave; Mary picked up the remaining stave and brought it to the ready. The orcs twirled the staves and brought them to the ready. Mary attacked without hesitation and in seconds, all four were on the ground and she held the end of her stave against the leader's throat. "Perhaps you were not ready. I will give you a second try. Plan your attack." She turned her back and walked over to the goblin and checked on him. It had used virtually the last of its strength to protect her. It was asleep, or unconscious, but breathing, so she left and returned to the orcs.

The leader nodded and its followers spread out around Mary. She held her stave down and brought it to the ready position only after the leader motioned. She waited for the attack and the battle was over in moments, all of the orcs on the ground and the end of Mary's stave again against the leader's throat. She spoke slowly. "I let you live because I wanted to know why your kind comes, murdering innocent men, women, and children. I think that an evil man has used your own legends and traditions to cause you to commit evil acts. Know this, I, and others like me, will try to protect the innocent against any and all evil that comes against them. I will also remember the story you told and seek a course that allows all to live at peace with all others."

The orc rolled to his feet after Mary moved the stave. "Me listen. Woman is mighty warrior. Is woman one legend tells will come with man and restore the world?"

Mary looked the ugly creature in the eye. "I will not answer that. I do not know your legends. Go in peace, maybe we will meet again in peace." She did not intentionally use the magic form of the word, but the small clearing was filled with a pure light. She could see small dark sparks detach from all of the orcs and the goblin and disappear in the light before it faded. For a moment the orcs were confused, then the leader shook its head and looked at Mary with wonder in its eyes. It fell to one knee and laid its ugly twisted sword on the ground between them, the others did the same.

"You have freed us from an evil touch. You are mighty in the power. We will not tell the Evil One of your presence. Now we must hide until the power of your blessing fades with time. Never will we take back the curse. We repay some day. We take little one with us." They rose and were fashioning a litter when Mary left.

CHAPTER TEN

Mike walked through the camp and smiled to himself. It was beginning to look like a military camp. There was order, and the sentries were well set and were becoming more effective. The men were being drilled each day, and he was even able to send patrols through the surrounding area. He had sent the elves to find the second horde, but they had not returned. He had a force of about three hundred men; more arrived each day. They had begun to supplement their supplies by careful hunting and were actually doing quite well. Word had reached them that the king of the middle kingdom was sending a thousand troops to garrison Blackthorn Hearth and was readying a large force to move against the horde. The King of the Dwarves had also promised a hundred soldiers for the defense of Blackthorn Hearth.

Lieutenant Norris had been promoted to Captain and had taken command of the militia. Mike had quietly faded from the command circle and was prepared to resume his journey once the King's forces arrived. His destination this night was the command tent, where he was often summoned. He allowed the two Captains to formulate plans and did not offer advice unless it was requested. Norris was competent enough, and Gandy usually did not interfere. It was clear that his title was honorary and had more to do with the fact that he had financed the original militia than any training or experience on his part. It was a credit to the man that he had accepted his status without rancor. Mike secretly thought it best that Mary did not have to deal with the man though. The man had an almost overbearing coarseness about him whenever females were mentioned.

Their meeting was brief. Captain Norris had a solid plan for engaging a force numbering more than a thousand. Mike could find no major fault with it and thought there was an excellent chance it would succeed. He was slightly concerned that the scouts had yet to report. There was also a mild concern in his mind that Mary had not returned. She had left after speaking with Bardwind, and Mike was not overly worried, assuming that she was still scouting. He left the command tent and returned to the tents that had been set aside for "the Pair," as they had become known. Mary was there and he waited outside as she sponge bathed, amused by the running tirade about the lack of bathing facilities. She called him in as she was combing her long hair.

Mike embraced her for a moment, earning a rebuke for mussing her hair. He again marveled at the strength in her body. Muscles had been hardened by long hours of practice and sparring. Her face was a beautiful as ever, and Mike thought that her skin almost glowed. The dark eyes in the oval-shaped face were staring into his, and he had only to lean forward slightly to kiss the full, rich lips. He drew back instead and held her at an arm's length. "It is good to see you. Did you find what you were searching for?"

A hint of a shadow passed behind Mary's eyes as he drew back. Was it disappointment, or relief? He could not tell from her voice. "I found many things, including our elven scouts. I wanted to tell you first—we face a much larger force than we anticipated. Three thousand goblins and orcs, and about a hundred trolls. They have siege engines and some of the goblins ride wolves as though they were horses. I have discovered that the goblins believe this to be a holy war. They even have a human holy man of some sort that is pushing them into battle. They are more than just vermin; they have a culture of sorts, and laws. They are being influenced by the Dark Lord as pawns in his schemes." Her face glowed in anger as she finished.

Mike thought about this for a few seconds, troubled more by the last revelation than the others. "Captain Norris must know the strength that he opposes. We must tell Bardwind the rest. I want to know more about the enemy's culture. There may be something there that will stop this war before it begins." Mike waited and talked with Mary as she finished fixing her hair. The Pair walked to the command tent and found Captain Norris studying a map.

The captain's expression was grave after he listened to the news. "How much of the original plan do you think is still valid?" he asked Mike. He was reassured when Mike endorsed the original tactics with one added mission: to destroy the siege engines. He was less enthusiastic about how that could be accomplished. "Part of our strategy is that the men will see you fighting with them to bolster their resolve!"

Mike shook his head. "If standing between their homes and this evil horde is not enough, then no deed of ours will suffice. Think of this though; when the men see the smoke from the burning siege engines, they will be filled with hope. You know that Mary and I, as well as the elves, walk in and out of your camp easily. It is not your sentries' fault, they are good enough. The horde will not even be as good. Destroying the siege engines will add to the confusion, and you will be able to cut into their ranks." The captain reluctantly agreed and the battle plan was adjusted. The Pair slipped from the camp and joined the elves in their small encampment.

There were now twenty elves in the force, and they knew of 'Sir' Michael and 'Lady' Marilyn. They listened with approval to the plan to destroy the siege engines; an animated discussion evolved as to who would support the infantry and who would accompany the Pair. They were less enthused about what Mary had discovered about the culture of the goblins. They agreed to send word to Bardwind after the battle. Naroin, the eldest and defacto group leader, was of the opinion that the wizard would appear during or after the battle anyway.

The next two days were spent with the militia as they marched to meet the horde. They received regular updates from the elves about the horde's progress. Everything seemed to progress more or less according to plan. The Pair spent most of their time with the elves or taking a turn scouting the advance of the horde. They were mostly able to avoid contact with the goblin scouting parties; if not, they destroyed them so they could not report. The night before the militia was to make contact was spent discussing the plan, calming the nerves of Captain Gandy who would have made wholesale changes to the battle plan. The Pair returned to their tents after midnight and sat outside talking for a while. They had a few laughs at the expense of the unfortunate Captain Gandy before sliding into their bedrolls. Just before she felt herself falling asleep, Mary asked, "Are we really heroes?"

Mike answered through the tent wall." I don't know about me, but you are my Hero. You amaze me all the time.

The day that our paths first crossed is one of the happiest in my life since, well, one of the happiest days I can remember. Now, go to sleep, we have a battle to win later today. You want to look your best." He rolled over to face the opposite wall. "G'night love."

Mary lay in her bedroll smiling. He had often called her his hero in various degrees of seriousness. She had started it though. On a cold New Year's Eve when her car died downtown, she had called a man she barely knew as a last resort. He had driven through snow and sleet to work on her car in the light of a street lamp. He had discovered that a mouse had chewed through a wire was able to patch it and get the car started. Mary had been so relieved that the problem was no more serious than that and had declared Mike to be her Hero of the Year. The year had ended only minutes later, but they had found a coffee shop that was open and talked until sunrise. Tonight, on the eve of battle, his words held a ring of sincerity that comforted her. She heard his breathing even out. "You have always been my hero. When will you see that?" Only then did she allow herself to fall asleep.

The next morning was busy, and Mike lamented that the horde must surely hear the racket the militia made. The Pair joined the elves and made their way around the huge encampment of the horde to approach from its rear. There they waited for the militia to begin its attack. They saw the activity in the horde camp before they could see the attacking cavalry. Then they waited a half-hour and slipped into the camp. All of the raiders wore cloaks with color patterns designed to shift and blend into the background, far more effective than any camouflage Mike could remember. The guards were taken with less than lethal matters, as Mary insisted, and bound. The group set the skins of oil that would fuel the fires on the war machines and gathered under a large battering ram.

Mike's attention had been drawn to a nearby tent that had been heavily guarded. He had the others wait as he checked it out. Inside were two locked chests. Mike simply broke the hinges on the first and was shocked at the contents. The chest was filled with crude black gunpowder! He quickly set an oilskin between the two and rejoined the others. He quickly whispered instructions and the group slipped out of the camp. When he and Mary were beyond the edge, they paused and Mary spoke the word that ignited all of the oil pots. The fires burned for a few seconds before any in the camp noticed. Outcries of "fire" began just before the powder in the tent ignited.

The explosion was not large by comparison to the gunpowder that the Pair knew, but it was terrifying in this land that had no knowledge of such things. There was a huge quantity of smoke and fire that created havoc among the horde. The battle across the valley paused as the shockwave reached the militia. After a moment's silence, the Pair could hear shouts and cheers from the men as they renewed their attack. The Pair had to press hard to catch up with their companion elves and take their position for the attack on the enemy flank. They fought beside the dwarves and the friction between the races turned to competition. It was hard to determine which group was the more efficient fighting force.

The combination of confusion and the pressure of the multiple attacks were too much for the horde. Huge portions of their lines broke and ran from the battle, leaving the small force of trolls to fight to the last creature. The Cavalry, Dwarves, and Elves harassed the fleeing horde for several hours to keep them from reforming immediately and then returned to the camp. Captain Norris seized the opportunity to plan cooperation between the three races to share information and to patrol the edges of the wilderness as an early warning for when the horde again marched to battle.

Abstidian paused his journey near a small village and waited for reports from the horde. The news of the disastrous defeat of the first horde reached him the same day as a summons from the Dark Lord. He was near the Dark Mountain when he received word that the second horde was defeated. He expected the Dark Lord to be furious when he arrived, but was surprised to be received and sent out again with new instructions. The second stage attacks were ordered, and Abstidian was sent to find the chosen Pair at Blackthorn Hearth.

CHAPTER ELEVEN

It was nearing noon as the livery stable keeper finished his chores. There was very little to do; most of his stock was gone and few citizens were brave enough to travel very far beyond the town's boundaries. Newly constructed fortifications surrounded the city, sentries, and an almost daily influx of families from the countryside. He idly wondered if he could rent some of the stalls to those families when he heard a pair of horses approach. He turned to see the couple who had bought his best bay gelding. He quickly calculated in his mind the increase he would see if he bought it back at the price they had paid. He greeted them warmly, but before he could ask about buying their mounts, the big man riding the bay spoke. "We were to meet someone here today to return his property. Do you know where he is?" The keeper thought for a moment and then pointed towards the Town Square.

"I don't think he'll be taking it back," the stable master said as the Pair looked towards the gallows that had been erected. "The chamberlain don't take kindly to the misuse o' tha King's name." He waited as the Pair recognized one of the figures hanging there. "Probably best ye weren't here to give a sword to a condemned man. Now aire ye wishin' ta sell them mounts?"

Mary shook her head, "No, just to board them a few days." She and Mike dismounted and completed the arrangements. They walked the few blocks to the Inn where they had left their belongings. Mike wandered farther down the street towards a knot of men who were talking excitedly. As Mike approached he could hear that they were talking about the battles with the horde. He smiled inwardly as almost miraculous feats were described, but he became serious when the talk turned to the mysterious pair who had appeared from nowhere and disappeared when the fighting was over. He was heartened that they had not recognized him; he returned to the inn where he found Mary arguing with the innkeeper. Only one room was available for them. Mary stomped her foot and turned to Mike. "You talk to him. I want my bath!"

The innkeeper turned apologetic eyes to Mike and spread his hands. Mike waved away his apologies and asked about their belongings. They were safe in the room, untouched since the river men had delivered them. Mike bargained for a reduced rate and pocketed a fair amount of the coin that he had already paid. He returned to the room to find that Mary had not returned from the bathing room. Changing into different clothes, he went in search of his own bath. When he returned he found the room just as he had left it; Mary was still taking every advantage of civilization. He stepped behind the dressing screen to change into the clothes of a nobleman. He heard the door open and called out, "Be out in a minute." He was surprised that she did not answer so he stepped from behind the screen still in his under tunic. Bardwind was seated on the room's couch, unlighted pipe in his teeth.

"You are as good as your word, truly an action worthy of a hero. As were your actions in saving this town! Thirdly, you do not seek recognition for your deeds. Were you this selfless in your world?" Bardwind lit his pipe and blew a large cloud of smoke. "The dwarves have the best leaf, except perhaps for the gnomes. You do not smoke do you? A shame really. You should be prepared for the dwarves, as they might not understand. They do enjoy a pipe after dinner, or any other activity for that matter"

"I'll remember that. I spoke with the leader of the dwarves contingent, Alexar. He'll meet us beyond the border in two days. I hope to leave during the celebrations of the militia's return. We'll seem to be just two travelers, of some means of course, who have business in Blackthorn Hearth. I hope to leave before any of the soldiers can recognize us. From the stories I've heard in the town, no one would give us a second glance." He was interrupted by a knock at the door and Mary's voice. She entered and warmly greeted Bardwind before retiring behind the dressing screen to change clothes. Bardwind and Mike waited patiently for her to join them.

Mike could only stare when she emerged. Bardwind snorted and said, "I sincerely doubt you will go unnoticed anywhere, my dear child." Mary only smiled and walked to the couch; she sat beside him in a whirl of skirts and rich fabric.

"I know I cannot go out like this, but I have been dirty and grime encrusted for too long. I am glad that you think I am memorable. I think that Mike, or Sir Michael, has lost control of his tongue, a rare occurrence I assure you. What's the matter, Big Boy, too much woman for you?" Mary stood and walked around Mike, who turned to watch her. She strutted for a moment and then collapsed into a chair laughing. "The expression on your face is priceless, Sir Michael."

Mike laughed and tried to be suave. "You clean up real

nice, Doll." His smile could not be suppressed. "Who am I kidding? You look gorgeous, Mary. Bardwind is right, though. No one would remember anyone else in the room."

"Oh stop," she said. "No, go ahead, tell me how marvelous I look, *dahlings*." She struck a dramatic pose. "So tell me, Good Wizard, why are you here? We know the Dark One is searching for us. Surely we did not do wrong in helping these folks."

The old man shook his head, "No, of course not. I am here for an entirely different matter. Did you learn anything about the goblins on your foray? Actually, I should ask, what did you learn about the orcai, that is the term for goblin and orcs together?"

Mary sat up straight and smoothed her skirts around her. "Yes, I did. They are not the sub-human vermin that most of Heavenshire believe them to be. They have culture, history, and even laws. One of the strongest laws apparently involves hospitality. I found a goblin, too exhausted to run any further. I gave him water and a crust of bread. This led to an actual dialogue." Mary spent the next hour talking with the wizard and answering questions, especially about the dark sparks that she apparently banished. Mike listened more to the way that Bardwind asked questions than the questions. He caught Mary's glances toward him and thought she had picked up on the same undertones. He was not surprised when she asked a question of her own. "Do you have any legend of the orcai living above ground?"

Bardwind pulled the pipe from between his teeth, rose, and walked to the fireplace. He knocked the ashes into the fireplace, turned, and spoke. "That is the most troubling. I have reexamined some of the sacred writings. The oldest tell that the chosen people were commanded to take the land from those who had inhabited it. There are legends of older writings, but they are very vague. I must make a search of the archives of the elves. Look for me when you return to Elvhome, as this might have a bearing on your destiny. You have done well so far. You must not become over confident. There is still much to this world that you do not understand, even as I do not understand. There are events in motion even greater than I first believed. Maybe I will have answers when we meet again." The wizard took his leave and the Pair prepared to dine in the common room after Mary changed clothes.

The next morning when Mike woke from his place on the floor, he immediately noticed that the bed was empty. He quickly found Mary in her bedroll near the fireplace, evidently more comfortable on the floor than in the bed. He rose silently, dressed, and attempted to slip out the door. Mary's' voice stopped him. "Leaving so soon, big boy? Is my company that, ah, distasteful?" She rolled over and slipped out of the bedroll, dressed in the clothes she had worn to supper the night before. "Or is there some other damsel in distress that needs a hero's aid?" She walked up to him and reached up to embrace him to remove any sting her words may have held. "Do you have a little time for this fair maiden?"

Mike returned the embrace and tried to think of a snappy comeback. The truth was that he would gladly spend the day within the confines of the room with her. The softness of her touch and the scent from her hair encompassed him and all thoughts of their quest, of the dangers they had faced, and the threat to Heavenshire faded into the background. He lifted her and effortlessly carried her to the couch where he gently sat with her in his lap. She tilted her head back slightly to look into his eyes, and he looked full into hers. There was not a sound in the room, as if reality held its breath to see what would happen next.

Their eyes were locked together for several long seconds, and it seemed so natural for Mike to lower his head and allow his lips to brush against Mary's. His world contracted to consist solely of that touch. He felt the softness of her lips in contrast to the hardness of her well-muscled body. He drank in the sweetness of her breath as they kissed lightly and then with more force, as if a hunger had grown so large that it must be assuaged. After several moments Mike became aware of a growing clamor outside the Inn that demanded his attention. There was true regret in his eyes as he released Mary and slid her from his lap as he stood. He did not miss the longing look on Mary's face when he walked to the window. It shuttered against the chill of the early spring morning, and he opened it only a tiny bit.

The street was filled with the militia as it marched towards the town square. The sidewalks were filled with cheering civilians—men, women, and children. The cavalry led the procession followed by the infantry. Mike could see that the gallows had been converted to a reviewing stand that was filled with dignitaries. Mary joined him and the two exchanged glances, knowing that they would have to depart that night. She left to dress for the day, and Mike watched the Army's arrival. The mayor made a speech recounting the militia's victory and praising Captain Gandy for his exploits. The mayor's speech ended and those assembled waited for the Captain to speak.

"Left to my own, there would have been a monumental disaster, and Blackthorn Hearth would be in the hands of the enemy." These words quelled all conversation among the crowd. "Had we not been graced by the appearance of a pair of forest rangers, all would have been lost. They trained and taught the militia and fought with such bravery as is the stuff of legend. They left us for a quest of their own and forbade us from using their names. This wonderful and mighty Pair was the salvation of Blackthorn Hearth. Let our thanks ring out to them, wherever they are." There was a short pause as the crowd digested the meaning of these words, but then the militia began a cheer that was taken up by the crowd and lasted for many minutes.

Mike turned to Mary who had rejoined him at the window. "That will make things difficult," he said. His eyes widened as he saw Mary had dressed in her finery and was laying out similar clothing for Mike.

"Perhaps we should not look like warriors, but be remembered as something else?" She laughed as he could only stare. "Don't worry, I shall let no other knight ride to my rescue."

CHAPTER TWELVE

It was three days later when the Pair met Alexar at a dwarf outpost. They were once again in their Ranger garb and were greeted warmly by the dwarves. "Ye need nae worry about spies here. This bae all one clan, and we don't hold wit' anything tae do with tha Dark One." They traveled on foot with the dwarves for a week until they reached a mountain deep in the dwarven lands. Heavily fortified walls and gates set into the mountain were the entrance to the King under the Mountain's hold.

They were escorted through a maze of tunnels ornately decorated with metals and gems. They were shown to apartments where they changed into formal clothing in preparation for meeting the King. They emerged a short time later, and Mike again enjoyed Mary's transformation from warrior to beautiful woman. She paused and took time to straighten the collar on Mike's formal blouse and to tuck a wayward strand of hair into place. She smiled and told him that he looked wonderful, to which he snorted and would have made a retort except their escort was waiting. Instead he whispered, "Guess you're just stuck with this for now."

They were escorted to a silver door that opened into a fantastic hall that seemed to be made entirely of silver. They waited at the door to be announced and then walked side by side to the dais that held a golden throne. They paused and bowed their heads to King Kextar, and Mike spoke the traditional greeting, "Greetings, King under the Mountain, may your halls be ever straight and strong and may your forges ring with the sounds of the smiths forever."

The King rose and welcomed them to the dais where they were seated while the King addressed those assembled, giving a brief history of the Pair's activities in Heavenshire. He concluded, "These Heroes have now come to us for a great quest to return the Hammer of Silverthorn to its rightful place in the hall of the King Under the Mountain." The hall erupted in cheers, and the King waited for silence to fall again. "Our own favorite son, Alexar, has dedicated himself to this quest and will accompany the Pair." There was even louder cheering and the King waited patiently for it to end. "Now we will show the *Pair* how dwarves entertain their guests." This signaled a long evening of dinner and dancing.

The Elves' dances had been formal and reserved, but those of the dwarves were fast and unrestrained. There was no shortage of dance partners for either Mary or Mike, and both were exhausted when they finally returned to the apartment and retired to their separate beds.

They were served breakfast in the common room of their suite where they found more books. Most dealt with mining, refining ore, or working metals. Mike noted that steel was rarely mentioned in the books and made a note to ask Alexar why this was so. They were left alone for most of the day until Alexar arrived late in the afternoon laden with maps. The trio poured over them and chose a route that would keep them from passing too close to the Dark

One's strongholds. Their destination was a mountain that was part of the range where the Dark Lord reigned. Silverthorn's hammer was in a city long abandoned by the dwarves because of the presence of the Dark Lord's minions. Alexar showed them the location of a gate that had been sealed magically many decades before that the orcai would not bother to guard. Once the gate was opened, it would only be a matter of time before the breach was discovered. They would have to travel fast and avoid fighting when they could.

The journey would last well into the fall and perhaps winter. They would have to be out of the mountains before winter set in; the prospect of being caught on the mountain in a blizzard was not pleasant. Plans were made to leave in the morning, and the dwarf bid the Pair good night. Mike would have retired to his room except that Mary caught his arm.

"Is there something wrong between us?" she asked. "Since that morning in Blackthorn Hearth, you've pulled back from me. Are you ashamed that you kissed me?"

Mike turned to the worried woman. "Absolutely not! I would not trade those few moments for any other in my life."

"I sense a 'but' coming. I do not need magic to see that," Mary said wryly.

"Yes, there is a 'but' and it is this: But there is too much at stake for me to lose control of my feelings like that. You remember that Bardwind said we must work as partners. I am afraid that to…to change. I think.…" He faltered and then proceeded, "Mary, you are my dearest friend in this or any other world. There is nothing in any world that could entice me to ruin that friendship. What we have is special, deeper than some 'loves' I have seen. If we change that now—"

"But," Mary started and then thought better of what she was going to say. "I know what you mean. There is too much at stake for personal feelings." She turned quickly so that he would not see the tears in her eyes and strode quickly to her bedroom, slamming the door behind her.

Mike called her name and started for the door, but she did not hear. He hung his head and slowly turned to his bedroom. For the first time be began to question the task before them. Why him? Why should he be denied happiness at just the moment it seemed in his grasp? He had almost forgotten that he had ever had a different life, but then the memories flooded in on him. The image of his first wife floated before his eyes, just as he had seen her on that fateful day. She had only been going to town; she had not planned on stopping at the bank. She had not planned on being the victim of a senseless crime.

> He prepared supper that night, complete with candles and soft music. The knock at the door was unexpected, but when Mike saw the Sheriff's face, he knew the news the man bore. The shock drove Mike into a kind of insanity. He descended into the dregs of society and tracked his wife's killer to a meth lab in a run-down part of town. No one, not even Mike, knew what had taken place in that seedy house. The investigators knew there had been a fight and that the criminal had shot Mike. There was an explosion and only Mike survived. His

broken body healed but he was changed, withdrawn. He remained so until he met Mary.

Their meeting seemed to be coincidence. They both tried to hail the last cab from the airport on a frigid Christmas Eve. In the end they shared the ride, and Mike gave Mary a business card that he thought she would never use. She probably would not have, except that her car broke down late at night that New Year's Eve. She saw the card in her purse as she searched for someone to help her and remembered that he said he was good with cars. He drove to where she was stranded and was able to get her car running. She insisted on buying him breakfast, for by then the sun was rising, and they immediately became good friends.

He turned back to Mary's door and walked over to it. Just before he knocked he could hear her sobbing. The sound tore at his heart like a physical blow. He knocked and called out to her. She replied that she wasn't dressed, and he just said, "I'm sorry." There was something in the tone of his voice that touched her. Even though she was fully dressed, she swept the coverlet from the bed, wrapped it around her, and opened the door. He was halfway across the room, and his face looked haunted when he turned to her. His pain was obvious, and she could not be angry.

"Let's talk tomorrow," she said and watched him enter his bedroom. His shoulders were sagging, and it seemed that he bore the weight of the world. She resolved that she would not push him, but to trust in the dream that she had dreamed at the Haven.

The next morning when Mike tried to speak, Mary shushed him. "I know how you feel about me. I will endeavor to rest secure in that knowledge until you can come to me. Just don't wait too long!"

CHAPTER THIRTEEN

Abstidian arrived in Blackthorn Hearth to find the city still celebrating its victory even though word had arrived of the fall of much of the southern kingdom. He found the citizens eager to recount the exploits of their militia and to point out the heroes of the battle. He began to work his way closer to the one identified as the great leader who had defeated the orcai. After a period of two weeks, he had become a regular at the man's favorite tavern. Abstidian could hardly believe that this man could have led troops to defeat his hordes; the man seemed barely capable of leading the tavern patrons in a song.

The alchemist bided his time and made himself familiar with the man's routine. There was a certain woman that the man visited often, and Abstidian deduced that this must be the woman of the prophecies although she was no beauty and did not seem capable of bearing more than children. The alchemist chose a time for his attack and carefully set a trap.

He took a piece of split firewood, carefully hollowed it out, and filled it with the last of the explosive potion he carried. The man always gathered an armload of wood when he arrived, always from the same end of the stack. Abstidian had noticed that the smoke from the fireplace always increased soon after the man entered, so he knew the logs went directly on the fire. The alchemist was waiting in the shadows when the man arrived and grabbed the armload of firewood. Abstidian cast a silence spell around the cottage and held it until the flash of light came from inside. Soon the interior of the cottage was filled with flame and neighbors were gathering.

Someone from the crowd called out, "Captain Gandy's horse is here. He must have been inside!" Several men tried to enter the cottage, but were driven back by the flames. Abstidian joined the crowd in lamenting the loss of the Hero of Blackthorn Hearth, leaving only after the flames had burned out and the remains of two bodies were pulled from the ruins. He left the city secure in the knowledge that the Pair had been destroyed.

Days later he was enjoying the hospitality of the Kingdom of Raimbre as he wove his web of deceit around its king. It took less than a week for him to convince the King to join the Dark Lord and send troops to consolidate the victories the hordes had won. He found it more difficult to spread his darkness among men, but he did find some who unwittingly accepted the darkness. A few setbacks to the Dark Lord's plan still remained—not all of the objectives had been reached—but the tide had turned toward the dark forces. He returned to the Dark Mountain to again meet with his master.

CHAPTER FOURTEEN

The land of the dwarves was mostly wilderness. A majority of the dwarves lived underground, and only a few men lived within their borders. Still there were scattered farms where men and dwarves raised crops or livestock to support the underground cities. These small farms welcomed the travelers warmly and provided food and shelter in exchange for news. Alexar was well known, and it was apparently not unusual for him to travel among the towns, so few questions were asked. Mike and Mary were worried about the news of the war, but the dwarf kept them convinced that they must continue their quest.

They were forced into long detours by the fall of Raimbre to the Dark Lord. They had to approach the Dark Mountain from a treacherous wilderness that was the home of many trolls and ogres. These creatures were evil and fought often among themselves, but they were not hard to avoid; the small band found themselves in the foothills of the Dark Mountain as fall began. One night as Alexar regaled the Pair with legends about the mountains. Mike asked him about steel and was very surprised at the dwarf's answer.

"Aire ye daft, man? The entire reason for this quest is the key to producing steel! Silverthorn was tha greatest of all tha Dwarven metal smiths. He discovered how ta add charcoal ta iron tae produce steel, but his arrogance cost him, and our entire race, tha secret. He set his forge in tha range o' tha Dark Mountain and eventually awakened the servants o' tha Dark One. They destroyed his clan and set his hammer inside a stone on tha forge where he had created steel. It is said only one who is pure o' heart and strong o' both mind and body can retrieve it. Once in every generation a dwarf is sent tae attempt tae retrieve it; I have been selected from this generation. Some of tha prophesies mention a pair o foreigners who will aid in the recovery of Silverthorn's hammer. I pray tha' ye be tha' Pair. Tomorrow we will reach the gate, and you will see the result of Silverthorn's pride."

The next morning was cold; the group traveled quickly. They had walked the entire way; dwarves rarely used horses. This had served them well in the lands of the trolls and ogres. Mike secretly feared it would be their downfall on the return journey. They would undoubtedly be pursued and would also be racing against the onset of winter. He never mentioned his misgivings to either Mary or Alexar, but he felt that Mary shared them. They had regained much of their closeness, although the memories of those days in Blackthorn Hearth were never far from Mike's mind. They halted a half-mile from the gate, and Mike scouted the path. He encountered a dead body in dwarven armor. It had been nearly ripped apart. Its armor was shredded and the bones mangled. Mike silently slipped past and reached a vantage point where he could see the gate.

The gate stood open and bones and debris littered the ground in front of it. Mike could identify pieces of dwarven armor and weapons strewn around the entrance. He did not have to wonder for long what sort of creature could cause such destruction. It exited through the gate and stood, nose to the wind. It was huge. The lower body was that of a massive bull, but it had a torso of a man and the head of a jackal. Mike could smell its stench on the wind that blew in his face. The creature looked downwind towards him and then began to pick through the debris in front of the gate.

Alexar's expression was grave at the news. "This bae a creature spawned in the lowest depths of Hades. It was probably created tae hunt dwarves, so we have tha advantage. I will give it what it seeks, and the three o' us will kill it." Mike had some suggestions to modify that plan and Alexar accepted most of them. He remained adamant that he would face the beast and draw it out.

The next morning they were in sight of the gate at the same hour the creature had emerged the day before. Only, to their dismay, a figure on the ground was bound hand and foot. Alexar roared and sprang forward, slicing the bonds with his ax. The figure scrambled to its feet, and Alexar shoved it away from the gate as he backed towards his original position. It was a dwarf child, and she was almost too terrified to run. From inside the mountain the drumming of hooves could be heard, and the beast burst through the gates only seconds later.

Alexar stood his ground and shouted a challenge at the beast. It was startled for an instant then its lips curled back in a sneer. "So the chosen of the dwarves arrives today. I thought that too much of the year had passed. I will dine well today." It charged Alexar, and the dwarf met it with ax and shield. The impact threw the dwarf ten feet and the beast laughed. "Do you run or fight? Each time, that was the question. Each time the result was the same." It reared up on its hind legs and an arrow blossomed from the juncture of man and beast. Another arrow struck its chest, and a third hit just below the second. Alexar was back on his feet and charging the creature. Mike had covered most of the distance between him and the beast when its feet hit the ground. He struck at the shoulder of the bull and found that the creature's skin was nearly as hard as rock. Its screams were deafening as Alexar struck with his axe. Its flailing arms knocked dwarf and man to the ground as other arrows found their mark. Nothing penetrated very deep; all three warriors pressed their assaults, keeping the creature off guard.

The dwarf's helmet was gone, and Mike felt as though a tree had struck him. The creature was bleeding but did not seem to tire at all. It reared once more as something brushed past Mike's leg. It was the child; she carried a spear nearly twice her height. She ran under the beast and knelt, holding the spear braced against the ground. Alexar and Mike screamed with one voice, "No!" The beast turned towards them and did not see the girl beneath it. Its hooves crashed to the ground, and the spear pierced it from belly to back. It roared in pain and outrage, then rose again on its back feet. Mike rushed in and grabbed the child as Alexar swung his ax with all his strength, splitting the chest of the beast. Both warriors sprung away as it crashed to the ground with Alexar's ax still embedded in its chest.

Silence reigned for several long seconds, and Mike became aware of the child struggling in his grasp. He released her, and she ran to Alexar who gathered her in his blood-stained arms. "Is it dead?" she asked as she buried her head in the dwarf's beard.

"Aye, Lassie, ye have killed tha beast. As it is written, 'a child shall deliver them from tha beast.' What aire ye doing out here?" Alexar held the sobbing child until her tears slowed. "We have ta get ye inside, Lassie. Come on, no one will harm ye." He carried the child through the gate and inside the ancient underground city. He did not let her look as they passed the beast's lair, and they traveled a good distance farther before they stopped.

Mike had lit a torch, and Alexar chose a door set in the side of the tunnel and ushered the group inside. He found a chain and pulled it, opening louvers that flooded the chamber with light. The dwarf child turned her head away when Mary tried to speak to her, and Alexar spoke gently. "These bae friends, child, they will not harm ye. Now show yer manners and speak to them."

The child kept a firm grip on Alexar, but stood and whispered, "Thank you for saving me, my name is Niatia." She curtsied and retreated to Alexar, eyes still wide in fear.

Mary lowered to her knees beside the dwarves and spoke gently. "Niatia, what a special name. You are a very brave girl to attack the beast like that. I am Lady Marilyn, and the big man over there is my friend Sir Michael. Are there any other children near here?"

The child began to cry again. "I was the last one. They said they were gonna git more. I don't know. Something was going to happen. A man, like him," she inclined her head towards Mike, "came and told the orcs a story. They cheered and screamed and danced a lot. Then a lot of them left, and I was took to the beast." Mary offered her water and the child drank deeply. Mike brought some of the elven travel bread out and offered it to her. At first she was reluctant to take it, but after she tasted it, she thanked him and asked for more, adding please to her request.

Alexar was finally able to disentangle himself from the child, found some bedding, and convinced the girl to sleep. Once the girl was sleeping, the three discussed their options. Alexar had only his belt knife for a weapon, and Mary had expended nearly a third of her arrows. They knew time would be against them now, and the child was an entirely new factor. "Do nae worry, she'll be able ta keep up. She'll hide when we tell her to. She's brave enough, we all saw that. We'll just have ta make do."

They allowed the girl an hour's nap and then they were on their way. The chamber where Silverthorn's hammer was enshrined was several hours' journey into the mountain. They traveled silently with all three taking turns carrying the girl. In a chamber similar to the one they had rested in, they found clothing and a pair of boots that fit the girl. They allowed her to walk for short periods, but still carried her much of the way. Finally they reached the city. The louvers that allowed sunlight into the underground city were open, but the light was failing as night fell outside of the mountain.

Alexar led them to a building within the great cavern that was obviously not dwarf's handiwork. It was built into the side of the cavern and was crude and simple. They entered and found that it was just an entrance to another small cavern. The scent of orcai was heavy in the air, and they were very cautious. In the center of the cavern was a stone table that was carved from mountain itself. At its center was a forge hammer, the handle of which was set deep into the table. There was another door on the far side of the cavern. Mike approached that door as Alexar approached the hammer, Niatia at his side.

The dwarf rubbed his hands together and grasped the head of the hammer and pulled, but the hammer did not budge even though he exerted all his strength. He just fell to his knees and dropped his head. Niatia walked around in front of him and drew his hands back to the hammer, this time on the handle. She then grasped it also and pulled. The hammer moved slightly. Alexar raised his head and then lifted with all of his strength again. The hammer rose with a rasping noise as dwarf and child, together, withdrew it from the stone. In that instant, Mike heard a noise from the other side of the door and drew his sword. The sound was that of a bolt being withdrawn, and Mike shouted over his shoulder, "Run!" The others sprinted as the door in front of Mike burst open and disgorged a stream of orcs. He fought as he retreated, but there were already over fifty orcs in the room with more coming.

Mary was at the far door, shouting for him to hurry, but Mike could see that there was no hope for him to reach the door. "Go, you must bolt the door behind you." He turned to the fight and cleared some room in front of him and glanced at the door. Niatia and Alexar were dragging Mary through the door, which slammed shut. He turned back to the battle and fought furiously, knowing that every minute he delayed this force would give them a much better chance to escape. In the end, the orcs overwhelmed him by piling enough bodies, living, dead, and dying, on him that he could no longer breathe. He woke a few seconds later to the sound of the orcs pounding on the door the others had escaped through.

Mary screamed at the dwarf as he dropped the heavy beam into place to bar the door. "We can't leave him." She drew her sword as though she would force him to open the door.

"Thar bae another way!" Alexar screamed back at her. "We must hurry, but we can ambush them." Mary sheathed her sword and he turned; they began to run through the city. Niatia was amazingly swift on her feet, and it seemed they would reach the ambush in time. Disaster struck as they careened around a turn right into the midst of a force of at least a hundred orcai.

Alexar and Mary placed Niatia between them, and she drew her sword while he raised Silverthorn's hammer. There was silence. An orc sheathed its sword and stepped forward. It removed a water skin from its belt and tossed it to Mary. She recognized the orc, uncorked the skin, and drank, handing it to Alexar and telling him to do likewise. She used her left hand to pull a ration pouch from her belt and tossed it to the orc. He took a small bite and passed it around to the other orcai. Then he said, "Woman, we meet again. Must come quickly." As Mary began to protest he repeated himself. "Save big man later. First you come!" Mary shrugged and sheathed her sword, motioning him to lead on.

They traveled a short distance; the orc leader stopped and opened one of the small chambers set into the tunnel walls. He motioned to Niatia, and she peeked through the door; she squealed and ran inside. Mary followed to find five dwarf children gathered around Niatia.

The orc leader spoke. "This all we save. Beast not know difference between dwarf child and wild pig. We sad we not save more." Alexar stepped forward and reached out his hand. After a moment's hesitation the orc clasped forearms with the dwarf.

Alexar spoke. "Tha' ye saved this many has earned my thanks."

The orc leader dropped his hand. "Little one, stay here, safe. We go save big man. Must hurry." Niatia did not protest for long as the other children hugged her. The armed group then ran through a series of tunnels and paused outside a small chamber. Mary and Alexar were loosely bound, and the group entered the chamber and waited.

The orcs were unable to force the door open, and their leader stood over Mike where he lay bound. "You meet Dark Lord now. Him wait long time for chosen man. Now all Overworld see that Dark Lord not be beaten." Mike was kicked and punched to his feet, then led by a leather thong around his neck. He tried to delay by stumbling, but the orcs just pushed him back to his feet and shoved him along. He had been warned that he would have no magic this near the Dark Lord, and he found it to be true. He was led through dark tunnels and caverns until they were met by another group. This group had two prisoners—Mary and Alexar.

CHAPTER FIFTEEN

The two bands of orcai mingled while the leaders spoke. One squad leader turned away from the other for a second while it drew a dagger, and then turned and plunged it into the other's heart. This was a signal for Mary's group; soon there were none of the first group left standing. When it was over a shocked Mary asked, "Why?"

"Them kill childs" was the only answer. "We must go now, take childs with you. You must be out of mountain before day. Hurry!" When Mike would have thanked him, he pushed him towards the exit. "Go. We meet again, talk then."

The children were ready to go when they reached the chamber. The orcai had given them clothes and boots, so there was no delay. The entire troop ran until they reached the gate where Mike insisted that he and Mary scout the area. Vultures and a wild boar contested for the body of the beast, but no sign of other activity was visible. Mike drove the scavengers away long enough to retrieve the spear and the remains of Alexar's ax. They returned and ushered the group out as far as they could travel by daybreak. The small band took shelter under a rock outcropping and rested. At about midday a great flock of ravens could be seen spreading out across the countryside.

"Those are the Dark One's spies," Mary whispered. "We must be careful until we leave the lands of the trolls and ogres. If we are spotted they will hunt us down." The next day brought snow and even greater hardships for the group. A week later they emerged from the badlands and sought out a small outpost where they left most of the children. Alexar insisted on bringing Niatia with them and even consented to riding the rest of the way.

The corridors of the palace of the King under the Mountains were packed with dwarves in all manner of finery. The crowd parted as if by magic as the quartet rushed towards the throne room. They paused only long enough for a hurried announcement and strode towards the dais. King Kextar rose and Alexar ran up the steps to place the hammer in his King's hands. He then motioned Niatia forward. "It was the hands of this child that drew forth the Hammer."

The girl was trying to hide behind Alexar and to see the King at the same time. King Kextar knelt and took her by the hand. "You need never fear again. We know your parents were killed when you were taken, and I have sent messengers to find any relatives that you might have. You shall always have a seat at my table, and I shall be glad to call you my daughter if you will allow it." A mighty cheer erupted from those inside the throne room and spread throughout the palace.

Mike stood at the bottom step of the dais and spoke into the silence that followed. "Oh Mighty King under the Mountain, here is the spear that Niatia used to mortally wound the beast, and the pieces of Alexar's ax that brought its reign of terror to an end." He bowed and laid them on the top step and backed away.

There was silence in the room for several seconds and then a great cheer erupted from the crowd. The Pair slipped away and made their way through the crowd to the apartments where they had first stayed. An hour later they rejoined the celebration, ate, and danced long into the night. The dwarves were still going strong when they retired to their rooms. Mike desperately needed silence, and Mary just wanted to rest. The celebration was still going on the next morning when they woke and met in the common room of their suite. Mary summed it up. "Just think, something that has been denied them for hundreds of years has been restored. Even more than that, one of the oldest of their prophecies has been fulfilled." Mike nodded and was nearly dozing when she slapped him hard on the arm.

He shook his head. "What?" His puzzled expression earned him another slap on the arm.

"That is for making me leave you behind! Do you have any idea what that did to me, seeing you facing certain doom? I was ready to fight Alexar!"

Mike reached out and took Mary's hand. "I cannot imagine. If the roles were reversed, well, I do not think I could let you go. I probably would have foolishly rushed in without counting the cost. It is good that you have more sense than me. Today I am tired. I wonder if this quest will ever be fulfilled. I wonder if I have the strength to follow through." He released her and stood, facing a tapestry that decorated the wall. "You are my strength, and I am such a fool!"

Mary stood and wrapped her arms around him from behind. "You are no fool. If anything you are too noble a man for one such as me. You always seem to know what is right, and you do it—no matter what it may cost you. I would have gone insane in this place long ago if it wasn't for you. This is so fantastic and, well, in a way I don't want it to end. When our task here is done, what then? My old life could never be as fulfilling, and you. You cannot possibly know how much you have changed! You are confident, bold, and strong. You are so handsome that I will never be able to compete for your attention."

Mike turned to where he could drape an arm around her. He smiled as he said, "I doubt that I would notice anyone but you. You have changed as well, and talk about a—" He was interrupted by a hurried knocking at the door. A messenger had arrived with disturbing news. Captain Gandy had been killed in a freak accident. Captain Norris suspected that there was more to it than a simple cottage fire. He was informing the Elves in hopes they would contact Bardwind. In the meantime he requested that the rangers, Mike and Mary, return to Blackthorn Hearth to look for clues.

They discussed these events and sent a return message that they would come as soon as possible. Then Mike began to search for Alexar. He was nowhere to be found in the celebration; Mike finally located him at his forge. He was stripped to the waist and sweated over thin plates of metal that he repeatedly struck with Silverthorn's hammer. Mike watched as the dwarf worked charcoal into the metal and then heated it and folded it and worked it back into plates. When the Dwarf had finished he showed Mike the result. "Stronger than plate, four times as thick. This will make armor fit for heroes." He listened to Mike's story and replied, "I'll need ye both for two days to take measurement and make molds. Then ye can leave for a fortnight while I forge enough steel for the armor. Then ye should come back for the final fitting. It will be tha height of winter by then, and ye'll not enjoy travel, but I think ye'll best return to the Elves. Come back in tha morning, first thing."

Mike started to leave and then remembered something. "King Arnyea said that there was Elven Silver to be added to the armor and that Mary and I would need to perform a spell as the metal was forged."

Alexar nodded. "Aye, that bae called the shinin.' It makes the plate reflect e'en tha smallest amount o' light. In light o' wha hae happened in tha town, ye shud go. Thar bae clerics here tha can say tha words. Now off wit ye, yer woman friend will bae wantin' tae see ya no doubt. Can't say I understand why, the way ya string her along…" The dwarf's words were lost in the ringing of the hammer as he began forging another billet of steel.

The next morning was filled with activity. Alexar had several assistants ready, including Niatia, who measured, checked, and rechecked every conceivable aspect of their bodies. The Pair were sent away and told to return late in the afternoon. When they did return they were met with sculptures that were almost embarrassingly exact. Mike joked that they had missed a mole on his back and had to spend several minutes explaining that there was no mole, that he was joking. Mary asked the dwarf if she had to maintain the exact weight she was now and he laughed. The armor would adjust to a few pounds in either direction, but that she should make sure that Mike did not develop a taste for rich food and mead.

They returned for the final check the next afternoon and found that the dwarves had created stiffened leather mock-ups of the armor, complete with helms, boots, and gauntlets. Alexar fussed with the fit just like a tailor and eventually proclaimed them adequate. He promised to have the armor complete in two weeks, and the Pair was soon on their way.

CHAPTER SIXTEEN

Blackthorn Hearth had changed greatly in the time they were gone. The city walls had been reinforced and a palisade erected a bow's shot beyond the walls. The defenses were manned, and there was evidence of continuous patrol activity. The Pair avoided the patrols out of habit and were challenged at the gate to the palisade. They were quickly escorted to a redoubt where Captain Norris was overseeing the construction of a catapult. He immediately left the project in the hands of a subordinate and escorted them to a burned out cottage. He showed them to a section of wall that had not burned completely. Mary looked closely and noticed small splinters embedded in the wall as though driven into it from the room. The surface of the wood was burned, but she was able to dig a few splinters out with her knife.

Mike poked through the fireplace and was puzzled by a faint sulfurous odor. He asked Captain Norris, who explained that the odor had been heavy during and after the fire. The fireplace had collapsed, but was fairly free of ash. The local constable had theorized that a gust of wind had swept down the fireplace and pushed burning embers into the room. "Something pushed fire into the room all right, but it was not a natural wind," Mike said. A few moments later he found a charred end to a piece of firewood. "Look, there was a hole bored in this log, and it was stopped with wax. There are probably some traces of wax on the side of the fireplace. I believe this log was hollowed out and filled with gunpowder." Captain Norris just gave a blank stare.

"Gunpowder, an explosive mixture of sulfur, saltpeter, and charcoal. It is the substance that caused the explosion at the orcai camp. Are you not familiar with it?" Mike had assumed that gunpowder was used in this realm since the orcai possessed it.

"No, I do not know this magical mixture," replied Captain Norris. "I thought the blast at the orcai camp was your magic. I know of sulfur and charcoal, but saltpeter is unknown to me, perhaps the elves or dwarves know of it. You believe this magic was used here?"

"Yes, someone bored a hole in a piece of firewood and filled it with the powder. They used wax to stop the end of the log and probably left it on the pile outside. Gandy probably brought it in and put it on the fire. The wax melted and the fire ignited the powder. It exploded and threw burning coals throughout the cottage," Mike explained.

"Yes and it also threw wood splinters through the room. Gandy and whoever else was in here were probably injured. There seems to be blood on these splinters I dug out of the wall. This was no accident. It was murder!" Mary exclaimed.

"Yes, it would appear so. Gandy was not the object of this scheme either. I believe that whoever did this thought he was killing the two of you!" Captain Norris said. "The town's folk had been calling him 'The Hero of Blackthorn Hearth,' buying him plenty of mead and meals. The widow who owned this cottage was quite interested in him. Her son is a teamster who took freight north every week. Gandy would show up here an hour after he left the gates, every week."

Mike and Mary looked at each other for a long moment and then Mike grinned slightly. "Likely the Dark One believes us to be dead. That at least is to our advantage. We must leave quickly before anyone recognizes us. You must swear all who we have spoken with to secrecy. Let the town believe that their hero died in this fire. Maybe he can be more inspiration in death than he was in life."

Captain Norris accompanied them to the gate. "I wish I could provide you with hospitality. I am gravely concerned about this gunpowder. Even if it is a crude mixture, it is something that we have no defense against."

Mike frowned, "I may be able to show you the ingredients, but I do not remember the correct ratios. Saltpeter can be found anywhere that carcasses have been allowed to rot. It can also be made from dung. I will show you how that is done. I do not think that it is readily available here. With any luck we will have destroyed all the gunpowder that the enemy has produced. I did not hear any stories of it being used in other battles. We will camp for a day outside of town. Come, and I will show you what I know."

Mary turned several interesting shades of green as Mike described a method for creating saltpeter. Captain Norris was amused and predicted that he knew some alchemists who could perfect a better method. The captain was somewhat reassured that gunpowder was not easy to produce and left to return to the defense of Blackthorn Hearth.

"Dung and urine? That was the best method you could remember!" Mary exclaimed. "That is so sick that I cannot begin to tell you." She was cut off by Mike's laughter. "What is so funny? Oh, you're impossible, you're such a, such a man!" She stomped her foot and glared at Mike. He began to feel a little warm, then hot. He swept his hat from his head as it began to smolder. Mary clapped her hand to her mouth and gasped. "I was only thinking the word. I did not even whisper it."

Mike looked at her in admiration. "You have become a full sorceress, my dear. Remember that in this realm, looks can kill. Remind me that I want to stay on your good side." His humor was infectious, and she was soon joking with him about the things she would do to him if he really made her mad.

CHAPTER SEVENTEEN

The dwarves were happy that they returned early. Mike immediately asked Alexar about saltpeter; the dwarf referred them to an old patriarch of the clan who took Mike to the slaughterhouse. There he led Mike to a chamber that had several hundred pounds of a white salt-like substance. He said it was a by-product of the rendering process. The dwarves wasted nothing of the animals they used for meat and had found that this substance could help preserve meat for travel. He also showed him another chamber where there were piles of a yellow powdery substance. He explained that some veins of coal produced a foul-smelling smoke and had to be refined. The yellow powder was a by-product, and they had found limited use for it—treating certain wounds to prevent them from festering.

Mike asked to borrow several pounds of each and a place to work. Through trial and error he discovered ratios that would flash when ignited; he knew he had the crude beginning to gunpowder. He knew that the mixture was more stable if it were mixed with a reagent and formed into cakes, dried, and ground into powder. After a week of further trial and error, he had found a workable method and produced about five pounds of passable gunpowder. He used some scraps of parchment to make the equivalent of firecrackers and asked if he might demonstrate for the king.

The demonstration was held outside of the city on the surface. Mike began by igniting loose powder to create a flash of light and worked up to the firecrackers. The King was amused but he really did not see an application for this noisemaker. Mike's final demonstration was to blow a small boulder to pieces. He explained that this could be used for better efficiency in mines, if done with care. The King was enthused at this prospect and asked what other uses there were for this powder. Mike only told him that there were as many uses as the imagination could create, but would not go into details. He knew that this place had little need for the advanced weapons that could now be created, and he did not want to introduce them. The Dark One's advantage would be nullified, and that was all he wished to do.

The armor was soon ready, and both Mary and Mike were astounded. The suits were works of art with intricate etchings as decorations and articulated joints that moved effortlessly. Mary's helm gave her face the look of a great lion. Mike's gave the impression of a great eagle. The fit was perfect; it looked as though the Pair were creatures of metal who moved with the grace of animals. Alexar regarded them with pride.

"Tha' bae my finest work. Tha only problem is that you'll bae recognized as the Chosen Ones at first sight. I recommend that ye pack this away until yer time o' greatest need, or until the war begins in earnest. Get ye on yer way. Tha elves don't wait well, fer all their braggin' about patience! We shall meet again my friends." At that moment Niatia zoomed into the room and wrapped herself around Mary's neck.

"Tell me you'll come back. I helped with the armor, you have to come back, you have to." The young girl regained her composure and continued. "The King sends his compliments and bids you farewell. He shall meet you at the appointed time and place. He says that you must make haste for the snows come and your journey will be difficult." She bowed, hugging Mary again, and timidly wrapped her arms around Mike's neck.

They were soon outside of the mountain and the air was chill. A few flakes of snow were on the wind; they hurried north towards Blackthorn Hearth. The bypassed the city and struck out along the river. At the trading post where they had first encountered the orcai they were surprised to be greeted by the woman they had saved. A barracks and a company of infantry were stationed there. Their lieutenant had bad news; most of the waypoints were in enemy hands and few supplies could get through. Occasionally the army would clear the way for a convoy to make it down river, but they could not hold the entire river. It was a one-way trip, the boats and rafts were dismantled, and the crews would make their way back over land. A crew had passed through earlier that day, and it would be safer to travel in numbers. Mike smiled and said they would leave in the morning. They enjoyed the widow's hospitality and were on their way early the next morning.

They quickly caught up with the crew, and Mike was pleased to find the same river men they had traveled down the river with. Their journey was uneventful with Mary and Mike scouting for the party. They avoided trouble and traveled swiftly. A week from the trading post, they encountered snow and the captain reckoned that they had made their last trip for the season. Another week later they parted ways just one day's travel from the King's city. The river men could not understand why the pair wouldn't join them for the winter, but they bade warm farewells, the only warmth Mike and Mary would know for some time.

CHAPTER EIGHTEEN

Three weeks later they reached the entrance to the valley that sheltered Elvhome. They were nearly frozen, and the horses were so weak they could barely walk. The Pair had lightened their load to only the essentials: food, weapons, and armor. Their meager supplies were in a makeshift sled that Mike now pulled as he walked in front of the party to break an opening in a foot or so of snow so that the horses would continue to stagger forward. When the elven sentry appeared, his dulled mind prompted him to reach weakly for his sword, nearly collapsing on the elf. The elves quickly brought help and carried the travelers inside Elvhome.

The King insisted that they remain in bed for several days with constant attention from the healers. They were fortunate that they had been well prepared and did not lose fingers or toes to frostbite. Once they were able to walk about a bit, they were chagrined to find that their new armor hung loosely on their frames. The King and Queen laughed and informed them that their next quest could not be accomplished until spring, so there was ample time to regain their strength. The days passed swiftly, and they did regain their strength and continued their training. Mike demonstrated the blasting powder and showed the elves how to find the ingredients. They were reluctant to consider trading with the dwarves even for such a powerful substance. The King insisted that Mike preserve his small cache, saying it might be useful on their quest.

Mary spent much of her time working on magic with the elves until she had learned all they could teach her. Very few ever attained the level where they could will the magic without speaking the words. Many times the elves alluded to their quest, but never told them what it was. They continued to drill Mary in defensive and stealth spells until she was able to pass their most difficult tests with ease. Elsharone became a close friend; the two spent many afternoons together while Mike tried to find a way to produce blasting powder that did not involve decaying flesh, dung, or trade with the dwarves. The days quickly drew to a close, and the Pair again prepared to travel.

King Arnyea called them to his private study. His face was serious as he began to tell them of a prophesy that had never been shared with non-Elves. He revealed the existence of an ancient book that contained the great spells of Heavenshire. It had been hidden centuries before because of the extent of the power of the magic spells it contained. It was said that the spells that created the foundations of the world were contained in the book. It was written that at the time of the great battle that the book would be retrieved by the Chosen Pair. Their final task would be to cast one final spell that would allow the Elven race to ascend to their eternal reward. Only one who possessed great ability with magic would be able to decipher the ancient runes and start the great exodus. The book was hidden far to the west in a wilderness that once was the land of men and elves. They had been driven from the land as the result of a great sin. Mystical creatures guarded the book in a Grand Castle constructed of precious gems. Only true heroes who had demonstrated their love for the land and creatures of

Heavenshire would be able to enter. As a final test they would have to face the Guardian of the Tome.

No one knew what sort of creature the Guardian was. They only said that the Chosen Pair would have to choose correctly or they would be destroyed. There were clues in the castle, and it was predicted that the pure of heart would understand. Once the Pair obtained the book, they would have to fight the great evil that sought to attain its power. A servant of the Dark Lord slept in the wilderness and would be awakened when the Guardian was defeated.

The King finished and Queen Ilsidora spoke. "This is a quest that you must freely accept. If you do this for any but the purest of motives, you will be doomed, and all of Heavenshire with you. Please return to your quarters and discuss this quest with this thought in mind." The King and Queen rose and escorted them to the apartment. "You have all the time you need to decide. We cannot, indeed we would not, coerce you in any way. Remember, prophesies are very difficult to understand. You may not be those who are destined to perform this quest."

After the door closed Mike walked over to the sofa and sank slowly onto it. He laid his head back against the cushions and stared at the ceiling. He did not speak even when Mary sat beside him and put her head against his shoulder. They sat in silence for many minutes before he spoke. "This has to be your decision. We will have to rely heavily on your skill with magic."

"I know, and that scares me. The magic is so new, and I still find it hard to believe that I can do the things I do. What if it's not genuine? What if I can only perform like this in places like this, where there is no evil?" Mary rolled her head slightly and buried it against his chest. "What if

I cannot protect you? Leaving you in the clutches of the orcai back in the Dark Mountain was too hard. I would not have left unless Alexar and Niatia drug me away. What if I have to make that same choice when there is no one to drag me away? What if I have to choose between the quest and leaving you behind?" She stopped and just lay there against him, feeling the steady rise and fall of his breathing.

Silence reigned in the room for many minutes. "You would make the right decision," Mike said softly. "You do not give yourself enough credit." He wrapped his arms around her. "You have never given yourself enough credit. Always thinking some other woman is prettier or more talented. Have you ever looked at yourself? I mean really looked? Your picture could be on the cover of any fashion magazine, but more importantly, you are intelligent. You learn so quickly, and you know so much. It just seems that when the moment comes for you to really shine, you second guess yourself or you hesitate. If not you, then who can? They say you are the most adept sorceress of this generation. You are the prettiest woman I have ever seen. As for all the 'what if' questions, most of them will never come to pass. The only way to know is to take on the quest. "Do you know that I have asked myself most of those questions?" Mike paused, then continued. "Especially the one about leaving you behind. What would be better—to go down in an epic and glorious defeat, or to win the battle against impossible odds? I think that the bottom line is faith. This fantastic land was created by a power that I cannot imagine. That Creator has predicted that we would come. Surely He knows the outcome, and if He wants this world preserved, He would not send us on a futile quest. It may not be so important that I believe in you. It is important that the Creator believes in you."

Mary sat up. "Does He? I guess there is no other explanation; this place does not exist by chance. If we are not the Prophesied, then we cannot succeed, and it would be better to find that out before so much is committed to a final battle. If we are, then maybe we need this test to prove ourselves ready to fight the Dark Lord. Oh, Mike, what should we do? What should I do?"

"You must decide. Leave all doubt behind and choose. I believe in you, and I will go wherever you go." His eyes were so earnest that Mary was almost embarrassed. He believed in her. He wasn't like the boys in junior high who teased her because she was a chubby girl and slow to develop. He wasn't like the seniors in high school who wanted to date her when she grew slender and well developed. She did not know what it could be about her that he believed in, but he believed in the person she was. She could still hear his voice as they trudged through the snow. *"One foot in front of the other. Right, left, and repeat."* She could not guess how many miles they had walked with only his voice to guide her. Maybe he was right; maybe something unseen had kept him beside her.

Her thoughts turned to another man, one whom she had almost married. Her ex-fiancé, Rusty, had been very accommodating and always ready to compromise. There were few situations where he did not declare that a win-win situation had been achieved. Looking back, Mary wondered who had really won most of the time. Rusty had a way of convincing people that there was no black or white, just varying shades of gray. This was never more apparent than when Mary caught him with her maid of honor.

Mary could see the scene when she closed her eyes.

> She walked the short distance from her apartment to her best friend's house. There were some final details of the wedding to be worked out. Rusty's car was parked out of sight, so Mary was completely unprepared when she stepped past her friend and encountered him in the living room. There was a nearly empty wine bottle on the coffee table and two half-filled glasses. There was no mistaking where the evening had been headed. During the confrontation that followed, he had almost convinced her that she was wrong to be angry. Almost. In the end she had seen his carefully crafted arguments for the lies that they were. She had literally chased him to his car, brandishing the wine bottle. That was the final time she had seen him or the girl who would have stood beside her at her wedding.

Mary glanced at Mike and decided that there were many advantages to having a strong sense of right and wrong.

"Just promise me one thing," she said softly. "Promise me that you won't ask me to leave you behind!"

"This may not be the wisest promise you have asked of me. It could be your doom as well, but I promise." He was not joking now; his face was as serious as his words.

"I accept. Look, it is morning already. Let's go and tell the King and Queen of our choice."

CHAPTER NINETEEN

Their journey began with the onset of spring, and they were accompanied by the twins, Alsharon and Elsharone. Elves could not enter the castle grounds, but they would show the Pair the way to the gates. The snow was newly gone from the land, and the trees were just beginning to show their spring leaves. The quartet traveled quickly to the west and had soon left Elvhome a good distance behind them. The land was wild and untamed. The twins proved their usefulness almost immediately. They kept the group from invading the hunting grounds of the great bear, Ursa, and thereby earning its wrath. Alsharon had disappeared and upon his return ushered them silently to another path. Later that night he explained.

"I saw signs of Ursa along the path. He is perhaps the largest bear to have ever lived. His hunting grounds change with each season, and he is very protective of them so soon after hibernation. He was willing for us to pass, but we had to be gone before sunset. This is the way of the Elves—to cooperate with nature instead of conquering it. If I had not sought him out, he would have watched for a while. If we had taken game without his consent, he would have acted. I doubt that even your strength of arms would have prevailed for you would have been the unsuspected hunted. He may still visit our camp this night—he is curious about men who would show him respect." Alsharon smiled, "It would be a most memorable event."

Mike could see that Mary's eyes were large, and he had an uneasy feeling about facing a bear that wanted to see him. After the twins had bedded down, Mike asked, "Mary, which watch do you want? I am sure that I will not sleep unless I know someone is watching for this Ursa."

Mary shivered. "I would like the first watch. You will be asleep in a minute, but I doubt that I would sleep a wink. You are aware that elves posses a sense of humor, aren't you? This could be a joke, just like a snipe hunt."

"I hadn't thought of that. I hope it is a joke, but just in case, let's keep watch." He rolled his blanket out and, as Mary predicted, was soon asleep. It was a fitful sleep, filled with dreams of giant animals chasing him and trying to examine him. He woke instantly when Mary put her hand on his foot. She pointed to the far side of camp, and he saw the twins rise. Then the largest bear he had ever seen rose from the underbrush in front of them. The elves bowed, and the bear returned their bow.

The conversation was entirely silent, conducted by gestures. After a short while, Alsharon spoke. "Lady Marilyn, Sir Michael please come forward." The Pair exchanged glances and approached Ursa. They bowed when they reached the twins, and the huge bear bobbed its head. The massive bruin bent forward and sniffed each of the Pair in turn. Mike held his breath when Mary pushed the huge snout away after the bear's nose came too close to a sensitive area. He could have sworn the bear was laughing as it settled on its haunches. It extended a huge paw and showed its sharp claws. Mike responded by sliding his sword partway from its sheath and then back. Ursa nodded and spoke in a series of grunts and growls. Elsharone translated.

"As it is with forest creatures, you have met with me,

neither allowing excessive familiarity nor showing fear of tooth or claw. I meet you as equals, and you may walk my lands when you return. Your enemies shall be my enemies. There are strange creatures walking the night now. They have become allies with the wolves and jackals, even to the point where the great wolves allow them to ride on their backs. There are other creatures that I do not know of, old abominations of nature. I think the Dark One seeks to create new servants by combining the traits of ancient creatures. Beware these." Ursa waited.

Mike glanced at Mary and nodded slightly, asking her to respond. She drew a deep breath, bowed and spoke. "We are honored by the privilege that you grant us. We will do nothing to betray your trust. We cannot speak for all men of this realm, but, as far as we are able, you will not be troubled. Do you stand with us against the Dark One?"

Ursa replied, with Elsharone translating, "The affairs of men are of no importance to me. I will protect my land, and beyond that, I will do no more."

Mary bowed again. "As you will, it shall be. We shall speak to the King of the neighboring Kingdom on your behalf. I believe that an accommodation can be made that no man should enter your hunting ground unless he seeks your leave, and any that do are subject to your punishment."

The great bear shook his head in surprise and spoke with Elsharone at length. Finally he turned to Mary and again spoke through Elsharone. "I would never have expected men to behave with such honor, but the Elf assures me that such bargains are often struck between men and other creatures. I am pleased. I will seal our bargain as men do." He extended a massive paw to each of the Pair who placed their hands in it as best they could. "I will go now. You need fear nothing in my domain." With those words, Ursa rose and slipped away into the night.

Alsharon regarded the Pair with interest. "I was not aware that you were such a statesman, Lady Marilyn. You did well tonight, not only for yourselves, but for your entire race. Ursa is a powerful creature and not easily impressed. We need not fear for anything while in his realm. This will save us at least two days. This is good since the Dark One has servants even here. Sleep well tonight. You have earned it."

The Pair returned to their sleeping area, and Mike touched Mary's elbow and she turned to face him. "Lady Marilyn, you were awesome! I could think of nothing to say, but you knew exactly what was right." He hugged her. "You really are one in a million." He released her and turned away, but not before Mary could see the brightness of his eyes. She wanted to call out to him, but she held back, almost hating him for his personal code of honor. Still that was who he was, and she knew how much compromising it had cost him. So she slipped into her bedroll and was soon fast asleep.

Mike sat for a while, just looking at the stars and at the sleeping figure a few feet from him. He asked himself again why he could not tell her how he really felt about her. The future was so uncertain; there was no guarantee that they would survive to fulfill the prophesy. It could be fulfilled, and they could become martyred Heroes. This was so unfair. He had been comfortable; he had come to grips with the death of his wife, and his actions afterward. He and Mary had been the best of friends, and he was beginning to hope that they had a future together. Now they were in a crazy world on a crazy quest, and he could not see how he could take any more. He knew this was no dream; he had too many new scars and bruises for that.

He wondered if he had gone insane and was locked inside his own mind. Could the insane question their insanity? He knew the answer—somehow this was real, and there was no escape from it. He watched Mary turn in her sleep. Her face was relaxed, and her beauty seemed intensified. He knew he was hopelessly lost in love with her. Still, he could not succumb—he had to remain distanced or he feared that all would be lost. That he would not be able to protect her, that she would leave for just a simple errand and not come back. He snorted slightly; that was an irrational thought. It wasn't Tammy's fault that a man had decided to rob her bank. It wasn't her fault that she had been there.

He looked up into the night and drew a deep breath and let it out. There were no answers in the night sky. He could hear the hunting cry of wolves in the far distance and the song of night birds closer to hand. He turned to his bedroll and prepared to sleep. After a few moments he did something he had not done since the day of Tammy's funeral. He prayed. He knew that, somewhere, God listened. He felt truly relaxed for the first time since that horrible day and slept through the night.

CHAPTER TWENTY

The morning dawned gray and the clouds looked as though they could discharge a great deluge at any moment. Alsharon led the way, keeping to higher ground without exposing the group to the unfriendly-seeming skies. Before nightfall they discovered a long-abandoned farm with a corner of the farmhouse that was reasonably intact. The storm began just as they had settled in. The wall gave protection from the wind, but the roof was long gone. The travelers huddled under a makeshift tent constructed from their cloaks. They spent a long, sleepless night listening to the rain. At one point in the night, Mary stiffened and peered into the darkness. The others watched her, and Mike's hand strayed to the Sword of the Ancestors. When Mary did not react, he began to slide it from its sheath. He stopped when he noticed that the blade was reflecting light that was not there. Mary whispered, "Put it away quickly." And he immediately complied. The Elves were watching with interest, straining to listen.

Mike opened his mind as he had been trained, allowing it to passively search for magic that was nearby. He had detected a shadow when Mary's hand grasped his. His eyes seemed to open at that contact; he could see in his mind a shadowy figure not far from them. It was looking for something and roamed back and forth across the path they had taken earlier that day. The rain seemed to confuse it, and it passed the point where the travelers had turned from the trail. Mike could not make out any features, but had the impression that this was a malevolent creature and that it meant them no good. It wandered further and further away, and Mary released Mike's hand. The image was immediately gone, and he was looking at the Twins.

"What was that?" he asked. He was not at all sure that he wanted the answer, judging from their expression.

Alsharon answered, "I believe that was an Elf bane. I thought it was an imaginary creature that was conjured by parents to scare their children into obedience. It is said to be a terrible creature that feasts on the very essence of an elf. Once an elf bane has the scent of its victim, it cannot be turned away except by the fiercest of spells. It can detect an Elf's magic at great distances and will come."

Elsharone continued, "The Sword of the Ancestors is rumored to have tasted of the blood of these dark creatures, but they cannot be destroyed through purely physical means. I do not know if it poses a threat to you humans, but it is a great threat to we elves."

Mike looked to Mary, who thought for a moment before she spoke. "That was truly an evil creature. When Mike began to draw his sword, it stopped and looked directly at me. I believe it will follow us wherever we go. It would be best to face it at a place of our choosing. It has immense power, but I do not detect any great sense of purpose. It is as though it is a powerful beast, driven by instinct, not reason. As a beast, it is vulnerable to our intellect if we keep our wits about us. Its greatest weapon will be fear. It will make us believe there is no hope and will gain strength through our despair. We must make an end of it."

The Elves agreed and they huddled under the cloaks the rest of the night. The creature did not return, but they knew they were not free of it. Before daylight the storm ended, and they got a fitful hour of sleep. Once the sun rose and quickly banished the remaining clouds, Mary drew Mike aside while the others prepared for the day's journey. "Mike, this beast may concentrate its attack on you. Forgive me, but this must be said. It will find the hurt from your wife's death and any guilt that you are harboring. I know you always say that you know it wasn't your fault, but I have seen the pain in your eyes for years. I know the pain of her death is as fresh as though it has happened yesterday. You can't abandon her memory; you wouldn't be you if you did. Please understand that any thoughts about her and what happened afterwards are coming from the creature.

"The only way to kill this creature is with the Sword of the Ancestors. It has many weapons, and not all of them are magic. When the battle is at its darkest, and when all seems lost, when there is no hope, that is the time to think about love. Then you must think about the years that you did have, all of the good things that happened to you." Mary reached out and brushed his hair out of his eyes with her fingers. "Remember, you must feel all the love you've ever had if you are going to prevail. We will fight its magic, but you must destroy its body."

Mike looked down into her dark eyes and read the concern there. He felt a cold fear begin to grip his heart; if Mary was afraid of this creature, then how could he possibly prevail? He stepped closer, embraced her, and whispered, "I know you'll be all that we need. Thank you for warning me, which is an advantage it will never suspect that we have." He hoped that his bold words covered the trembling that he felt in his heart.

He looked up and saw Mary packing the last of their gear;

he must have been lost in thought for a moment because he did not remember her moving away. He quickly helped her finish, and they joined the twins at the trail. They had just finished an incantation and a dark purple mist seemed to seep from the ground. It formed into footprints on the ground and led away from them. The elves glanced at the Pair and started following the purple prints.

The trail meandered and switched directions several times. It was clear that the beast was circling, searching for them. They stopped to eat a quick lunch, and Mary asked Mike, "You were very pensive this morning, what was on your mind?"

"I was thinking about what you said about the beast." Mike had not been able to ease his sense of foreboding. He wondered how he would know when to strike. His thoughts were interrupted by a comment from Alsharon.

"It is good that you warned him, Lady Marilyn. Anything of elven origin will draw it to us. We have been using certain dampening spells, but we will only know how effective they were when we confront the beast. You must remember to allow us to use our magic when the battle comes."

Mike nodded to the Elf and his discomfort rose as he realized that Alsharon greatly feared the creature. How could he fight a creature whose magic caused elves to fear? His hand found its way to the pommel of the Sword of the Ancestors, and he felt somewhat reassured. They soon resumed the trail and even he could feel the presence of the beast. They stopped and discussed the situation. It was decided that they would make their stand there, before sunset. The others began to pile their gear and remove everything that had elven magic worked into it.

Mike joined them. "What about the Sword of the Ancestors? When will I strike the beast with it?"

All three looked at him with expressions that ranged from surprise to horror. "That would be disaster, that would be—" Alsharon was interrupted by a great shout from the edge of the clearing. The beast was upon them.

Mike had only a moment to ask Mary, "But this morning. You warned me? What am I to do?"

Mary was completely surprised. "We didn't speak this morning. You were lost in thought, and I did not want to disturb you."

"No, you warned me that it would attack me. That the only way to kill it was with the sword."

Mary looked into his eyes. "No. It wants the elves and their magic. That is what it feeds on. The Sword would only make it stronger. It is attacking you; it wants you to undo our strategy." She turned and cast a spell that broke up a deadlocked exchange between the elves and the beast. She turned back to him. "It cannot be hurt by a magical weapon now, and we must keep it from feeding. Fight it, weaken it enough for me to banish it." She turned and ran to stand next to the elves.

Mike sank to his knees, horrified that he had nearly doomed his friends. Despair engulfed him like a raging flood. He could barely keep from falling. He began to think of his wife and the despair deepened; he couldn't recall the good times. He heard one of his friends cry out in pain, and he began to berate himself for being unable to help them. Then, like a drowning man grasping for anything that would float, he thought of his dearest friend.

He could see before him the last five years of his life and the one person who had always been there, the one person who had never asked too much of him. Mike could feel his spirit rising as though from the depths of the ocean. He locked on to the memory of a distant New Year's Eve and the tradition that it had begun between him and Mary. He remembered outdoors concerts and Broadway plays they had attended. Soon it felt like he broke the surface of the water and he could breathe again.

He glanced across the clearing and saw Elsharone bent over her brother and Mary between them and the beast, the Grybon. He did not know how he knew the name, but it was there. Along with the name was an idea. He knew what he had to do.

He quickly stripped out of his leather armor and mail. Clad only in his breeches and undershirt he circled around behind the beast. As he approached he could tell that it was unaware of him. He paused for a moment and wiped his hand across his chest. There was a lump under the cloth and he remembered the silver cross that Mary had put on a chain for him. It had become almost a part of his body. Not understanding why he did it, he quickly removed the necklace and wound the chain around his hand and held the cross in the palm. He lightly kissed the cross, then drawing a deep breath; he whispered a prayer and charged the beast.

He slammed into the scaly body as though sacking a quarterback in his college days. The beast was knocked forward slightly, and Mike could feel its fetid breath as it turned its head to him. The beast's body was hot and solid. It began to laugh until Mike's palm pressed the silver cross against its side. It suddenly cried out in pain and spun around, swinging Mike like a rag doll. Mike clung to it with all of his strength as the beast screamed in agony.

A scalding hot liquid poured on his hand and wrist, causing Mike to gasp in pain. Still he clung to the beast and was battered as it fell to the ground and rolled. This caused the scalding ichor to splatter his body; the searing pain forced him to let go. He thrust his hand against the beast as it rolled away, and it howled in pain again. It struggled to its feet and turned on Mike, raising clawed hands above its head. It began its strike just as it was encompassed in a brilliant luminescence. The ball of light shrank down to pinpoint size and was gone, leaving nothing in its place. Mike's hands were burned, and it felt as though many embers had been sprayed on his chest.

He staggered to his feet and waved Mary towards the twins who were struggling to rise. They were even more pale than usual, and Mike knew that they had been grievously injured. He ignored his pain as he helped to set up camp and make them as comfortable as possible. They were barely conscious but were able to instruct the Pair in preparing a restorative. As soon as the twins were resting, Mike grabbed some burn salve from his pack and left the clearing. He ignored Mary's calls and walked a fair distance before he found a fallen tree trunk to sit on.

CHAPTER TWENTY-ONE

Mike hung his head and let his mind flow on a river of pain and regret. The image of his dead wife floated before his eyes again. He knew she would never have stopped at the bank on that terrible day; she would have had no reason to if he had made a different choice. His career had ended with the failure of the manufacturing company that had employed him since his graduation from college. He had used his severance pay, retirement, and savings to start a business. It was slow at first, but it was profitable almost from the beginning. The profits could not replace the income he had lost with the failure of his employer; yet everything was improving—albeit slowly. The start-up debt for the business seemed to loom over them and threatened to crush them with its weight.

They were able to pay all their bills, and the business was making just enough to keep up with the loan payments. Mike had just negotiated a long-term contract with a new client and would soon be bringing in enough income to pay off the debt and then to expand. That was where the trouble started. Mike agreed to accept some overflow work from a competitor's manufacturing business. Their businesses were similar, but did not actually overlap. Accepting the overflow work meant that both shops were able to contribute according to their strengths.

The alliance initially paid off until Jackson, the owner of the other shop, began to sign contracts for more work than Mike could keep up with. Then he convinced Mike to again borrow money and expand his shop. Over his wife's objections, Mike hired more workers, and the business continued to expand. The work continued to flow in, but trouble arose when Jackson took a long vacation without arranging for Mike's shop to be paid. It was an oversight and only delayed payment for a month, but it forced Mike to again borrow money to meet his payroll and payables obligations.

Jackson returned from vacation and immediately brought a check to Mike's house. He had overlooked an important detail before leaving on his trip, and he was truly sorry. Mike's wife had seen the prepared deposit on his desk and had decided to take care of it with her other errands. It was all very innocent, but it had deadly consequences. While she stood in line at the bank, a masked gunman had burst in, waving a small caliber pistol and demanding money.

The gunman was a drug addict who was badly strung out. He had surprised the bank guard and herded the few customers up to the counter. The teller was so frightened that she dropped the bag of money as she handed it to the robber. This caused the dye pack she had slipped in it to explode and panicked the thief. He fired the gun blindly as he ran from the bank. Tammy was the only casualty; a stray bullet struck her in the heart and she died instantly.

Mike sat and shook his head; he knew that in giving an outsider some measure of control of his life, he had lost everything that was important to him. By the time he met Mary he had ended his association with Jackson and was out of debt. He could not count how many times he had wished he could go back and stop the entanglement before it started.

The police had been unable to get any leads on the murderer, and Mike dropped into a deep depression, at least as far as his friends knew. He had started going to bars and had withdrawn from most everyone who knew him. He let his foreman run the shop, only going there once or twice a week. He began to associate with petty thieves and drug dealers until he had tracked down the addict who had killed his wife.

The man was cooking meth-amphetamine in a dilapidated house in a run-down neighborhood in the worst part of town. Witnesses said that Mike had entered the house and they had heard shouting and then breaking glass. The ruckus was punctuated by a gunshot and followed by an explosion and fire. Firefighters had found Mike just outside the door with the other man on his back. He had apparently tried to carry the man from the burning house, but had been overcome by the smoke and fumes. Mike had a gunshot wound and the other man had a sliver of glass lodged in his heart. He was probably dead when Mike picked him up to try and save him.

He sat alone with his thoughts for a long time, well after sunset. There had been murder in his heart when he entered the crack house. Something had happened to change that, so he apparently tried to save the life of a man he desperately hated, or thought he hated. The memories were interrupted as he became aware of something moving in the woods, and he reached for the sword that was not there. The pain that shot through his hands again reminded him of what had almost happened. Ursa was lumbering towards him, and he rose to greet the creature. Ursa sniffed at his hands and looked back towards where the others were, as if to ask a question.

"Yes, Ursa, the Grybon is gone. Little thanks to me. I nearly got them all killed," he said bitterly. "They are safer without me at the moment, especially since you are here."

The mighty bear shook its head and again sniffed Mike's right hand. Mike had almost forgotten the silver cross that he still clenched there. The bear shook his head in an affirmative, but Mike did not share the sentiment. "I am afraid that I did more damage than even this can atone for."

Ursa growled and then made as if to lick the burns on Mike's hands. Mike shook his head and reached for the burn salve. He methodically worked it into the burns on his hands and right arm. When he was finished, Ursa gently nudged him towards the camp. When Mike refused the bear again shook its head and then left. The bruin returned in a very short time with a gnome riding his back.

The Gnome addressed Mike. "Sir Michael, Ursa has asked me to speak for him. Your friends are very worried about you. While nothing will molest you here, they fear for your, ah, mental state. The Lady Marilyn thinks that you are, well, she said, 'moping around blaming himself for things he couldn't control.' Ursa says that you showed extraordinary courage and wisdom in fighting the beast. He says that few could conquer the fear that surrounded it like the stench of death. He has never heard of a man that had the capacity, and few elves. Please return to the others. Your wounds must be tended properly; otherwise they will fester and consume you."

Ursa motioned with his massive head, and this time Mike rose and followed the unlikely couple to the campsite. When they arrived he could hardly believe his eyes;

the campsite had been transformed. A number of gnomes moved about; they had built shelters over Alsharon and Elsharone, made a cooking area, and apparently prepared a meal. Gnomes attended the elves, and several approached as Mike entered the clearing. They ushered him to a seat near the fire and stripped away the gore-covered undershirt. They soon had the filth cleansed from his upper body and were engaged in a tug of war with him over his breeches. They eventually prevailed, and he tried to keep a blanket in place to preserve some measure of modesty.

Mary was enjoying his discomfort from across the clearing. Mike noticed that her hands were bandaged and again felt a pang of guilt, although not as strong as before. "Yes, the Grybon still clouds your mind as long as any of his taint remains. That is why we must cleanse your body as well as your wounds. Sit still, no one here is offended. These are experienced healers, please let them work." The gnome who had translated for Ursa spoke from beside him. He tried to relax, but kept the blanket close at hand. The gnomes finished their work and most of them slipped away into the night. A few remained near the shelters that had been built for the twins.

Mike held his blanket around his waist and walked towards where he had last seen his gear. His tent had been set up, and he found his pack inside. He dressed as well as he could, but all he was able to manage were clean breeches. He carried a fresh undershirt and his mail outside and looked for Mary. She was sitting with her back to him staring into the fire. "Hello, Doll."

Mary was nearly exhausted as she sat staring into the fire. She resisted the urge to check on the twins and poked at the fire with a stick. She thought of the spell to cover it and laughed at herself. Ursa had scouted the area and there were gnomes on guard in the forest. They were as safe as was possible outside of Elvhome or the Haven. She sighed and wondered how the creature had been able to get past their defenses to attack Mike. She knew she had failed him, and that they had all nearly suffered a fate worse than death. The Grybon, as the gnomes called it, had proven much more intelligent that she had guessed. She silently promised herself to never again underestimate one of the Dark Lord's servants.

She did not hear Mike until he called to her, and she rose quickly. He was standing there holding his shirt with an amused expression on his face. "A little help?"

Mary laughed and helped him into the shirt. It was a clumsy endeavor with both of them bandaged. Eventually they got the garment on and settled, and both sat down facing the fire. At the same moment they both turned and began. "I'm sorry, you, no I—" and dissolved into laughter.

When they had recovered somewhat, Mary put her finger on Mike's lips and spoke. "I get to go first because I know you are probably blaming yourself when it is as plain as day that I let you down. No, don't say a word. Ursa told me and you are just wrong. He agrees that you did all, even more than could be expected. I, on the other hand, didn't even know that the Grybon thingey had begun its attack before we left the cottage. I don't know how I missed that. I almost let you get killed, or consumed—they say it's different. Now no arguing, you need to rest." When he started to speak she interrupted, "Nope, you can't have the blame. Its mine. I called it." He tried to speak again and she again cut him off. "Nope, not sharing."

She stared defiantly at him until he slumped his shoulders and mumbled, "Apology accepted, but I—"

"But nothing. Just go to bed. We may not be leaving for a while, so get some rest." She smiled as he turned and gasped as he swiftly turned back and swept her up in an embrace. They clung to each other for several minutes, not needing words to express their relief. As he released her, she held up her hand. "No talking, just sleeping." She returned to the fire for a short while. A gnome approached from the shadows.

"Lady Marilyn," he began. "You have no blame in this. The Grybon has hunted elves for hundreds of years. Their bones litter the landscape from here to the Jewel Castle. You have cost the Dark Lord an important servant, and you have freed a people from a terrible curse. You will encounter other horrors along the way, and it is imperative that you and Sir Michael find out why it was able to deceive you both. Talk to each other and find out what happened. It is truly an ill wind that blows no good."

Mary smiled at the little creature and said, "Thank you, we will do that—tomorrow. Tonight I think I must rest." She rose and checked on the twins, and then made her way to her tent. Weariness claimed her, and she slept far into the morning. She again dreamed of a knight on a hilltop and again awoke before his face was revealed. "Who are you kidding? You know who it is. Let's just get on with it," she muttered as she sat up in her tent. Outside there was dried fruit and hot tea. On the cook fire there was a pot of boiled oats. It was a welcome break from trail rations, and Mary ate slowly, savoring the taste.

The last morsels of fruit had been washed down by the fragrant tea when Mike entered the clearing. "Hey, Sunshine! There is a beaver's pond just down there. The water is still a little chill, but it feels good to be able to wash. Just watch out though. When you leave the water, the gnomes'll ambush you and spread salve on your burns. How are your hands? Mine are much better, thank you for asking." Mary smiled at the cheerful tone of his voice; he sounded recovered from the battle, but she knew how well he could hide his true feelings.

Not from me though, she thought to herself, he really sounds happy. "Did you have breakfast? I thought you were still sleeping."

"Sure, an hour ago. I could hear your steady breathing, so I let you sleep. The twins were awake for a while, but our healer friends insisted they remain in bed." He sat beside Mary and refilled his tin cup with tea. "It's not so bad, the pond. I think it is worth it to be clean."

Mary punched his arm. "Are you trying to say something, mister?" She laughed. "Whoa, I guess you don't have to." She rose, retrieved a towel and some soap from her tent, and then made her way to the pond.

She noticed a beaver watching from the shadows under a willow tree, so she called to it. "Good day to you, Sir Beaver. I wish to make use of your most excellent pond." She bowed, and the beaver ducked under the water. Mary laughed and entered the water. It was chilly, but the sun was warm, so she rinsed out her garments and spread them on some bushes that grew from the water. She took her time bathing and swimming in the pond. The cold water was soothing to the burns on her hands, so she was in no hurry to leave it.

The beaver joined her as she swam laps around the pond. He would swim close and then burst ahead of her, splashing under the water only to reappear near her. She laughed at the creature's antics, and he rewarded her with new tricks. Soon she was tired and exchanged her wet inner garments for clean ones, and sat on the bank while the beaver played in the water. His family joined him, a female and two cubs, and the four of them played in the water as long as she watched.

A gnome appeared and examined her hands. The last burst of magic had been so intense that it had burned her hands as she maintained the spell until the Grybon was gone. The salve the gnomes applied was very soothing, and she did not resist the healer's ministrations. Her outer garments were nearly dry so she finished dressing and returned to the campsite. It was her turn to be amazed; it seemed a village was sprouting from the site. The crude lean-to structure was gone, and a one-room shack stood in its place. Her tent sat behind a small cottage-like structure. It was tall enough for her to enter without stooping, but the ceiling was very close to her head.

Mike was acting as scaffolding for a pair of gnomes who were working on the gable of his cottage. A gnome approached and took Mary by the hand to show her the inside of her cottage. He explained that the gnomes would build a proper shrine on the spot and that the worker's would use the structures after they left. They had built a bed frame with a straw-tick mattress, a table, and a chair. He showed her a type of mirror that employed a very thin sheet of water flowing down a smooth stone. "No magical spies here, and you will be able to sit and dress proper-like. Not that you're not proper…" Mary smiled at his sudden embarrassment and assured him that she took no offense.

As they left the cottage, a female gnome spoke in hushed whisper to her guide, who turned to her and said, "Good news. The Elves are awake and have eaten a good meal. Let us go and speak to them."

They hurried across the compound and entered the new infirmary building. They found Alsharon and Elsharone both sitting on their beds. They were still very pale, but some color had returned to their faces. Both smiled and greeted Mary warmly. Elsharone looked at the door and then asked, "Where is Sir Michael? He was not badly injured, was he?"

Alsharon took up the conversation. "He showed extraordinary courage, as did you, Lady Marilyn. You also showed an incredible mastery of magic. Tell me, was the creature destroyed, or banished?"

Mary laughed. "First question first. The last I saw Mike, Sir Michael, he was performing as a human ladder for the gnomes." Her face became serious. "I was only able to banish the creature. Bardwind warned me that this could happen. That certain dark servants, products of ancient magic, were very difficult to destroy. If not for the addition of your power at the very end, we would not have prevailed." Mike entered as she was speaking, and Alsharon had a puzzled expression on his face. He exchanged glances with his sister.

"We were too far gone at the end to aid you, perhaps Sir Michael?"

Mike held up his bandaged hands. "No, Sir Michael had

his 'hands' full. It was Mary—somehow she reached a little deeper and kicked butt."

It was Elsharone's turn to look puzzled. "I thought you banished the creature with a spell, not physically."

"It's an expression from our home," Mary grinned as she replied. "It can mean 'to banish' so it is appropriate. I think we had help from an unseen ally. I do not think I did it on my own." She held up her own hands. "None of us are unscathed. We have much to talk about, we barely escaped disaster, and I am the most to blame!"

This prompted a heated discussion and soon a clearer picture of the battle emerged. The engagement had begun when Mary first detected the creature, the Grybon. The twins knew of the legends surrounding this ancient bane to the elves. The Grybon had realized that the twins were aware of its presence, so it had retreated while it probed the minds of all four. It had decided that Mike was the least proficient in magic and had concentrated its attack on him, at first. Once it had planted doubts in his mind, it had planted the suggestion in the others' minds that they all knew the battle plan. It could not really enter anything into their minds, but it could affect thoughts that were already there. That was why it could convince Mike that Mary had spoken about his pain over the loss of his wife. Deep inside Mike wanted Mary to tell him she understood his pain.

While the quartet thought they were trailing the Grybon in order to attack it, the beast was actually leading them to an ambush. The ambush had been foiled in part when Mike asked about using the Sword of the Ancestors. The Grybon had to attack before the web of deceit it had woven began to unravel. The twins had been affected most due to its long history of consuming elves. Mike and Mary were new to it, and it had thought they posed little danger to it, perhaps because it had not been truly tested in over a hundred years.

The key to victory was a special kind of magic that no one in the battle could have thought of beforehand. It was simple; the act of creating the necklace and the reason that it was worn created a bond that was pure and strong. The silver that the cross and chain were made from came from another world and was unique in Heavenshire. Not that the metal did not exist, rather the symbol simply had no meaning here. The result was an icon of the purest friendship, built entirely on nothing more than the desire to be together—no demands and no expectations. The Grybon had no defense against such purity, and it became a weapon that destroyed its foul flesh.

Alsharon, Elsharone, and Mary had held the upper hand at first, but the beast was able to counter the elves' magic. Mary was able to shield them, but was not strong enough to press an attack alone. Mike's attack on the beast broke its concentration on its own attack, freeing Mary for one great stroke. Her spell had encompassed it so quickly that all she had needed was to hold it. It was in essence cut off from its source of power, the darkness that had infected the surrounding land. The only mystery left was the surge of power that Mary had felt that closed the ball of light around the Grybon, either destroying it or sending it back from whence it came. Either way, it would not walk in Heavenshire again soon.

The gnomes returned and demanded that the elves rest, and the Pair left the twins reluctantly. They walked and talked for a while, and Mary unconsciously led them to the pond. The beaver family was playing in the waters as the sun set. The sight reminded Mary of a painting she had once seen, and she sat with Mike at her side for a long time just watching. The male beaver had disappeared some time after they had arrived and reappeared at the waters edge just before the sun slipped below the horizon. He held something in his front paws so Mary rose and walked to the bank. The beaver crawled from the water and sat upright and held the object out to her.

"Thank you, kind sir! This is a welcome gift from such a noble beaver." Mary bowed and took the object and gasped. It was a carving of intricate detail. It depicted a young woman standing in a battle pose. She held her hands in front of her, palms nearly touching, between them a crystal was inserted; as it caught the last rays of sunlight, it glowed just like the spell that Mary had cast to banish the Grybon. She bowed again to the beaver. "I shall treasure this. Thank you again." The beaver turned and dove into the pond and his family also disappeared.

Mary turned to Mike and displayed the carving. It was perhaps six inches tall, and there was no doubt that Mary was the subject. "That's you destroying the beast," Mike whispered. Mary could only nod; she was filled with a flood of emotions, some conflicting and some almost overwhelming. She was humbled because she still felt that she was not the hero of this battle, yet she felt a great wash of gratitude to the beaver for the gift. She was even more than a little awed by the craftsmanship of the figurine. The little face showed intense concentration, and the figure's hair was swept back as though a wind were blowing into its face. It was a truly remarkable work of art.

"I know that I did not do it alone, but I will treasure this gift for as long as we are here. Do you think we'll be able to take anything back? You know, when it's over, and we can go…home?" She looked over the carving and into Mike's eyes. "Do you ever think of home? I don't mean your little house in the country, or even my apartment. I mean home, where the animals don't speak and create works of art, and where there is no dark force tracking our every move." She paused and waited for him to answer.

Mike did not speak. His hand went to his chest, and he brought out the silver cross he wore. He had meticulously cleaned both the cross and the chain to remove all traces of the Grybon's blood. When he spoke, his voice sounded far off. "I suppose that we can take what we can carry. The real chore will be in choosing. What will hold the greatest memories of this place?" He placed his hands over hers and slowly turned the carving. "Just think, when we look at this carving we will remember a momentous battle, where we fought our own doubt and fear as well as a powerful enemy. Our friends will just see a fantasy figurine. What a perfect irony? I think I will remember…" he stopped and no amount of prodding from Mary could get him to continue.

They returned to the camp and to their new cabins. Mary placed the figurine on the windowsill and sat on the bed and looked at it for a while. Occasionally the light from the fire would be reflected in the crystal, and it would glow as though with an inner light. She continued to reflect on what Mike had said, and on what he didn't say. She knew that they had never made formal commitments to each other. In fact, they had both emphasized that they were friends. Mary had not questioned their relationship because she knew it would change when he was sufficiently healed from the tragedy of his wife's death. Well, it seemed he was healed, but was holding back. She did not understand why. If they survived their quest, then they could have a good start on their life together. If they didn't, or if only one survived…

Mary paused in her musings. That had to be it! He was afraid of surviving alone. She could see how horrible that would be for him, to have lost twice to death. It wouldn't matter, he either loved her or he didn't. He would feel as much pain either way if he loved her. "I will just have to survive," she whispered into the darkness as she lay down on her new bed. On the windowsill, the crystal glowed brighter for an instant and then was dark.

The following day dawned bright and warm. Mary had been up early and was practicing shield spells in her mind when she heard Mike's door open. She quickly opened hers and joined him for breakfast. The gnome healer appeared and informed them that the elves would be able to travel in a few days, but that they needed to be left to themselves until then. The Pair promised to allow them the privacy and discussed what they should do in the mean time. Mary suggested that they continue to train and offered to show Mike what magic she could.

The next days passed quickly, and Mike made good progress in defensive magic. He was able to erect a shield that would deflect powerful bursts of hostile magic with little effort. They were not able to test the limit of his new skills, but Mary was confident that he was better prepared than when their journey started. The elves joined them for breakfast one morning, and the four of them made plans to resume their journey. There was one more interruption before they departed—Ursa returned.

The mighty bruin had scouted the lands far to the west

and reported that many of the dark creatures were moving towards the Jeweled Castle. They should be able to travel quickly and avoid any but a few small groups. The elves would not be able to camp and wait for the Pair to enter the castle and retrieve the Book. They would keep moving to avoid easy discovery by the servants of the Dark Lord. Ursa showed them a place that would be safe for a rendezvous a few days after they had to part ways. Their plans made, they slept one more night in the gnome-built accommodations.

They traveled fast, covering many miles in the next few days. Too soon they stood before a stone covered in Elven runes. It was a warning to all Elves that they could not enter the land before them or they would face certain destruction. The castle was only a half a day's journey away. The twins could accompany them no farther, and it was with a great amount of sadness that the Pair continued their journey alone.

CHAPTER TWENTY-TWO

They were barely out of sight of the twins when harpies—birdlike creatures with bodies that resembled human women—attacked them. The resemblance was in form only; the harpies' faces were the personification of evil. They attacked in a group of five, each carrying a different weapon—sword, mace, spear, sling, and quarterstaff. They possessed a natural magic that defended them from the attack spells that the Pair dared to use. The battle was mostly a stand off; the Pair could not advance, but the harpies could not do them harm.

Mary had an idea; she quickly cast a language spell on herself. She called out to the harpies, "Why have you attacked us?"

"Well, you know why! We will not allow any stupid elf to enter the castle!" the reply came from the sword wielder.

Mary pulled the leather helmet from her head and shook loose her long, black hair. She continued, mimicking the harpies' coarseness. "Do I look like an elf to you, fool? And when have you seen a male elf that was so big and dumb looking? We ain't no stinking elves!"

"You don't have to get personal, doll face. The oaf carries an elf's sword, and with that face you could pass for one of those prissy pants." The leader alternately spoke to Mary and traded insults with the other four. Mike tried to follow the conversation, but all that he could hear was high-pitched shrieking. The confusion written on his face boosted the impression that he was not much more than an idiot, and the harpies ignored him.

Mary slipped her canteen from her shoulder, slung it into a tree, and backed away. The harpies fought over it until the leader beat them into submission and took a sip. She grimaced and muttered something about tasteless stuff and passed it to the others. While the others tasted the water, the leader tossed a water skin to Mary. Mary steeled herself and took a sip; the drink was surprisingly good—it was some sort of slightly fermented fruit juice. She looked at the leader and motioned as though offering it to Mike and the harpy shrugged. Mike took a sip and made a short bow in the leaders' direction.

The harpies descended and landed in front of the Pair. Mike reluctantly sheathed his sword after they lowered their weapons. The leader spoke to Mary. "We shared water. You go to castle? Others try, none come back. Maybe you leave man here and go? Not total waste then." The harpy smiled a broken-toothed grin and looked appraisingly at Mike. He could not follow the conversation, but he was beginning to get the idea.

Mary let him fidget uncomfortably for a few seconds, and then said, "No, I will take him with me. He doesn't get on well on his own. Maybe you could show us the best path to the castle. We have food to share." She unwrapped some of the elven travel bread, and the harpies crowed around, losing interest in Mike. Mary pulled the bread back and said, "Show me first, then I will give you the bread."

The leader bobbed her head. "Probably better than man anyway. We show, you give. Follow now." The five harpies rose into the air and flew to the northwest. The Pair trotted after them while Mary gave Mike a run down on the negotiations. He rolled his eyes at the thought of being used as barter, but kept his comments to himself, muttering, "I'll show them stupid all right."

The harpies landed after a twenty-minute run, and the leader pointed to a partially overgrown trail. "No troll or ogre this way. Go right to gate of castle. You get book, we be happy because dark servant leave land. Listen,

> 'To Enter Jewel, go by lesser door.
> To your quest be true, find your way through.
> To gain what you require, give in not to your desire.'"

Mary repeated the instructions and thanked the harpies, giving them the travel bread. They flew away in a shower of feathers and dust.

Mary ended her spell as the harpies left; it was of no further use and might draw the servants of the Dark Lord to them. She laughed as Mike tried to brush all the debris from his travel cloak. "Do not judge them too quickly. They held the first clue to entering the castle, 'To enter the jewel, go by the lesser door...' We will not enter by the main gate. Oh, and there are trolls and ogres about, be careful. We should try to enter the castle by daylight, I think." They walked the path with weapons drawn and soon were in sight of the castle.

It was a magnificent sight—crystalline turrets and towers reaching high into the sky, reflecting the sunlight and glittering like a jewel. The stones of the castle were shaped like ordinary building stones but possessed the color and clarity of precious gems. It seemed that the entire structure glowed with reflected sunlight. They cautiously approached and located the main gate. Bones were scattered around it, so the Pair kept their distance. They made their way along the wall until they reached a smaller gate. The castle had once had a moat, but it was now little more than an overgrown ditch that held very little water. They approached the gate and found the portcullis down and no apparent door or access of any kind.

Mary and Mike discussed the clue, and Mike asked if they needed to be more literal. He walked past the gate and started around the castle. He noticed a mouse trail that led right to the wall and apparently through it. As he walked up to the wall he saw a narrow passage that lead obliquely into the wall. To Mary, standing by the gate, it looked as if he just disappeared. She followed after him; they found a small door at the end of the passage. It opened inward at her touch, and they found themselves inside the Jewel Castle. Mike closed the door and barred it, against what he was not sure.

They were in a hall more ornately appointed than any they had seen in Heavenshire. Mary repeated, "'To your quest be true, find your way through.' We are here for a book. I think we should ignore the riches of this place."

"I agree," Mike replied. "Let's move farther inside. These walls are translucent enough that we might be seen." They followed the hall towards the interior. Doors opened to the right and left, and Mike looked questioningly at Mary.

"Be literal; let's go to the end of the hall." They proceeded, and she glanced into one of the rooms and paused. A long-dead figure slumped before an array of gold and jewels. It seemed to have starved to death admiring the riches of the Castle. As the Pair penetrated further into the castle, the glow of reflected sunlight in the walls illuminated their way. They followed the wide, sweeping turn of the hallway until it ended before a pair of simple wooden doors. They looked at each other and Mary shrugged and pulled on the handles. The doors did not budge whether they were pulled or pushed.

Mary stepped back and studied the doors; they were very plain with only a few carvings adorning them. In the center of the right-hand door was a brass knocker. She ran her gloved fingers over it and glanced at Mike. The big warrior shrugged and motioned for her to try it. Mary lifted the striker and let it fall against the plate. It bounced three times, each bounce eliciting a different tone from the plate. For a moment nothing happened, and Mike reached forward to do it again but Mary grabbed his hand. A sound of machinery came from somewhere below them, and the doors creaked and began to swing inward, revealing a vast library filled from floor to ceiling with books.

At first Mary thought they were not alone; a figure was seated at a table with books piled around it. She quickly realized that it was long dead and the books were covered with a thick layer of dust. Mary approached the table and ran a finger through the dust, examining the books there. Mike wandered along the main aisle, glancing down each row of shelves as he passed. A crystal column stood in the center of the library and inside it, water began to flow. The long-dormant fountain received only a trickle of water at first. Mike approached it, then suddenly turned and shouted, "Get out! We'll be trapped in here." Mary hesitated as he started to run for the door. He swept her up into his arms as he ran. Mary could see that the trickle of water in the fountain had become a torrent. She turned her head as she heard a grinding sound and saw the doors swinging closed.

Mike threw Mary towards the doors and dived through

just behind her as they snapped shut. The Pair landed tangled up on the floor with Mary on top of the heap. She stared at the door for a moment, but there was no magic to be seen. Mike grunted, and she stood, examining the doors. Finally she turned to him and was angered by the knowing look on his face. "What?" she snapped. "Do you know the secret?"

Mike grinned. "I read an article once about ancient automatic doors. The mechanism is on the floor below. There will be counterweights and shafts and gears. The main counterweight is an empty tank. When the door is triggered, the tank fills with water and sinks, turning the gears and stuff to open the door. That is why there was a hesitation before they opened. One of the variations automatically closes, the counterbalance drains and the machine returns to its neutral state. I was asking myself why there would be water in a library when the fountain started. High humidity is not good for books. I just guessed that it was refilling in order to open the doors the next time. Then it occurred to me that our friend in there had been trapped, so I thought we had best leave."

"Why wouldn't there be a way out? Surely this is not just an elaborate trap."

"I think that the doors are supposed to lock open, but the catches may be broken, or stuck," Mike answered. "We should be able to open the doors and look for it before they close. The one thing that bothers me is that a little of the water will be lost each time the doors open. There will come a point where they won't open unless more water is added. It is probably designed to be replenished from a rain gutter or something. I would not want to risk being trapped and depend on an ancient gutter that has not been cleaned in hundreds of years. Until we get the doors blocked open, one of us should stay outside or very near the door, just in case."

Mary was not pleased at that thought but agreed. "I don't think the book is in the library." Mike looked astonished and she repeated herself. "The books on that table were construction and engineering books. I think he was looking for a way out. The riddle said to find our way through. That could mean that our destination is through the library. When we open the door, I will run to the other side of the room while you look for a way to hold them open. I will watch the fountain and return before the doors close."

Mike nodded and lifted the knocker and released it. The same three tones sounded, each a different note. After a short pause, the doors began to open. As soon as she could squeeze through, Mary pushed in and ran to the far side of the library. A similar set of doors opened there as well. She checked the floor and saw a stone that was a different shape than the others. She quickly drew her dagger and tried to pry one end of the rectangle up. It resisted at first and then popped up, locking in place. She glanced at the fountain and saw that it was still dry. She checked the other side and found a similar stone, and it pried up easily.

Mary ran back across the room, noting that water was beginning to trickle from the fountain. Mike had found the stone and was still trying to get the first one up. Mary slid to a stop at the other side and frantically dug at the check stone there. The door was beginning to move when it finally locked into place, and she heard Mike exclaim in triumph as he got his opened. They stepped back as the doors moved and stopped against the stones. They hugged each other and reentered the library. They approached the table and the corpse; the books indeed were mostly about the sciences. There was what appeared to be a map of the castle, and they studied it. They had entered the backside of the castle and much of it was on the other side of the library.

They saw that the King's living quarters were on the second floor and guessed that the Book would be there, always near the King. The map was too brittle to move, so they both memorized a route to the King's Chambers and as much else as they could.

The other item of interest on the table was a plaque with a flat metal bar and a small brass hammer. Mike struck it experimentally, and the resulting note was distorted and flat. He examined it closely as Mary checked the remaining books on the table. He could see that the plate could be removed, if it were done just so. It was like dissembling a machine; the obvious was not always right. He got it apart and scraped away the dirt and grease that had built up in the channels. A dead beetle was also in the center, where the resonance would be greatest. He reassembled it, and this time a clear tone issued from the plaque.

Mary looked up. "That was the opening note of the sequence that opened the doors. I think you found the key. I wonder if our friend here was tone deaf?" She noticed that the room had fallen quiet and that the fountain had stopped flowing. She took the key from Mike and let the hammer fall just as they had the knocker. The same three notes rang out and the water from the fountain basin drained away. Nothing happened for several seconds, and then the doors opened a little wider. The stops all fell back and the Pair realized that it was time to leave. They went to the far doors and watched as the fountain began to flow again and the doors closed behind them.

"Impressive," Mary said and then turned to the corridor. "We go left and up the staircase. I do not see any indication of magic, but we should still watch for traps. 'To gain what you require, give in not to your desire.' That is not particularly helpful. I can think of a dozen desires right now."

Mike smiled and started down the left-hand corridor. It opened into a large room with a central staircase. He carefully examined the room before entering, as did Mary. They entered together, and Mike slipped along the wall while Mary walked directly to the stair. She stopped as he called to her and joined him at a painting. She could see that it was oddly shaped, wide and not too tall. At first it appeared to be a painting of a country road, then she realized that it was the view through the windshield of Mike's 'Vette. The dash and interior were perfectly reproduced. Mary just stared. Mike quipped, "This can't be right. The speedometer only shows it going twenty-five. I never drive that slow." He reached out as if to tap the instrument, and his hand entered the painting. He quickly drew it back and looked at Mary.

It was several seconds before she could speak. "This is a way home. We can get back in the car, and we will be home. Do you see what this means? We can go home, right now!" The excitement in her voice was infectious. She noticed a shadow pass behind Mike's eyes. It was only a flicker, but there was no mistaking it.

He tried to sound excited. "A way home. Back to Earth in time for Christmas." It was clear that there was a conflict raging inside him. "What are we waiting for? It's right here. Let's go."

In that moment Mary saw the self-sacrifice in his nature. She knew every bit of his being screamed at him to continue the quest, but he thought she wanted to go home—he would do that for her. Emotion welled up inside her as she also felt the turmoil, then she heard the harpy's words. *"To gain what you require, give in not to your desire."*

"No, that would not be right! An entire world needs you, needs us. We will find our way home without abandoning those who are counting on us." She quelled the protest on his lips by placing a finger there. "No argument! That is the last of the riddle. We go up the stairs!"

He shrugged and turned back to the staircase, but it was gone. In its place was a huge creature. It looked mostly human except it was over ten feet tall and its skin glowed with a golden light. Its voice filled the room like thunder, "You must now prove yourself worthy to take the book." The creature addressed Mary and Mike, both of whom seemed frozen in place. "I am Alothen, the Guardian of the Tome."

CHAPTER TWENTY-THREE

Alothen gestured towards Mary, and she was nearly swept off her feet by a magical wind. She countered the spell and let the wind sweep past her. "Why must we fight? Is there anything in this world that doesn't require bloodshed?" She did not attack so that Alothen could answer her.

The huge creature gazed impassively at her for several seconds. Then his thunderous voice again rang through the hall. "I think your companion has the answer in his mind. 'That which we obtain too easily, we esteem too lightly.'[2] He quotes Thomas Payne. I do not know this Payne, but his words are filled with truth. I cannot just give you the book."

"But look at all those who have died already! Even in the next room, death captured one who sought the book. We passed the tests, we defeated the Grybon, our friends were nearly killed! Mike had to relive the most painful portion of his life. I destroyed a creature that hated us just because we were not evil!" Mary paused as she noticed light collecting on the creature's right hand. She was ready with a counter spell when it cast the fireball at her. She deflected several attacks in rapid succession. Still she did not retaliate.

"You will not fight? Then how could you protect the book? An evil greater than the Grybon is waiting for you. The book of Ages cannot fall into the hands of the Dark Lord; with it he would be able to control the ancient magic that created Heavenshire. Perhaps you need more relevant motivation." The Guardian waved his hand; Mike disappeared and reappeared against the ceiling. "In ten minutes the levitation spell will fail, perhaps less if he struggles. No, you will not save him so easily." He easily blocked Mary's attempt to free Mike.

"I did not want this. You have given me no choice," Mary replied grimly. She sent a bolt of pure magic at the creature. It struck with enough force to drive it backwards a step. She quickly followed with a levitation spell of her own and flung the guardian against the wall. She dodged the counter spell and managed to spin him and drop him on his back. She immediately threw a suppression spell over him and held it with all her strength. The guardian was trapped and fought back fiercely, filling the area inside the suppression spell with light and multi-colored flashes. Mary recalled a containment spell that she had read about and an opaque box formed around the suppression spell. Once it was fully formed, Mary released the suppression spell and waited. The box shook, but it held. Quickly she turned to face Mike and was able to cast a spell that caught him as he fell lightly to the floor. She ran to him; he appeared unhurt.

"Well done, daughter of Eve!" Alothen's voice rang through the hall. "You have passed your test. You were not required to defeat me. You cannot match power with the ancient magic that created me. You just had to do your best. Now it is time for your friend's test. Alas, you cannot aid him!" Suddenly she was again at the painting and turning to look at the room. The grand staircase was again there, and she heard Mike saying he would go ahead and that she should stay. She tried to protest, but could not utter a sound.

Mike was a little amused by the painting; he could not imagine driving so slow on an open road. He started up the stairs and paused at the first landing to look back at Mary. She had not moved, and he was puzzled. He drew the Sword of the Ancestors, and the room was instantly bathed in golden light. The stairway above the first landing vanished, and he heard the sound of an armored figure entering the room. A knight in golden armor stood opposite him. The knight was huge, probably ten feet tall, and the broadsword he carried had to be six feet in length. His helm concealed his face, and he made no sound.

Mike began to descend the stair, his sword held low before him. "Are you the Guardian of the Tome, Sir?" The armored figure made no answer, merely standing with his sword partially raised. "We were sent by the elves to retrieve the Book of Magic so that they can complete their journey. Their King presented me with this blade." He dropped to one knee and presented the sword to the knight.

The knight lowered its sword and walked forward. It struck as swiftly as lightening with its gloved fist. The blow would have sent the Sword of the Ancestors flying across the room—had it landed. At the last moment, Mike gripped the pommel and spun away from the blow. He was ready to meet the broadsword as it descended in a blow meant to split him in half. He grunted and slipped from under the blow and aimed a slice at the giant knight's torso. The blow connected, but did not pierce the armor. The knight staggered, and Mike spun counter to his first stroke to impact the other side of the massive body. The golden armor rang like a huge bell but held.

Seeing that he was too close for the knight to strike with his sword, Mike attempted to grapple with him. He crooked a leg behind the knight and drove his shoulder into his midsection. The knight was leaning back; Mike thought that he may have toppled him. Then he felt the gloved hand grasp the back of his leather armor and lift him into the air. The knight raised him to eye level and caught the Sword of the Ancestors as Mike tried to slice at the base of his neck. Mike could not see the knight's eyes; only a golden light came from inside the helm. The Giant Knight began to spread his arms, and Mike felt as though his arm would be torn from its socket. Desperately he cast a levitation spell that barely lifted them from the ground. He threw his weight backwards, and they began to topple in the air. He held the spell until they had rotated through the vertical and the knight's back was to the floor. Mike released the spell. They crashed to the floor, and the knight released his grip. Mike rolled away and quickly regained his feet.

The knight's arms and legs thrashed as he tried to roll over so that he could regain his feet. Mike grabbed the huge broadsword and lifted it above the knight's head, his muscles straining. "Do you yield, sir?"

The knight was still for a moment. "Yes, to you I yield, son of Adam." Then the knight vaulted to his feet as lightly as any acrobat. "You have passed your test. You and your companion may retrieve the book. Go as you planned, and then return here." Mary had been released the moment the knight yielded. She retrieved the Sword of the Ancestors and handed it to Mike. The Pair turned to find that the staircase had again reappeared.

Mike halted abruptly at the top of the stairs. "I just remembered watching you face Alothen. The memory was not there while I fought him. How strange!" He looked into Mary's eyes and reached out to brush a loose lock of hair from her face. "It was the most amazing thing I have ever seen. When the guardian threatened me, you fought like a tigress." He was smiling, but she could see that the smile was covering a profound sadness. "You are well qualified to protect those you," the pause was very small as he searched for an alternate word, "care for. I think that our greatest challenge is before us—the servant of the Dark One." He turned; Mary raised her hand, then let it fall as he started towards the King's chamber.

Mary wanted to scream or throw something at him as he walked away. *"Why is he holding back? Doesn't he think I can take care of myself? Haven't I proven that? Is he unsure of my love?"* She could hardly stand the questions rushing around in her head. She was slightly distracted as several objects rose into the air. She laughed to herself at how easy it would be to make him pay for rejecting her. Only he had not really rejected her—but he hadn't accepted her either. The night they had discussed their feelings in the Dwarf's mountain seemed a lifetime away.

She forced herself to relax, and the objects settled to the floor. Mike looked back over his shoulder, and she started walking after him. She couldn't resist dislodging a small piece of an overhead candelabra and guiding it to gently strike the top of his head. He jumped at the impact and drew his sword; Mary laughed and pointed to the jade-colored stone on the ceiling. "Looks like the caretaker has been a little lax. Watch yourself." Mike gave her a suspicious look and turned back towards the goal, eyeing the ceiling as they went. Mary used magic to push a carpet runner into ridges, and the big man stumbled over them. He muttered about a sudden attack of clumsiness, and Mary offered to lead the rest of the way.

Mike let her pass and carefully followed behind her, watching both floor and ceiling. They reached the King's quarters with no further incident and entered. The apartment was lavishly decorated and consisted of several rooms, including a library. A book was in a glass case along one wall, which opened easily to Mary's hand. She retrieved the book and stopped, puzzled by the expression on Mike's face. "Don't you think that was too easy?" he asked.

"Yes, it was a little obvious. But there is great magic in this book. Let's look around a little. I wonder why Alothen sent us after the Book? Do you think this is still part of the test?" She looked around for a moment, glancing at the bedroom. She laid the book on the table in front of the case and walked into the bedroom. "This book will be safe here for a while. It has a strange feel to it. I think he would want the real book near, but not necessarily in plain sight."

Mike stood in the door between the library and the King's bedroom. "Look at these walls. They are not true to each other. There is a void near the far wall, behind the glass case where we found the book."

Mary came and stood in the doorway and saw that it was true, "I wonder," she said. She walked back into the library and stood in front of the glass case. She stepped to the side and began to examine the books on the shelf. She softly read the titles aloud until she found one titled *Gateway Gardens, Past and Present.* She turned to Mike.

"This book doesn't belong here. The rest are volumes of the law, royal decrees and things like that. It is the only book that doesn't deal with governing."

"Take it down. Maybe it is a clue. Can you tell anything about it magically?"

Mary pursed her lips. "No, it does not appear to be magic, although it does seem a bit strange." She reached up and carefully removed it from the shelf.

Nothing happened. She stood on tiptoe to look behind where it had stood on the shelf. She saw a scrap of parchment and had to remove another book to retrieve it. Two symbols were scratched on the parchment: an omega symbol and a script "A." She looked at it for a while and asked, "Mike, were you ever in a fraternity?"

"No," he answered. "The Greek alphabet made my head hurt." He looked over her shoulder; his nearness was vaguely unsettling. "Omega and Alpha. Wait, what did Alothen say to you when you won?"

"He said 'Well done, daughter of Eve!' and he called you 'son of Adam,' both biblical references from our world. Is this a clue? What do Omega and Alpha stand for?"

Mike smiled and quoted, "'I am the Alpha and Omega.' A reference to God. It was also thought to be a code or cipher."

"A cipher, a code, how would that apply?" Mary opened *Gateway Gardens, Past and Present*. "This has a lengthy foreword. Let's see, 'G' is the seventh letter of the alphabet, so I'll look at the seventh word, 'hail.' 'A' is one, and the first word of the next sentence is 'chosen.'" She stopped talking and her brow furrowed as she concentrated. After a few minute she exclaimed, "'Hail chosen ones, ye have discovered the tome!' It is a cipher, now does it continue?" Some time later she said, "Hail chosen ones, ye have discovered the tome. Open ye not the book of spells in solitary lest ye be destroyed. Open the companion and let it lead."

"A warning! Cryptic, but still a warning. The elves will probably understand. We knew that the book was dangerous. It evidentially has powerful protections. Let's take both books." Mary handed the *Gateway* book to Mike. "Wait. You are taller. Look into the hidden space."

Mike was able to stick his head into the space. He could see a panel in the bottom. Reaching in he slid it aside to reveal a handle in the bottom. He reached in and lifted. The section of the bookshelf in front of them swung open and revealed a large book. It was a little larger than an encyclopedia volume and maybe twice as thick. He could feel the power within and automatically cast a shielding spell, feeling Mary do the same.

Mary gasped. "That is The Book. The other must be the Companion." Mary turned aside to retrieve the first book and paused as she looked at the open case and the bookshelf. She pushed the bookcase closed and shut the door to the glass case." Let's go and see what Alothen has to say."

"Gladly," Mike said as he led the way, watching for falling pebbles and wrinkled carpets. They returned to the staircase hall without incident and found the Guardian waiting for them. He no longer wore armor and seemed happy to see them.

"Well done! You have proven worthy to carry the book. It is useless without the index, and you discerned the truth without aid. I have prepared a meal and rations for your journey. There is one favor I would ask." He ushered them into the next room where a table was set. As they ate he spoke. "I cannot leave these walls. Indeed I will sleep until the Elven King again requests my services. It pains me that there are servants of the Dark One just beyond my reach. A Troll and an Ogre trouble the paths leading to the castle. They might have served a purpose if they were not completely evil. They bargain with travelers for safe passage down the path and then turn and kill them after collecting their toll. Rid Heavenshire of their treachery.

"Now I have one final warning for you. You go to face the Grybon. It will attack you on many levels—"

"Did you say the Grybon?" Mary interrupted the guardian. "We have already faced this creature, and banished it. The Gnomes are building a shrine on the spot."

"Impossible! I would know. Come, show me!" Alothen strode quickly to the painting that had tempted the Pair. I became blank at a wave of his hand. He stared at Mary, and an image began to form. It was just lines at first, and then colors began to fill in. The image of the clearing where they had fought the Grybon became clear on the canvas. Then, in the center, the scaly, reptilian figure of the Grybon formed. A man, only half its size, grappled with it, holding fast to the creature's waist. Both were splattered in blood and gore, and the creature's clawed hand was reaching for the man's throat.

A woman stood to the side, braced as though to push a heavy object. Her arms were stretched out in front of her, and her hands were cupped around a brilliant ball of light that was bursting away from her. Two elven bodies lay limp on the ground behind her. The entire scene was as detailed as a photograph. The woman's hair was streaming back from her face. A face that held a fierce expression, which was almost terrible to look upon as she cast the spell that banished the creature.

"It is true, but how can it be? I am bound to this place as long as the Grybon walks the land." Alothen turned and ran from the hall towards the front gates of the castle. The doors opened as he approached, and he paused at the threshold. "Perhaps this has been my prison so long that I have forgotten what freedom feels like." He turned to Mary and bowed, and then he turned and stepped through the gate unhindered. Outside he raised his hands to the sky and turned in a circle.

From nowhere a dark bolt of lighting struck the Guardian. For a moment the image of the Grybon was superimposed over Alothen. The giant began to glow as the darkness merged and was drawn inside him. A great shout issued from his lips and beams of light began to pierce his skin. The light seemed to flow into the castle walls, which began to glow from within. The Guardian's form seemed to explode in a final burst of light; when it was gone, a middle-aged man stood where the Guardian had only a few moments before.

He was an imposing figure—an elf but tall even for that race. His blonde hair had a golden tinge and curled around his face. To call him handsome would be to miss the beauty of the elf. His blue eyes seemed to pierce through Mary into her soul, and she was lost for a short time. He was dressed in rich clothing that seemed archaic even by the standards of Heavenshire. The light from the Castle grew brighter for a moment, and then seemed to wash outward into the land, cleansing the dinginess that one would not have realized was there. The only sound was the whisper of the Sword of the Ancestors sliding back into its sheath. Mike had started to draw it when the bolt struck Alothen.

Mary asked, "Don't you remember? We spoke of the Grybon during my test?"

Alothen turned away from Mary and spoke. "I did not think it possible. I assumed it was something else. I do not know when I last felt the sun. It has been even longer since I was complete. Let us go back to the dining hall, and I will explain." He placed a hand on her back and guided her back into the castle. "Long ago I discovered that everything has characteristics of light and darkness. I found that it was possible to separate out the darkness and contain it. I started with this castle and found that its stones transformed to gems when the darkness was removed." He spoke as they walked back to the banquet hall.

"I thought my crowning achievement would be to remove all traces of darkness from within myself. I was blinded by arrogance, and my mistake has cost Heavenshire much grief. When I placed my darkness into the containment spell, the Grybon was created. It was a creature of total evil, and it escaped the castle. I was trapped within these walls. It fed on the elves of my kingdom and drove them far away from the castle. It was still bound to me and could not pursue them beyond a certain distance from the castle." Alothen hung his head in shame. "Too late I learned that evil must be confronted, that it cannot be contained. We must daily confront the darkness within us and subdue it. Only the Creator has the capacity to destroy it completely.

"The Dark Lord will know that you have dispatched his servant. He will send many more to attempt to stop you. You must deliver the book to Elvhome and then prepare for the final battle. I must walk a different path, but we will meet again on the plains before the Dark Mountain. We may start together, but our paths must soon part." Alothen turned his attention to the food on the table. "It has been hundreds of years since I sat to table. How appropriate that I break bread with those who have given me a second chance."

CHAPTER TWENTY-FOUR

Mike lounged in the grass waiting for Mary and Alothen to complete their preparations. He was leaning against his pack and was sharpening the Sword of the Ancestors. He had noted that there were birds investigating the trees, something that had been missing when they arrived. He checked the edge of the blade and decided that it was sharp enough. He laid it aside and put the sharpening stone back in his pack. He glanced at the gate and lay back with his head against his pack and closed his eyes. A few moments later he thought he heard laughter and opened his eyes but there was no one there. This happened again and he sat up.

He noticed that the Sword of the Ancestors was lying where he had left it; he put it in the sheath where it belonged. He lay down again and when he heard laughter, he did not open his eyes. He could make out five distinct voices and waited until one was very close and stationary. He grabbed and caught a leg; when he opened his eyes, he saw that he held a small, winged female. He quickly released her, and she flew a few feet and hovered over him, laughing. She was joined by four others.

The creatures looked like human girls, except for the wings. They were dressed in floral colors and all seemed to be trying to get his attention. He finally asked, "Who are you?"

"Don't you recognize us?"

"We led you to the path."

"Don't you wish you had stayed with us?" It was hard to follow their conversation as they flew up into the air and then perched on anything that would hold them.

"Would you like to play hide and seek?"

"Bet you can't catch me like you did my sister?"

"Stop! Be still!" he bellowed. "One at a time. Are you saying that you are, or were, the harpies who guided us?" They all landed and nodded vigorously. "No, I cannot play now, and I am sorry for grabbing your sister like that. What happened that you are changed, and what exactly are you?"

One of the creatures, dressed in a deep rose red, flew close to Mike and said, "We are forest fairies. When the evil was unleashed, we were transformed into those, harpy things. When you destroyed it we were changed back to our true selves. You are our hero!" The other joined with cries of "our Hero."

Mike tried unsuccessfully to get them to quiet down to no avail. The all seemed intent on getting close and kissing him on the forehead or cheek. Finally he shouted, "I didn't do it! All I did was distract it so Mary could banish it."

A fairy dressed in blue whispered in his ear. "We know, but you are more fun to kiss." She kissed him on the ear and flew beyond his reach. A new note of laughter reached him, and he turned to the castle gate to see Mary nearly rolling on the ground as she laughed. The fairies noticed Alothen and flew to him, landing and falling to their knees.

Alothen bowed to them and bade them rise. He held out his hands to them and embraced all of them as they giggled and blushed. Mary was not ignored; they all embraced her as well. Mike straightened his tunic and threw his pack over his shoulders and settled it there. He belted on his sword and turned toward the path. This was a serious mistake as it allowed the fairies to approach unseen. They tackled him and bore him to the ground where they held him for a moment so that each one could kiss him. Then they flew away, their laughter floating on the air for several minutes.

Alothen tried to maintain a solemn expression as he said, "Fairies are most unpredictable." He barely suppressed a giggle as he motioned to Mike's face. "They have left their mark."

Mary was right there with her mirror; prints of fairy lips were stained on his cheeks. "Here let me get that for you," she said.

"No, I think I must bear my mark for a while," Mike said as he rolled to his feet and started marching down the path. He wasn't sure if Mary had set him up or if the fairies were just capricious by nature.

Events were rolling along quickly, and they had been out of touch with the rest of the world for several weeks. He knew there was one more quest for them to fulfill before they could face the Dark Lord. They had served the Dwarves, and now the Elves—next they would serve Men.

He was lost in his thoughts and barely noticed that he was outdistancing the others when he came to a small stream.

They had not crossed a stream on the way in, so he was slightly surprised. It was too early in their journey to need to replenish their water supplies, but he thought that it would be a good place to rest a moment and wait for the others. The path crossed the stream at a stone bridge, so he angled a ways upstream to where he could get a drink. He stopped and took a tin cup from his pack to dip in the water. With hand on his sword, he knelt to get a cup of water from the brook. A large stone slammed into the water inches from his hand.

He straightened, drawing his sword in the same motion. A troll now stood next to the bridge. It had a second stone in its hand and called to Mike. "You must pay for water!"

Mike knelt again and ignored the stone as he dipped a cup of water. He rose and faced the troll. "I have never heard of anyone who would deny a thirsty traveler a drink of cool water. Maybe you will include the price in the toll you wish to charge for crossing the stream?"

The troll eyed the sword in Mike's hand and said warily, "Could, or could knock water out of you!" It reached for the club it had laid down to pick up the stones. "Maybe not want toll from trouble maker." It took a menacing step towards Mike.

The troll was small for its race, standing less than seven feet tall. It was heavily muscled, as were all its kind. The club it held was a dangerous weapon, heavy and spiked on the end. Mike knew his mail would probably prevent it from puncturing him, but the force of the blows could still injure him severely. He held the cup out towards the troll. "Share water?"

The troll lowered the club and reached towards the cup. Mike relaxed slightly and was completely unprepared when the troll knocked the cup from his hand and swung the club in an overhand arc towards his head. He managed to get his sword up in time to deflect the club, but the force of the blow left his entire side numb. He twirled away and backpedaled out of reach of the club. The troll was already pressing its advantage, and the next blow was a horizontal sweep that Mike had no hope of avoiding. He fell away, and the club did not connect directly. Mike was sent tumbling and barely managed to hang on to his sword.

He let himself roll until he was well out of reach and his momentum brought him to his feet. He gripped the sword with his off hand and was able to raise it. He struck towards the troll, keeping it off balance. The exertion of the swing proved that Mike had several broken ribs; he again retreated, barely able to keep from gasping in pain. He rushed the troll and swung his sword over the top, forcing the troll to block the blow. Mike was able to force the club down, but the troll surprised him by releasing the club with one hand and backhanding him.

Mike was sent flying and landed on his back, forcing the air from his lungs and causing the broken ribs to move. The force of the landing and the pain caused him to loose his grip on the sword. He weakly tried to roll away as the troll brought the club down in a savage swipe. It grazed his back and sent new waves of pain through his broken ribs. He continued the roll and saw the club rise again. His hand found the dagger in his belt and he drew it, hoping to at least draw blood. The club did not strike, and Mike rolled once more and tried to regain his feet.

Mary and Alothen walked along the path, and he answered many of her questions about the land they traveled. He could tell her what it had been like before his downfall. The entire race of elves had lived there, creating small towns and large estates. They were long lived, but bore few children, so the population did not grow quickly. They served goodness, but stayed within their borders. They had very few dealings with the other races, hardly needing anything from them. Mary thought that it sounded like paradise. Even in paradise, it would appear, problems could arise. Alothen had grown tired of arbitrating the few disputes among his people, and that had led him to seek to drive out all darkness from their lands.

After the disaster, the Grybon had consumed the essence of many elves, and the survivors had fled far from the jeweled castle. The Grybon had not pursued them beyond the borders at first. Alothen had remained in the castle alone, seeking to undo what he had done. He realized that the Grybon was bound to him and would not venture far from his location. The creature could not come too near him either. To save his people, Alothen had cast a great spell that bound him to the castle as the Guardian and bound the Grybon even more strongly to him. This prevented the creature from pursuing the elves and was Alothen's penitence for his sins.

The spell was one of the ancient spells from the time of creation that had established the prophecy of the heroes who would come to face the Dark Lord and attempt to free Heavenshire. Alothen had been immortal while free of his inner darkness, but was now once again a mortal creature. Alothen suddenly stopped talking and looked around. Mary instantly searched for hostile magic and could detect none. Then she heard the sounds of battle and ran down the path. She topped the rise in time to see the troll fling Mike through the air. He landed with a dull thud and a groan of pain. As the troll raised its club, Mary drew her bow and nocked an arrow. She took quick aim at the club and released. The impact confused the troll for a moment, and she saw Mike trying to rise, armed only with the dagger from his belt.

The troll was looking at his club, which now had an arrow embedded in it along with the spikes. When Mike rolled again it started to strike and stopped when it felt the impact of another arrow in its club. It finally turned to the path where Mary and Alothen were charging towards the battle. It recognized Alothen and charged towards him, roaring in incoherent rage. The former guardian stopped and clapped his hands together as he spoke a word of magic. There was a deafening roar, and the troll just disappeared in a burst of black smoke.

Mike had made it up on one knee, but his vision was ringed with a red-tinged blackness; the pain from his broken ribs pulsed and threatened to engulf him. He saw Alothen stagger slightly, and then the entire scene tilted and he was looking at the sky. There was a roaring in his ears like a raging river, and he could not hear anyone else speak.

CHAPTER TWENTY-FIVE

Mike was barely conscious when Mary reached him. He looked battered, but there was only a slight trickle of blood from a split lip. He was gasping for breath and did not respond to her at first. A hand grasped her shoulder, and she nearly threw Alothen before she recognized him. His face was ashen, and he needed support to kneel beside the fallen man.

Alothen closed his eyes and placed his hand on Mike's chest. He whispered a few words of magic as he concentrated on the wounded warrior. He straightened up and said, "He has several broken ribs, and the cartilage between them is torn. His lungs are clear, but his heart is beating too fast. Lift his shoulders and prop him against your backpack. I am too weak now to complete the healing spell. I shall summon help." He stood and raised his hand into the air, calling, "Come forth, little friends. The man needs your help." Almost instantly the fairies appeared. He spoke quietly, instructing them to gather several roots and herbs.

Mary had managed to get Mike propped against her pack, and he was breathing slightly easier. She looked around for his pack and noticed his tin cup lying near the water's edge. She looked at the scuffmarks and tried to determine what had happened. Pursing her lips she picked up a pinch of dust and grass, tossed it gently in the air, and spoke a word of magic. An image of the troll knocking the cup from Mike's hand appeared, as well as the first few seconds of the battle. She let the image fade as she collected the cup and filled it with water from the stream. She was only a few steps from Mike when she heard him groan. He was struggling against Alothen's hand, trying to rise. She quickly returned and spoke to him. "Be still! The battle is over. Here is some water, drink and rest. Alothen has summoned help. Be still and your ribs will stop hurting."

Mike's eyes opened and he nodded his head, accepting the water. He tried to speak, but Mary stopped him. She said, "I know what you tried to do. I am proud of you for trying, but the troll deserved his fate." After a few sips he refused more and laid his head back, closing his eyes.

Alothen had retrieved Mike's pack and was preparing a small fire. He had collected tinder and was clumsily attempting to strike a spark with Mike's flint. Mary motioned him back, pointed to the wood, and spoke the word for fire and the branches burst into flame. She quickly cast a shielding spell and watched as Alothen fed the fire.

"We will need to heat some water to make a potion that will ease his pain," Alothen explained. "I am so weak I cannot cast even a simple spell. It might be just as well, I cannot seem to control magic just now." The fairies returned, and Alothen went to work creating the potion. Mary watched carefully and took the finished liquid to Mike. She mixed a small amount of cool water with it and offered it to him. He spit the first sip out, and she had to convince him that the bitter drink was intended to help him. He drank and made several interesting faces. This elicited giggles from the fairies, and he noticed them for the first time.

"Fairies, just what I need." His voice was gruff but he managed a slight smile.

The fairies stood in front of him and bowed and recited their names.

"Ariel."

"Alexis."

"Alicia."

"Arica."

"Arrissa."

Mike inclined his head to them. "Are you going to attack me again? I am hardly in a position to fend you off." His breathing had slowed, and there was a hint of laughter in his voice. The fairies protested that they only wanted to help, but he cut them off. "I know. I know. That was my game with you. Thank you for your help in creating the medicine. I am in your debt."

"No, no. We are in your debt because you fought the troll. He can no longer trouble us." Ariel flew near to Mike. "We know that the others fought him also, but you were the first to engage it in battle. And you took the full force of its treachery."

"Very well," Mike replied. "Then you will steal no more kisses!"

The fairies were shocked and dismayed until they realized that this was part of his game. Then they flew in a circle around him, feinting as though to cover him in their lip rouge again. This continued until Mike laughed and was sent into a spasm of pain. Then they crowded around him in sincere concern until Alothen sent them away. Mike insisted they help him to his feet, and the pain lessened greatly. Leaning slightly on Mary they traveled a short distance down the path to a hut that was evidentially where the troll slept. All manner of junk was strewn about, the belongings of unfortunate adventurers.

Mary cleared away the filthy bedding and collected enough fresh material to make a bed for Mike. Alothen insisted he take another draught of the potion, and they helped him lie down. Once he stopped moving the potion took full effect, and Mike was soon sleeping. The others made the best beds they could and shared standing watch through the night. Mike cried out once just after midnight, and Mary made him drink more of the potion. When morning came they tackled the task of binding his ribs. They were traveling again by mid-morning and reached a crossroads. Alothen bid them farewell, saying that they would meet again in Elvhome, but that he must travel a different path.

The Pair turned their attention to the road before them and calculated that they would reach their rendezvous with the twins within a day. They reached another sign warning against entering the realm and knew they were not far from their destination. Mike paused at this and said, "We promised to dispatch the ogre as well."

Mary started to protest, but something about the look in Mike's eyes stopped the words in her throat. "It will require something other than brute force. You'd have trouble raising your sword even if something weren't trying to kill you." She stopped for a moment and a smile slowly spread across her face. "What if we use his greed against him?" Mike smiled as he began to grasp the essence of her plan.

CHAPTER TWENTY-SIX

The Pair camped just off another road that led to the Jewel Castle. Mike rolled and muttered in his sleep as Mary tried to keep a damp rag on his forehead. He was muttering, and she was trying desperately to keep him quiet. "Keep the gold safe," he would nearly shout. "Hide the treasure," he would whisper. His eyes would open wide, but they were not seeing the surrounding woods. Mary would lay her hand across his mouth but he would struggle and begin to shout. Finally she whispered to him.

"You hid the gold and jewels, remember? You would not even let me go with you. You were soaking wet when you returned and have been struck with fever since. Oh, I wish we had never found that treasure!" she cried.

Not far away an ogre—a large, hulking creature—listened. It was covered in coarse hair and had almost no neck. The creature's bushy eyebrows and beard gave the impression that its eyes floated in a sea of hair atop its shoulders. Those beady red eyes were focused on the man and woman who had been unfortunate enough to camp near its lair. It smiled to itself as the man rambled on about a treasure. The ogre's greed was fueled, and it began scheming.

The ogre knew of several swamps around the Jewel Castle where a man could catch serious illnesses. Some of the fevers were almost always fatal to them. The ogre feared that the man would die before it could force him to tell where the treasure was hidden. It made a decision and walked quickly into the makeshift camp.

The woman rose to face the ogre with nothing but a belt knife in her hands. It grinned, a horrible expression that usually sent human females running away screaming. This woman was different; she stepped between the man and the ogre. This caused the ogre to pause; he was certain that she was no threat, but fighting her would delay his plan, and the man had fallen silent. The ogre thought he might already be dead. It simply reached out a long arm and swept the woman from her feet, throwing her to land several feet away in a crumpled heap. Turning to the man, the ogre did not see the woman rise.

The ogre grabbed the man roughly and shook him. "Man, tell where treasure! Tell now!" The man's head lolled back on his shoulders, and the ogre grabbed his face, drawing him to his feet. When the man's eyes opened, the ogre spoke again. "Tell where treasure, not rip off face." The man's eyes widened so the ogre released his face and almost drooled in anticipation of finding the treasure.

The man spoke slowly. "You will find your reward at the feet of the Dark One."

The ogre was confused for a moment until it realized that the man was defying him. It raised a massive fist to strike and suddenly stopped. It looked down at its chest where the tip of a sword protruded. While it watched the sword disappeared back into its body and black blood poured forth. The man easily broke free of the ogre's grip and pushed hard against it. The creature toppled like a tree that had been felled by the woodsman's ax. The woman stood just beyond the body with sword raised. No finishing blow was required; the first thrust had pierced the evil heart.

Mike groaned slightly, and Mary rushed to his side as he waved her off. "I'm all right. Good timing on the blow, love. One more shake like that might have broke something. Are you injured? That looked like a hard fall."

Mary shook her head no as she turned to their packs and retrieved the pain mixture. "Here, take some, and we must get going. We are already a day late for the rendezvous." Mike sipped the potion while Mary gathered their packs. He retrieved the Sword of the Ancestors from where she had laid it and carefully cleaned it before sliding it into the sheath on his back. He then shouldered his pack and started resolutely down the road. Mary looked back one time at the dead ogre and then hurried to join her friend.

CHAPTER TWENTY-SEVEN

Mike breathed a sigh of relief when he saw the old outpost where they were to meet the twins. The elves showed an unusual amount of emotion when they saw their friends, even before they knew the quest was successful. They were dismayed by Mike's wounds and immediately stripped him of his shirt and mail. They placed their hands on his chest and back and completed the healing spell Alothen had begun. Mike felt warmth in his chest and most of the pain disappeared. Alsharon informed him that the bones were knit together and the torn cartilage repaired. The bruising would have to heal naturally, and Mike would be hindered for some time. This was not good news due to the fact that they had to move quickly; forces of the Dark Lord were already searching for them.

They allowed Mike one day to rest, and Alsharon drew some sketches of a few strange creatures that had been seen around the old elven kingdom. One creature was a twin to the beast they had killed at the Dark Mountain, and there were others that were equally fierce looking. It was early summer, so they would have no problem with the weather in the mountains, but they could not allow themselves to be ambushed by such creatures in the high passes. They would not be able to find mounts until they crossed the mountains; their plight seemed to grow more dire all the time.

The next morning was gray and overcast, which cast a

pall over Mike as he plodded along, feeling sharp stinging pains with each step. They still had the ingredients for the pain potion, but Mike did not like the way it dulled his senses. He needed to be alert with so many servants of the Dark One near. They encountered one of the strange beasts almost immediately. It had the body of a deer and the head and tusks of a wild boar. It charged Elsharone, but the elf easily avoided its flashing tusks and killed it cleanly with an arrow to the heart as it turned for a second pass. They burned the carcass quickly and hurried from the area. They heard a second beast before nightfall, but were able to avoid it.

Two days later they camped near the high pass. Mike was left at the campsite while the others scouted around the pass for signs of enemy activity. Alsharon insisted that the bruised muscle and cartilage were healing, but Mike could not claim any improvement. He heated some water and prepared the pain reliever, waiting restlessly for the others to return. As he scanned the mountains to the east, he saw something flying. He hastily found his sight glass, a crude telescope that Alexar had made for him, and saw a flying beast. It had large leathery wings and a serpentine tail and neck. It seemed to be searching the eastern pass, a route that they had abandoned—even though it would have been more direct—because it would have been too dangerous. Just as the sun set, the beast—Mike thought of it as a dragon—turned back to the south and dropped from view between mountain ridges.

When the others returned they discussed the flying creature. Mike was determined to press on even though the others did not want to make the crossing at night. In the end, he was able to convince them that he was physically up to the task, and they quickly moved out.

They jogged at the best pace Mike could manage and reached the pass before nightfall. A mixed band of twenty orcai was camped in the pass. This led to an argument between Mary and the Elves about negotiating or striking first. Mike listened for a while and then slipped silently away. He approached the pass and observed the orcai. They were eating their evening meal and did not seem to have posted a guard. Mike did not believe them to be so incompetent, so he searched further and discovered a well-concealed post overlooking the trail.

There was something odd about the gathering that bothered Mike. He realized that these orcai did not quarrel among themselves. They had the look of a well-functioning military unit. He could detect no dark magic or magical threat. He sat for a while and observed before returning to his camp. The three were still arguing when he arrived. He could see a dangerous glint in Mary's eye and moved quickly to defuse the situation.

He explained what he had seen and asked the twins if they had ever heard of such a well-trained orcai unit. They had not, and this raised their concerns greatly. Finally they agreed on a plan.

Mike strode the path as though he had not a care in the world. As he approached the lookout's post, he called out to the sentry and met him in the center of the trail. It was then that he noticed the second post on the opposite side of the trail. A goblin slipped from it and headed for the camp. Mike made a show of un-slinging his canteen and drank before offering it to the sentry. The sentry politely refused, stating they would wait for the commander.

Mary and the twins watched the second sentry enter the camp and go directly to the leader. The leader was a huge orc who quickly gathered the remainder of the band, and they marched towards the lookout posts. Alsharon followed while Elsharone and Mary swiftly looked through the camp. There was little to find except for a dinner plate that Mary recognized as coming from Silverthorn's keep. She signaled Elsharone, and they quickly caught up with Alsharon.

The orcai were arrayed in three ranks with the commander in front facing Mike. The elves and Mary took up flanking positions and waited. The leader just stood and watched Mike, who stared impassively back at him. Mary had seen Mike employ this tactic before. He would wait for the other to begin to speak and would then interrupt as though he had thought to speak at the same time. After a few false starts, the orc was getting frustrated. After another attempt he bellowed, "Speak!"

Mike made a small bow, never breaking eye contact and offered the canteen. The orc replied, "Why should I share water?"

"Because," Mike said softly. "I did save the children."

The response was immediate; the orcai turned to each other and whispered, debating whether this was true. The leader silenced them with a hard glance and turned to Mike. "Where is woman?"

"Behind you," Mary exclaimed as she stepped from cover with her bow drawn. "You are far from home. Will you share food and water again?"

The commander turned his head and then shook it slowly. "Once again you have advantage, woman. Yes, we break bread, but not here. The servants of Dark One are approaching. Let us be away from here." He signaled the troop and they performed a fair about face and marched back to the camp.

Alsharon and Elsharone joined Mike as he followed, and Mary joined them as they passed her position. The orcai leader's eyes widened slightly when he noticed the elves, but he said nothing. The orcai struck camp quickly and marched about three miles to a small plateau before pausing. The group entered an opening in the wall of the mountain. Inside was a small cavern, adequate for the group to set up camp. The orcai set guards at the entrance and did not prepare fires. The two groups shared their rations, and Mary explained how she had met this orc. It took several moments for her to remember its name—Cracktooth.

A sentry who whispered a message to Cracktooth interrupted them. The creature's expression was difficult to read, but it did not look pleased. It stood and bade them accompany him to the cave entrance. Mike could see the same winged creature he had seen earlier winging over the pass. The sentries retreated inside the cavern, and no one spoke. The winged creature flew over the pass twice and then back the way the company had traveled.

The creature had been out of sight for several minutes when the orc spoke. "This is not best. Dragon expected to find orcai guarding pass. It will alert nearest patrol, and they will come to investigate. We must push on and separate. The orcai will pursue, and we can do little for you. If we face dragon now it will sense that you have been with us. We must hide until your scent passes from us." They quickly gathered their belongings and departed.

CHAPTER TWENTY-EIGHT

Days later they approached the entrance to the valley where Elvhome lay. The pain of his injured ribs was constant; Mike could barely keep pace, the pain potion having long since run out. They had fought several battles with orcai patrols as they left the foothills and had barely rested. It had been over a day since they had seen any sign of the enemy, and Mike looked forward to allowing his abused body to rest. They were met by a large patrol of elves and escorted all the way to the villa.

Mike handed over a bag he had carried that contained the Book of Magic and turned towards the infirmary, leaving Mary to deliver the prizes to the King and Queen. Word of his injuries had preceded him; a healer met him, immediately led him to a heated bath, and helped him out of the leather outer garment and his chain mail. Mike paused at the healer's exclamation as he held up the chain mail. A large tear stretched across the back, and the healer said, "The blow that did this might have killed you. I will have to examine you for internal injuries. It is no wonder that you are in such pain. I can see that someone used a healing spell on your bones. Who was it? I did not think Alsharon versed in that magic?"

"An elf named Alothen cast the spell. It took a lot out of him." Mike paused when he saw the expression on the healer's face. "I am sure I pronounced the name correctly. He was the guardian of the jeweled castle and was set free when Mary defeated the Grybon." Mike was very puzzled by the expression of the healer's face. "What is wrong?"

"King Alothen is either one of the most revered or reviled of the ancient Kings, depending on the portion of his life one considers. It does not seem possible that you have encountered him. That said, the strength of the healing spell that was laid on your body could only have come from one as powerful as Alothen was said to be. He did not have experience with men, so he could not fully heal you. He did the best with what he knew but the differences in Man and Elf physiology are causing you much of the pain you are experiencing. There are soothing herbs in the bath water, and I will create a potion that will give you lasting relief. Then we will talk of Alothen." The healer turned from Mike and soon as he was settled into the steaming water.

Relief was nearly immediate as the warmth encompassed his body; Mike closed his eyes and let the tension and pain drain away. He realized that he had not relaxed for days, and his thoughts turned to Mary as he slipped into a light slumber.

It seemed that only moments later he was roused by voices at the far end of the room. They were hushed, but he could hear Mary's worried tones. He was so relaxed that he considered pretending to still be asleep. The healer was telling her about bruised organs and improperly knit bones. Mike opened his eyes and drew an experimental deep breath. There was almost no pain so he took another deeper breath. He had not caught their attention so he sat upright and spoke. "I would stand, Mary, but that might cause us both a good deal of embarrassment. What are you two conspiring over there? Do we have a few days to rest or must we journey immediately?"

"You can discuss travel plans later. Now you should rest in the water for at least another half an hour. If Lady Marilyn would be so kind as to sit with you, I must confer with others on how best to undo the damage to your bones. Someone will bring clean clothes when I am ready for you to leave." The elf's demeanor was no different than that of many doctors Mike had faced.

"I've damaged these bones before, and the universal treatment seems to be rest. Some times I listened, others I did not. I seem to heal well either way," Mike replied. He was surprised by Mary's sharp intake of breath. He asked a second question. "What have you not told me?"

The healer sighed and turned to face Mike. "While man and elf appear to be the same species, there are many profound differences. The most significant is the composition of the bones themselves. There are different minerals in the mixture and the bones have different properties. An elf's bones are more supple, flexing under conditions that would cause men's bones to break. When Alothen healed you he introduced some of the different minerals into your bones. The result appears to be that your ribs are not as rigid at the point of the fractures. I am not sure what this portends for you, but I believe that much of the pain you are experiencing is your body trying to reject these foreign minerals. It is possible, even likely that your body will repair the damage. As I said, I must confer with other healers on the best course of action." With that the elf turned and quickly left the room.

Mike mimicked the healer. "The best course of action." He contorted his face and made Mary laugh. He continued to clown until she was laughing so hard there were tears in her eyes. Finally she exclaimed, "Stop. You know he means well."

When Mike mocked her she slapped his shoulder and was horrified by the expression of pain that crossed his face, horrified until she realized that he was faking. Then she hit him harder and turned away. He was immediately contrite. "Mary, I'm sorry. It's just so good to not hurt for a while. Hearing you laugh is the best possible treatment. Please don't be mad at me?"

She turned back to him and her smile told him that all was well. "Did you know that the troll hit you hard enough to break the rings in your mail? You could have been—"

Mike interrupted, "But I wasn't. You were there in time, and I will mend. It's my fault for being irritated about the fairies. You know how I am when I get mad. I want to burn it out of my system. You have no idea how much wood I've split after an argument at the shop. Seems like this time, though, I got it beat out of me."

"You're impossible! I don't know how you can joke about that." She paused. "Although you do make a good point. Wonder where I can find a troll for the next time you need an attitude adjustment?" The both laughed and an elf arrived with fresh clothing for Mike. Mary left to wash the grime from their travels away, and Mike slipped into the pants and tunic. It was a tight fit and Mike needed the elf's aid with the tunic.

The young elf accompanied him to his quarters and handed him a small packet of powder. "When you are ready to sleep, mix this with water or wine and drink the entire cup. Then you are to go directly to bed. We wouldn't want to find you sleeping in the hallway somewhere." Mike thanked him and entered the apartment where they had stayed the last time. There were the same shelves filled with books, couches, and curtained windows. On a table in front of the windows lay a stack of parchment. Mike picked up the top sheet and began to read.

When Mary emerged from her bedroom later, he was pouring over the papers. They were an account of the situation in Heavenshire, and the situation was dire indeed. Most of the land around the Dark Mountain had been conquered. A great wall had been built across the approaches to the kingdom, and there were few places where men, elf or dwarf could travel in safety. Blackthorn Hearth and the Dwarven kingdom were completely cut off and under siege. The Northern Kingdom's armies had broken the siege briefly and resupplied the city. They had rescued many women and children who would be hard pressed to survive the coming winter in the makeshift camps they inhabited.

The wall that separated the Dark Lord's domain was well guarded and had at its center a massive gate over a hundred feet wide. The details were sketchy as there was an army stationed outside the gate. This force was made up of mercenaries and renegades, but had proven surprisingly hard to infiltrate. It was clear that the Dark Lord wanted the activities in his land hidden.

Mike looked up from the reports as Mary approached. She was dressed in the same gown she had worn when Bardwind had met with them. Her hair was piled up on her head and was held in place with a net of silver wire adorned with pearls. She walked up behind Mike and placed her hands on his shoulders. He rose, turning to catch her hands as his movement dislodged them. "You could steal the breath from a whirlwind," he whispered as they stood only inches apart. "I think dancing with you tonight would be like a promenade on air. You look absolutely stunning."

Mary stood for a moment looking into his blue eyes. "I wish that we could dance the night away, but I am to have an audience with the King and Queen, and you are to rest! No! Do not argue with me. Look into the mirror, look at the skin around your eyes, and at the whites of your eyes." She led him to the mirror. "I thought you were just weary from the journey and the pain of your wounds. See the yellow there. Your liver is bruised and is not functioning fully, and the burden of carrying the Book was more than just physical—it has taken a mental toll on you as well." She gently turned him so that she could look into his eyes. "A few more days and you would have slipped into a coma—" She could not go on and Mike knew then that he had been far closer to death than he could have imagined.

Mary read the realization in his eyes and laid her head against his shoulder, gently embracing him. He returned the embrace with only a small twinge of pain from his injured ribs. He spoke softly. "There will be another night to dance then, if you will accept clumsy me as a dance partner. I will dutifully take my medicine and sleep, rest, and maybe dream. Goodnight, my princess." Her eyes were shining with moisture as she reluctantly released him and once again looked into his eyes.

"Always, kind sir. I shall save my best dance steps for you." Mary turned in a rustle of skirts and rushed to the door, leaving Mike where he stood by the table. The closing door broke the trance, and he sank slowly into the chair. After a moment he rose, taking the packet of powder the elf had left for him; he mixed it with water and sipped the concoction as he walked to his room. Sleep came quickly and dreamlessly as the medicine did its work.

The next morning Mike was sore and his muscles stiff when he returned to the infirmary. He was treated to another herbal bath and very little information from the healer. He was ushered back to his quarters with more of the medicine and given instructions to rest there for the remainder of the day. He finished reading the reports and spent a long time considering options. It was apparent that the Dark Lord needed time to complete his preparations. There was no other explanation for the lull in the campaign. The Dark Lord would be satisfied with nothing short of the complete conquest of Heavenshire. Mike wondered if there was a way to use this knowledge to defeat him. It would be difficult to breach the defenses at any time, especially in the dead of winter, but they must find a way.

A thought came to him, and he began rummaging through the bookshelves until he found a book on the geography of Heavenshire. As he read a smile began to cross his face; winter came much later and was much milder in the southern areas around the Dark Mountain. The warriors from the northern Kingdoms would not be hampered by the weather and the southern warriors should be able to tolerate it. The orcai, on the other hand, were not used to being exposed to winter. They spent most of their lives underground, sheltered from snow and ice. Mike thought that it would be possible to mount an offensive in the early winter. Hopefully this would be before the Dark Lord was fully prepared, and thus give the forces of light some hope of success.

Mary was deep in thought as she returned to the rooms the elves had set aside for her and Mike. He was lying on the couch when she entered and he stirred. He swung his legs around and sat up, so she walked over and sat beside him. His eyes were much clearer, and his face did not look so tired. She brushed an unruly strand of hair away from his eyes and lightly kissed him on the cheek. "You look much better. Are you feeling better?"

He smiled and took an experimental breath, expanding his chest. "There is still some discomfort. I think that I am feeling better, but it is hard to tell how much of that is the medicine and treatments. I've looked over the situation reports, and I have a suggestion. I think you could detail it to the king so that he could consider it."

Mary shrugged. "If you want them to talk about it, then you'll get your wish. That is all they seem ready to do! All the while the Dark Lord grows stronger and innocent people suffer." She checked herself before she launched into a tirade. "The chamberlain of the Northern Kingdom is arriving this afternoon. He wishes to see us. I think the elves have not told him about your injuries, and he will be disappointed."

"Surely I can meet with the man!" Mike interrupted her, and she saw that he was indeed much improved. "He will not expect a wrestling match, will he? I bet you could take him at least two out of three falls!" He laughed at his own joke, and Mary saw him wince.

"Be careful. Do not undo the healing. Speaking of healing, the elves need to cast a healing spell to undo the damage from Alothen's attempt. It will weaken the healed fractures, and you will need time to heal naturally. It has to be done before too much of the bone—" she stopped abruptly. The healer had explained that Mike's body was at war with itself. The healing spell had produced new bone, but it was elven and not human. The new bone was trying to extend and replace existing bone while the human bone was attempting to replace the elven. The different type of bones grew through different mechanisms. Elven bones had no marrow and the cells reproduced linearly. This made for a strong and lightweight bone structure. Human bone cells were produced by the marrow and did not coexist well with the elven cells. The elven cells had to be removed or destroyed before they replaced too much of Mike's bone structure.

Mike was looking at her expectantly, so she tried to cover her concern. "I am sure I can't explain it, but they want to do it soon. You will heal quickly." She laid her head on his shoulder and sighed; she wished that he was well enough to sit in conference with the elven leaders. It was not fair, but they would listen to him because he was "Sir Michael." Sometime she felt invisible during the meetings.

They set in silence for several minutes until Mike stirred slightly. Mary immediately sat up and asked, "Did I hurt you?" She was looking for signs of pain in his face, but he was smiling.

"No, you did not hurt me. Actually I felt very warm and comfortable with you sleeping against my shoulder. I just had a strange sensation inside my chest. I didn't mean to wake you. It would be good for you to rest too." He drew a deep breath and reached out to lay his arm around her shoulders and draw her against him. "You need to garner your strength to meet with this chamberlain."

The invitation was appealing, and Mary relaxed against

him again. Absently she reached her hand to his opposite shoulder and settled against him. She did not know how long they sat there in their lazy embrace. Much later she heard a quiet knock at the door. She slipped from the couch and stole over to the door. A young elf waited with a message; the chamberlain had entered the valley.

The sight that greeted her as she turned back towards the couch stopped her in her tracks. Mike was standing and stretching, apparently without pain. He caught her expression, and then an amazed expression of his own crossed his face. "Hey, it doesn't hurt, well almost." He took a deep breath and twisted his torso gently. "A little stiff, a little sore, but not painful. Were you practicing healing spells in your sleep?" He was laughing—but in this place, it was possible that she had.

"I was sitting here wishing that you could be there and make them listen. That's it, I was *wishing*. It must have been enough to heal you over time. I wondered how I could fall asleep so easily. It is a powerful spell to heal and takes a lot of strength." Mary was filled with wonder. Mike crossed the room, grabbed her by the shoulders, and kissed her forehead.

"I am glad you did. Maybe they will listen to me. I'll get dressed, and we will meet the chamberlain. Together they will not be able to ignore us!" He twirled and rushed to his room, leaving Mary slightly amused at the transformation. She turned to her own room and freshened her appearance. He was waiting when she returned, looking very striking in the elven clothing. He bowed to her and offered his arm. She smiled and took it just as a knock sounded at the door. It was a messenger informing her that the chamberlain would arrive at the hall in moments. The messenger was surprised to see Mike, but thought better of making any comment. They were led to the reception room and were in place when the trumpets sounded a flourish and the chamberlain was escorted into the hall.

The man greeted King Arnyea and Queen Ilsidora warmly and thanked them for their welcome. Then he was introduced to Mike and Mary, and he was nearly overcome by emotion. "May the Creator bless you both. The people of my liege's kingdom suffer terribly at the hand of the Dark Lord. Please hasten to their aid as it is foretold. I have brought to you a gift; here in this bundle is the legendary Sword of Kings, forged by the hammer of Silverthorn himself. It shattered the day the Heir was foully murdered, but since the dwarves again have Silverthorn's hammer, you can have it re-forged." The man presented the bundle to Mike and turned to the King. "Forgive me for my haste, Your Majesty, but my people groan under the oppression of the Dark Lord, as will all of Heavenshire if the Prophesied Ones are not successful."

King Arnyea smiled and nodded. "We will talk of these things soon. First allow us to show our hospitality. We will speak at supper of our plans for this war." After the chamberlain was shown from the room, the King spoke to Mike, "It is good to see you on your feet, Sir Michael. I take it that the healers' spell was successful?"

Mary stepped forward and haltingly said, "Yes and no. The spell was a success, but I inadvertently cast it without the aid of the healers. I can explain."

Queen Ilsidora laughed, interrupting her. "No matter. It is enough that Sir Michael is recovering. It would appear that your final quest is set. Events rush forward without regard to schedules or seasons. Man has always been an impatient creature, and it would seem that he is no less impatient to face his possible doom." The Queen turned to Mike. "Sir Michael, perhaps you should visit the infirmary so that our healers can examine you. We are certain that you will want to be involved in our discussions later."

The Pair bowed and left the reception hall. On their way to the infirmary, they discussed what had transpired. Mary was relieved that the Queen had acknowledged the need for immediate action. Mike agreed; they were discussing the journey when they entered the infirmary. The Elven healer was astonished by the story of Mike's immediate healing; he warned Mary that she would need extra rest for a day or two. She promised; as they left she whispered to Mike, "Rest, yeah right, just like you do." Mike pretended to be shocked, and they laughed the rest of the way to their quarters.

CHAPTER TWENTY-NINE

One week later Mike and Mary were on their way to Blackthorn Hearth. They had briefly reunited with Alothen, who had arrived with news that he had contacted many small bands of elves unknown to Elvhome. They were marching to join their kin in the war against the Dark Lord. They had worked out a plan to join the remaining armies of men with the elven and dwarven armies to break the siege of Blackthorn Hearth. They hoped to accomplish this before the first week of winter. Mike and Mary's task was essential to the success of the plan. They were to travel to the King under the Mountain to inform him that the time for the final campaign was at hand. While there, they would have Alexar re-forge the Sword of Kings.

It was the first day of autumn and still very warm. The elves believed that winter would be late in arriving this year, a boon to the forces of light. The Pair traveled with the twins and two men from the chamberlain's escort, James and Peter. These two were reputed to be skilled warriors, and the chamberlain insisted that they be included in the mission. Opposites in nature, James was very outgoing and Peter was somewhat introverted. Mike noted that their weapons were well maintained and that they were well versed in woods craft.

They camped the first evening; Alsharon and Elsharone volunteered for the first watch. Mary sparred with James and Peter, if such an unequal match could be called a spar.

The men received a few bruises for their troubles and gave Mary a great deal of respect. Mike was under strict orders to avoid any contact until absolutely necessary. He practiced alone under the watchful eye of his friend. She was quick to point out where he fell short, causing him to redouble his efforts. He hoped he would be ready when they met the enemy. In the mean time he studied the maps of the area around the Dark Mountain. The Dark Lord was preparing for the final battle, that was clear. What he was preparing was not. Mike thought that maybe the Dark forces were preparing siege machines. That would allow them to break Blackthorn Hearth and completely isolate the dwarves and men. His tiny group had to reach the King under the Mountain in time to break the siege before Blackthorn Hearth fell.

Stealth was to be their main weapon on this journey. Discovery would doom the mission, as they had to cross many miles of enemy-held territory. They hoped to avoid the orcai by traveling through the wilderness far to the west of Blackthorn Hearth. This was the origin of the horde that had originally attacked the city, so it did not necessarily offer safe travel.

The days stretched into weeks, and they encountered little sign of recent orcai activity. Peter and James proved themselves adept at detecting the barest indication of the passage of any creature. Even Alsharon expressed admiration when they discovered the trail of an orcai patrol on bare rock. The men and elves followed the faint trace until they caught up with the orcai patrol. In the hope that it might be Cracktooth's band, Mary scouted ahead. She found the patrol camping near a stream. She noticed that they all wore a small bit of paint on their faces, a white teardrop under the left eye. As she watched, their leader emerged from the brush and the patrol formed ranks and began to drill. She recognized the techniques she had demonstrated on Cracktooth and his band.

Mary backtracked and found the sentry. It was a goblin that looked familiar. She approached with her sword drawn; she could not risk an alarm. When she was only feet from him, she squatted and picked up a pebble from the path, tossing it in front of the goblin. It started, and when it turned to look back, Mary's sword was at its throat. Its eyes widened, but it did not try to move. When she stepped back it bowed its head. "Lady, I take to Cracktooth."

"No," Mary said. "Wait for me to return with the others. Have Cracktooth meet us here at sundown." The goblin nodded, and Mary slipped away. She took care to cover her trail and reached the others well before sundown. They decided that Mike and Mary would meet with the orcai and the others would stay close but out of sight. They were all puzzled by the face markings; this seemed to be yet another evolution of their society.

They were in sight of the meeting place before sundown and found no one but the sentry. Shortly after they arrived, Cracktooth and two other orcs arrived. They spoke for a while, and then the two orcs left while Cracktooth sat watching the trail.

Once the two orcs were well out of sight, the Pair stepped from concealment and approached. Mary started to unsling her water skin when Cracktooth stood up, but he stopped her with a motion of his hand. He extended his hand when they were in reach. "You are friends now. Greet us as you would a friend."

Mike grasped the offered hand and shook. "Friends!"

Cracktooth smiled as Mary also shook his hand. "We have become our own army. Dark Lord started marking his troops. Different mark for different places at the final war. We chose white tear because we still cry for children we not save. You see mark of white tear, you know orcai friend. It good you not come to camp. We follow some who gave children to beast. We make them pay, maybe you not want to see how. It is for us to know. Why you not with elves? Big Man look much healed."

Mary laughed. "Yes, big man much healed. We go to the King under the Mountain. We will see the children you saved."

"Is good. Maybe we see you south of Blackthorn Hearth. Would dwarves let us see childs?"

Mary paused for a moment as she thought about the request." I will ask Alexar. It may be possible. Do you know how many other patrols there are between here and the Dwarves' kingdom?"

Cracktooth smiled. "Soon there be one less! There are few patrols. Most of the orcai have been called to Dark Mountain. Stay to what men call the wilderness, and you see no orcai except for those of the white tear. We find you, maybe, where man's army destroyed horde attacking Blackthorn Hearth, in two weeks?"

"In two weeks then, but we cannot wait—" Mary began and Cracktooth interrupted.

"No wait. Dark Lord not be ready to fight until leaves green again. Him have big plans for then. You fight him before."

Mary glanced at Mike and, catching his almost imperceptible nod, nodded in agreement. "In two weeks then, good hunting!"

The orcai was slightly startled by this last, but he grinned and nodded before turning and rapidly striding towards his camp. The Pair turned and jogged towards their own camp and were soon traveling south.

CHAPTER THIRTY

Alexar the dwarf rubbed his beard thoughtfully. "Let tha orcai see tha children they saved? On the surface tha' seems a small request, but few here 'ould believe tha' any orcai deserve anythin' but killin.' I know tha' we owe much to this Cracktooth and 'is friends. I think tha' I mae have an ally in this if Niatia were ta bae present when the request were made, well, to say she has tha King's ear is quite an understatement. First thing, though, we must re-forge the Sword of Kings. It will require tha elves assistance, as much as I hate ta admit it. It is their magic and our skill that made it a formidable weapon. Yer other two friends, tha men, will hae a hand in it as well." Mike and Mary left the group making preparation at the forge to speak with the King under the Mountain, King Kextar, about Cracktooth's request.

They found King Kextar walking with Niatia in a spectacular crystalline cavern. The little girl squealed and ran to Mary for hugs. They walked for a while with the King as he explained the various wonders of the cavern. Mary cautiously brought up the orcai's request; the King's response was a vigorous "Nae" until he caught sight of the sad expression on Niatia's face.

"What is it, my child?" the king asked.

Niatia wiped away tears. "Cracktooth saved many of my friend's lives. I never thanked him, I was too scared. He deserves to know that we are well and that we appreciate what he did for us. He was very different from the other orcai, he was good. I know you do not think an orcai can be good, but he and his friends have good in them, I saw it." At this last she crossed her arms and stuck out her lower lip, an obvious show of resolve.

The King knelt down and wiped away a tear that was starting to form in the corner of Niatia's eye. "How does one so young become so wise that she can teach a King? How does such courage grow in the heart of one so small? You shall go and see this orcai, and any of the others who wish also." Turning to Mike, he said, "Sir Michael, I will entrust you with a treasure that is more precious to me than this cavern. See to it that they are safe. I will provide an escort to take and return them after my army rendezvous with those of Man and Elf. I will make sure that every soldier knows that the orcai marked with a white tear are not foes."

They returned to their quarters and made preparations. Later that evening they were called to the forge to witness the final steps of the re-forging of the sword of Kings. The blade had been reformed under the blows of Silverthorn's hammer and glowed red hot on the anvil as Alexar made the final strokes to complete its shape. Alsharon and Elsharone stood next to the dwarf as did Peter and James. The elves began an incantation, and each of the five made a small cut on their hand and let a single drop of blood fall on the blade. The blood did not sizzle or dance on the hot metal, rather it was absorbed into it. Alexar then quenched the blade, and the resulting steam surrounded the quintet and rose in a column to the roof of the cavern. For an instant the figure of a mounted knight was visible in the cloud and then it was gone.

Alexar wiped the sweat from his brow and smiled at

those around him. "Well done, lads and lasses! Tha sword bae re-forged. I shall hae it remounted in tha grips before sunrise, and then we can embark to meet the Armies of Men and Elves. Now I shall find m'bed for a well-earned rest." After clasping forearms with the men and bowing to the Elves, he retreated from the forge.

The others made plans to leave for Blackthorn Hearth in the morning. They would arrive at the rendezvous a day early, but Mike wanted a chance to scout the forces besieging the city. Their last night under the mountain was quiet and peaceful.

King Kextar provided mounts for the group, and they were on their way at sunrise. Alexar had joined them, stating that seven was a lucky number and they would need all the luck they could get. The party traveled quickly but took time to rest the horses often. They were not far from Blackthorn Hearth as the sun hung low in the sky. Alsharon was scouting ahead of the party and detected a large orcai force in front of them. They turned to backtrack and go around a different way but ran into a second force. They melted into the low brush off the trail when a dragon arrived and caught them with too little cover. Mary and the Elves kept it at bay with their arrows, but the orcai forces were alerted to their presence. Finally an arrow found its mark just as the dragon opened its mouth to breath a fiery blast; the beast exploded in the air. By now they had no choice but to stand and fight. They were able to make their way to the base of a bluff where they could keep from being surrounded.

The orcai rushed towards them in a disorganized mass and were repulsed by the steel and resolve of the small band. The horde withdrew, leaving the ground littered with their dead and injured. They slowly formed a semblance of ranks and pressed the attack again. The defenders held an advantage of providing only a limited front for the orcai to attack. The orcai withdrew a second time, leaving the little band relatively unscathed.

The defenders were in dire straits; their supply of arrows was rapidly dwindling and they were vastly outnumbered. Their position at the top of a small rise with a sheer bluff to their backs gave them a defensive advantage but little else. They would eventually fall to sheer numbers if nothing else. The sun had set and a full moon was high in the sky as the orcai attacked a third and fourth time. Mike looked around at the others and saw exhaustion etched deeply in their gore-splattered faces. It was impossible to tell how much of the blood was theirs or that of the foe. They had time for a drink of water, and then the horde massed for another attack. Mike decided to expend the gunpowder that he had preserved as a last resort. There was little time to place the remaining gunpowder before the orcai charged. He worked quickly and returned to the small band of defenders. James was sharpening his sword while Peter sat writing on a small piece of parchment. Mike blanched slightly as he realized the man was using some of the blood that covered him as ink.

Alsharon was looking to the horizon, and Mike turned to follow his gaze. His heart fell as he saw the orcai streaming over the far hills. He turned to the elf and shrugged. "Can we break out?" Alsharon shook his head, raised his sword, and began to chant an elven prayer. Mike heard a faint sound on the wind, but dismissed it as the orcai began their charge. Mike waited until the charging orcai had begun to pass the gunpowder charges before he said the word to ignite them. The blast was devastating to the enemy and created a good deal of confusion. Their attack faltered slightly but did not fall apart. Disappointment seized Mike as the orcai regrouped and renewed their advance.

The orcai had seen the approaching force also and did not withdraw. They kept coming, and the world seemed to shrink down to the few yards surrounding the defenders. Mike saw that Mary was so weary she could barely raise her sword when he noticed a sudden increase in the sound of battle and a decrease in the pressure in front of him. The orcai were drawing back. When he looked beyond the carnage in front of him, he saw that the approaching force had attacked the rear of the former attackers. He also could hear the sound of a horn on the wind.

Alexar raised his head and reached for the horn slung across his back. He brought it to his lips and blew a long wavering note that was answered on the wind. The dwarf grinned at Mike. "Help bae ta hand, laddie. Let us mount up and break out while we can." Mike could see banners waving in the distance, in the direction of the Dwarves Kingdom. The orcai of the white tear had nearly split the attacking force, and Mike could see an opening to their right, in the direction of Blackthorn Hearth. He signaled the others as they swung into their saddles. The orcai flank disintegrated before them, and they rode in an arc around the enemy, turning them back on themselves. The front elements of the dwarven cavalry were driving into the far flank, and the orcai were in complete disarray. The white tear had spread out and now the attackers were pinned against the bluff in a wide front. The battle continued with no quarter offered or given until the last of the orcai attackers fell.

There was a pause as the white tear orcai faced the

dwarves, unsure of the reception they could expect. Mike rode his mount into the space between the forces and dismounted, looking for Cracktooth. He found the orc in the center of the lines, strode up to him, and clasped forearms, patting him on the shoulder. At first there was silence, and then a ragged cheer arose from the ranks of the dwarves as they realized that these were the orcai who had saved the children. Mike could feel the tension drain completely away as Mary rode up and embraced Cracktooth.

The two armies withdrew and hastily set up separate camps. A renewal of tension surfaced as the dwarves began to speculate as to how the orcai had been able to set their ambush. A single goblin had been captured and was brought before the leaders. It was defiant and vulgar, cursing and spitting at those who bound him. Mike drew the Sword of Kings and placed the tip against the goblin's throat. It screamed in pain, and Mike saw what looked like a black spark exit its chest. The goblin was suddenly calm, and Mike asked bluntly, "How did you know where to look for us?"

The goblin hesitated, but when Mike pressed the tip of the sword slightly, it spoke. "Dwarf tell."

"What do you mean?" Mike kept the tip of his sword against the goblin's throat, aware of the reaction of the dwarves behind him.

"Dwarf come to camp. Talk to Redshank. We come here, most die." The goblin eyed the angry dwarves behind Mike. "Men have spies, people have spies, same thing. Is war."

Mike nodded. "Is war. Cracktooth, he is your kind, you deal with him, just see that he does not betray us."

Cracktooth nodded and drug the unresisting goblin towards his camp.

The muttering among the dwarves in earshot rose, and Mike turned to stare at them. "Any of you who want to challenge me are welcome to do so," his voice was soft but it carried well in the silence. When no one stepped forward he continued. "There is no question that there was a traitor among us. It matters little now. The die is cast. We must break the siege of Blackthorn Hearth day after tomorrow. Go and rest." He found his companions, and after a small meal they slept.

The sun was high when Mike awakened the next morning. Mary had already stirred and had heated some water to wash the worst of the dried blood from his skin. She looked tired, and he dreaded telling her that they must ride again soon. "The goblin joined the white tear after they took him last night. The Sword of the Kings drove the taint from him."

She looked at him. "I was so glad that you turned him over to Cracktooth. It went a long way to helping the orcai trust us."

Mike turned to her. "Trust is a fragile thing. The white tear must take its place in the Dark Lord's ranks. They must trust that we will not attack them; we must trust that they will not betray us to the Dark Lord. The dwarves must trust the elves, and vice versa. And Men must trust them all. This is a house of cards, and the Dark Lord has now sown the seeds of mistrust. Maybe we will strike before they can take root." He hung his head. "I do not know. We can only go forward."

Mary forced a smile. "If forward is the only way we can go, then let's get to it." She rose and walked in the direction of their horses. Mike could only stare after her in admiration of her spirit.

The march was not long, and they were camped well before dark. No fires were permitted, much to the disgruntlement of the dwarves who were very fond of their after dinner pipe and tea. Scouts were dispatched and the army rested. Mike entered the white tear's camp and witnessed the meeting between Cracktooth and Niatia. He saw for himself that the orcai could cry. He kept to the shadows until the children left and the orcai leader had time to compose himself. Then he approached and sat beside him for a while.

After a short time Cracktooth spoke, "Big Man knows how to speak truth. I believe that you will defeat the Dark Lord. How can white tear help?"

Mike thought for a while before he replied. "Thank you. There is a way that you can help, but it may be too great a risk. I must ask you a question. Would the Dark Lord recognize that you no longer bear his mark, the mark of darkness, I mean?" Cracktooth looked puzzled and Mike continued. "You no longer bear the curse. Can the Dark Lord tell?"

This time the orc answered. "Never see Dark Lord, only see man he send to us. This man not look at people, just give orders. Other orcai not know."

Mike drew a long breath. "This will be dangerous, friend. " He began to detail a plan that would place the white tear where they would be of greatest use. Hours later Mike found Mary. She had found a place to wash most of the grime and gore from her body and was braiding her long, black hair.

"I saw you go to the orcai camp. Has Niatia met with Cracktooth?" Mary asked.

"Yes, it was a very emotional meeting. I can see that the orcai are not that different from men. I don't understand why they are so easily influenced by the Dark Lord. The white tear will be there when needed; I hope that I have not condemned them all." Mike removed his leather helm and threw it to the ground. "They trust me, the Elves trust me, the Dwarves trust me, the Men trust me, even the Gnomes trust me. Why don't I trust myself?" Even as he asked the question, he knew the answer. Tammy, his dead wife, had trusted him, and he had not been there to protect her when she needed him.

Mary could see where his thoughts had taken him, she could see the old pain begin to rise deep in his eyes. The pain had been gone for so long; she had hoped it would never return. She tied a ribbon around the finished braid, rose, and laid her hand on his shoulder. "You can not be everywhere at once," she began gently. "You have to learn to trust those who trust in you!" He was looking into her eyes now, thinking about what she had just said. "I never knew Tammy, but I know she was wonderful. That doesn't change the fact that—" Mary stopped for a moment. "I know this will hurt, but she lost her trust for a moment. She went into that bank because she didn't trust your plan. It was not your fault, it was not hers either. You have to acknowledge this. She was at the loan officer's desk. For whatever reason she was looking to borrow money! She put herself in that bank, but an evil man killed her."

Tears were flowing from her eyes, but this time she did not stop. "That man will never hurt anyone again, but the evil that was in him exists here. If you, if we, do not win, the evil will hurt countless innocent wives and children, and their husbands and fathers will be powerless to stop it! They all trust you, I trust you, and the stupid prophecy trusts you. Do not doubt yourself, just lead us." She stepped back. "There is no one else, and they would follow no one else. I would follow no one else." Emotionally spent she turned and entered her tent.

Mike stood for a moment and then leaned his head against the tree that sheltered their tents. He had evaded the truth for so long that it seemed foreign to him. He could not argue against what his friend had said. Tammy had made her decision, and only God could tell him why. His head was bowed as he whispered, "Why me, Lord? I forgot to involve You in my life long ago. Why do You believe in me when I hardly acknowledge Your existence?" There was silence in the camp, even the wind had died.

As Mike sat there he was overcome by a sense of grief and loss so profound that he was nearly driven to his knees. Then he heard a voice in his mind, and the grief was replaced by calmness. "My Child, even if you forgot to involve Me in your life, you never turned from My ways. You were pure in your marriage, in your business, and even in your friendship with Mary. You let anger and grief drive you to seek revenge for yourself, but in the final moment you turned from vengeance, and I took it up. It is not for any man to know his future, only that I will never leave his side. My Child, rise up and prepare for battle."

Mike raised his head and turned to a pack that he had carried with him since they left Elvhome. Mary had not closed the flap to her tent. She had collapsed on top of her bedroll and was fast asleep. He set the pack aside and sat and watched her for a while. Soon this would be over, he thought, soon he would be free to express his love for her. She stirred in her sleep and a smile crossed her face, erasing the fatigue that was etched there. He stood and closed the tent flap and took up the pack, removed their dwarf-forged armor, and spent an hour polishing it until it gleamed in the faint moonlight. Then he took his bedroll to his tent and slept.

CHAPTER THIRTY-ONE

The dwarf's camp did not stir until noon save for the sentries. They had only a few miles to cover to be in position for the attack the next morning. Carrying only their weapons and food for the evening meal, their only way was forward. Mike woke first and carefully wiped down the armor a final time. He quietly walked the short distance to Mary's tent. She just beginning to stir. His friend sat up, smiled at him through the tent flap, and then saw their armor laid out. Her eyes widened. "Is it?"

"Yes, it is time to reveal ourselves. We begin the march to victory, or doom, today. The Dark Lord would know soon enough anyway," he replied.

It was an hour past noon and most of the dwarves had begun to gather and form up into marching formation. Mike pulled back the flap to their tent and followed Mary into the open area at the center of camp. A few of the dwarves noticed them; soon all eyes were on the Pair as they strode in front of the formation. Mike could see a broad smile on Alexar's face as the dwarf began a cheer. Soon the entire army was cheering loudly, banging their weapons against their shields. As Mike looked into their faces, he could see fatigue and fear melt away. In unison, he and Mary placed their helms on their heads and mounted the horses that had been brought up. When there was silence, he spoke. "We must be silent from here until the appointed time tomorrow. When you see me raise the Sword of the Ancestors, then you cheer as you just did. Strike terror into the hearts of the orcai. We will free Blackthorn Hearth tomorrow!"

The dwarves cheered again and followed as Mike rode down the road to Blackthorn Hearth. They met Elven scouts almost immediately who informed them that the Armies were in place. Mike sent them back with word that all was ready in the south and confirmed the timing of the battle. They reached their destination just before sundown, and Mike met with the officers of the army. He reemphasized that any orcai with the mark of the white tear was a friend, even if they were in the opposing battleline. The white tear would appear to break first, hopefully setting up a general rout of the enemy. This would also allow them to return to the Dark Lord's encampment without suspicion—hopefully.

The night was warm even though it was nearly winter. The army slept in shifts so that all would be rested for the coming battle. Mike and Mary leaned against an ancient oak tree and dozed until about two hours before dawn. "Mike," Mary began, "All the old movies have a scene just like this; the morning before the battle when the leaders sit and question themselves. I just don't feel like that. I know that we done everything that we can. Somehow I also know that we will win today. Do you think that is wrong?"

Mike sat in silence for a moment before he answered. "No, I don't think it is wrong. I remember a story my grandfather told me. It was from the Bible, but I didn't read it until after he died. In the story, God gave a battle plan to a soldier named Gideon. First, He had Gideon send most of his army home. Then, what was left, each took a clay pitcher and torch with them and snuck into the enemy camp. When Gideon signaled, they smashed the pitcher to reveal the torch it covered and shouted. They beat their swords against their shields and made an awful racket. Well, this scared the enemy so much that they jumped out of their beds and killed a bunch of their own before they ran away. The whole idea was that Gideon relied on God for the victory, not on himself.

"The Elves, Dwarves, and Men, even the Orcai, all believe in the prophecy. For Gideon's people, they would believe in themselves, and credit themselves for victory unless it was impossible for them to win. Here, they all believe in the prophecy, and the One who gave it. They wouldn't even have fought if it had not been for the prophecy. I think that kind of belief is something that I have been missing. You were right to tell me to stop doubting. What I have to do is believe in something beyond myself."

Mary thought about his words before she spoke. "And maybe I just need one thing to believe in…" She turned and slapped his chest, making the armor ring. "You just ruined it. What Hollywood producer is going to buy that scene? Where is the doubt, the second-guessing, the unanswered questions?" Her voice softened a bit. "But it is real. I don't think I have ever—" Before she could say *loved you this much,* the sound of running feet interrupted her as a young dwarf messenger hurried up to them.

"Sir Michael, Lady Marilyn, the Army is assembled. It is almost time." The young man was clearly uncomfortable until Mike rose and returned his salute. He helped Mary to her feet and paused for a moment to look onto her eyes.

"We will have time soon," Mike whispered as they followed the messenger.

They took their places and rode silently to the edge of the plain outside of Blackthorn Hearth. They began marching onto the field just as the sun began to rise. Mass confusion spread among the orcai as they realized that the threat now came from their rear. They turned and formed clumsy defensive lines as the Dwarven Army formed up with precision. Cavalry Units backed by infantry and archers were soon spread across a wide front that stretched the orcai thin as they sought to face their attackers.

Mike and the band that he had traveled south with—Mary, Peter, James, Alsharon, Elsharone, and Alexar—were in the center. Mike and Mary had donned their helms, and their armor shone brightly in the early morning light. The seven were a magnificent sight as they rode a little ahead of the troops. When they were close enough for the orcai to hear, Mike halted and drew the Sword of the Ancestors. "We are the Prophesied Ones. Lay down your arms and you will live. Stand and fight and you will die." He could see a lot of movement in the ranks and was sure the orcai of the white tear were voicing their doubts.

Mike waited for a few minutes until it was clear that the orcai meant to fight. Then he pointed his sword at the enemy lines and shouted, "All right then, forward Lads, they've made their choice." The ground shook as a thousand mounts and ten thousand dwarves charged and the air was filled with their battle cry.

The orcai lines held steady until the attackers were within yards of them. Then the white tear turned and ran, taking many of the red-marked warriors with them. There was chaos, and the cavalry cut through the orcai lines like a scythe through wheat at harvest. The cavalry did not hesitate, but formed into a long column and sprinted for the southern gate of Blackthorn Hearth.

The gates swung open as they approached, and they

streamed into the city and to the town square without hesitation. There were mounted men in the square as they pounded through. Mike recognized Captain Norris and shouted to him. "Sally forth! Have the gates opened." He heard the orders relayed in front of them and kept pace. The gates at the opposite end of the City were barely opened wide enough for the Seven to pass as they reached them. The cavalry burst from the city onto the northern battlefield.

The Seven slowed slightly to allow the lines to expand behind them. Mike tried to make sense of the battle in front of him. The orcai force was much larger than they had faced in the south, as were the armies facing it. The army of Men was attacking in a column to Mike's right and the Elves to his left, leaving only a light force attacking the center. The plan had been for Mike to choose a direction and half the cavalry would follow him and the rest would attack the opposite flank. The Men and Elves armies were supposed to have attacked on a broad front to stretch the orcai lines and make them vulnerable to the counterattack from the city. As always, the most carefully laid plan had fallen victim to reality as soon as the battle had started.

Mike veered to the right so that he could seal off the escape route to the Dark Mountain. They crashed into the orcai rear and were engulfed in a melee of combat. They advanced quickly, and Mike was again puzzled—it was too easy. He reigned in and turned to look behind and was dismayed to see that the entire dwarven cavalry was behind him!

Catching Mary's eye he worked his way to the dwarf Captain who was to lead the second attack. He cut the captain out of the battle and pointed to the west. The captain shrugged and shouted, "The stinkin' Elves can take care o' themselves."

Mike leaned over, grabbed the front of the dwarf's mail, and drug him from his saddle. "You will follow orders! Get your men and follow me, or feel my blade."

The dwarf's eyes nearly popped out of his head and he stammered a reply. Mike flung him to the ground and quickly gathered ten dwarves to follow him. He could see that Captain Norris had led a hundred men to the left flank, but were in danger of being repulsed. They pushed their mounts hard to reach the embattled force, and a glance showed that at least a hundred others were following. This new force sheered through the orcai and reignited the stalled advance of Norris' men. The tide of the battle turned, and the armies of men, elves, and dwarves soon closed on the orcai like a steel trap.

Few orcai escaped and fewer were captured. As the survivors were rounded up, Mike sought out Captain Norris and clasped forearms with him. He gave the Captain instructions to arrange a meeting with the generals of the allied armies, but Mike wanted to question a prisoner first. Captain Norris bowed to Mary and galloped away, and the Pair went to where the orcai were being held. A type of corral had been hastily erected, and the orcai were herded in like animals. Mike grabbed two canteens from the guards and whispered to Mary, "Quickly, bless this water. I have an idea." Mary whispered a blessing she remembered and was amused by the glow of pure light from the canteens. Mike then took them and walked into the coral, glowering at the guards who were jeering at the captives.

"Water, I have water," he cried and began to give small drinks to the individual goblins and orcs who crowded around him. Mary had grabbed a staff and kept the orcai from pressing too close. Mike watched intently as each drank the water. In most cases he saw the shadow flee; he marked in his mind those who did not seem to be freed of the curse. It was one of these that he chose to question.

His target was a goblin that was defiant and vulgar. It kept a steady stream of curses and profanity directed towards Mike and refused to answer questions. It turned its profane attention to Mary; Mike drew the Sword of Kings and laid it against the evil creature's throat. It was only then that the black spark left the creature, yet it remained crude and vulgar, although not as defiant. Mike finished and walked the prisoner back to the holding area. A detachment from the city had arrived, and the orcai were being chained together for transport to the city jail. Mike was staring into the corral when an orc bowed to him and asked, "Can speak to Chosen?"

Mike nodded his head and the orc continued. "Belzar bad goblin. Choose Dark Lord when very little. Lastiter tell about Dark Lord. Him have man make big magic. Take long time but make overworlders weak. Two armies wait, small on outside wall, big army inside. When leaf turn green, overworlders too weak fight, People win."

Mike looked at the orc. "Why are you telling me this? Don't you believe the Dark Lord's promise?"

The orc spat. "Dark Lord is lord of lies. Dark Lord why people cursed, people forget Dark Lord cause people be cursed."

"Lastiter, come with me. I need you to tell the others what you have just told me." Mike led the orc to his mount where both orc and horse balked. Through bared teeth Mike's steed snorted at the orc and would have bit it except for the big man's hand on its bridle. Mike mounted and lifted the orc behind him. "If you try to betray my trust, I will let the horse have you." Mike could see real fear in the orc's eyes and knew he would not try to escape. They met the other commanders in the Town Square.

Mike could feel a cold rage building as he faced the commanders. He glanced at Mary, who nodded her head slightly, sensing his mood. He drew a breath and began, forcing his tone to be low and calm. "That was, without a doubt, the most unmitigated disaster that I have witnessed in this world. What was in your minds, or did you leave any room after the petty jealousy, stereotypical nonsense, and outright racial distrust? You nearly snatched defeat from the very jaws of victory today! The force that nearly routed us today is less than a third the size of the one guarding the gate, which itself is much smaller than the one inside. The Prophecy states that the Armies of Men, Elves, and Dwarves will battle the Dark One. How can that happen if you are ready to battle each other? Tomorrow, we will honor the fallen. You will honor each other's fallen in front of your troops. We do not have time to quarrel with each other. You were all created by the same Creator, the very One who gave you the prophecy!

"As I said, tomorrow we honor the dead. Then we rest and repair our equipment for one day. The next day we march for the Dark Mountain. Our order of march will be company by company, Man, Elf, Dwarf. Any fighting will be severely punished. If I have to shackle Man, Elf, and Dwarf together, then we will march in threes! There can be no dissension in the ranks!"

By this time the commanders' heads hung in shame. There was a long silence before one commander spoke up.

"It will not be my prejudice that sends Heavenshire into bonds of darkness." This was followed by heartfelt expressions of assent from the others.

"Very well, I will leave it in your hands. Now you must hear what we will face at the Dark Mountain. This is Lastiter, listen to him, ask questions later." The orc repeated the information he had given Mike and answered the commanders' questions as best he could. The commanders especially questioned the orc's assertion that the orcai had once lived on the surface.

"It is true!" a new voice boomed forth. Bardwind stepped into the center of the group. "You may know me as Bardwind, but my true name is DeauxEagles." Those assembled gasped in recognition of that name, which was at the center of many legends of Heavenshire. "The oldest records we have tell a story of a great evil deed at the Dark Mountain. A great curse was set upon the orcai, which means 'outcast' in the most ancient of tongues. A lesser curse was set upon certain others. I do not fully understand the details. What I have come to warn you of is that a dark spell has been cast and is growing stronger. We must press the battle with all haste."

Bardwind, or DeauxEagles, turned to Mike. "Sir Michael, your plan is sound. One day is all we dare delay. Alothen will soon join us with a thousand of the lost elves—those scattered by the Grybon. This is all the aid we can expect."

The services the next day were as Mike decreed. The elven general read a tribute to the fallen dwarves, the dwarven general for the elves, and DeauxEagles for the men. The rest of the day was spent in near silence, only the sounds of tools and the jingle of gear as it was manipulated to be repaired. The three armies were mixed together as the skills required for the many tasks did not reside equally among them. Mike was concerned at the amount of damage that had been done to personal armor.

When he questioned DeauxEagles, the old man was direct. "The spell that I detected is damping out our magic. Those who have been careless with the magic words will be the first to feel its effects. By springtime, we would have no magic at all. This is why we trained you so hard in physical combat; magic can be blocked, and if you rely only on it, you will perish…"

The night seemed all too short to Mike. It seemed he had barely laid down when Mary shook him awake. "Alothen has arrived, and he wishes to speak with us." He hastily drew on his armor, taking special care to set each piece with the word of magic. The former lord of the Jeweled Castle was eating when they arrived. He wore plain armor, and his helm had neither crest nor insignia. He rose at their approach and fell to one knee.

"Lady Marilyn and Sir Michael, Chosen of the Creator. We place ourselves in your service as you serve the Creator. Long has Heavenshire awaited this moment when all those who serve Good will ride forth to rid the land of evil." All of his men had followed his example and crossed their right arms across their chest as he finished. The ring of metal on metal brought all other activity in the camp to a halt.

"Rise, do not bow to me. If you would join us, you must pledge to fight alongside Men and Dwarves as one. There will be no distinction among us, only that we are Warriors for the cause of Good!" Mike waited for Alothen's answer.

Without hesitation the entire force of a thousand elves rose and repeated their salute, the sound rang across the valley and echoed back to be met with cheers, first from the men and then both elves and dwarves. Mike stood and smiled as the sound washed over him. He could feel Mary beside him, and he took her hand. She was smiling as she looked into his blue eyes. "They are united. You have succeeded."

"*We*," he emphasized the word, "have succeeded. I have seen you circulating through the camp, talking with all the groups. A significant achievement with nearly thirty thousand soldiers, I assure you." She smiled. They bowed to Alothen and his men once the sound had subsided and took their leave. Mike did not release Mary's hand as they walked; he was lost in thought about the coming march. It would take nearly a week to reach the dark gate. He did not know how great a wall the orcai could have built using slave labor, but he knew that it would be difficult to breach.

Mary watched his face as they strolled towards their horses. She could see the concentration in his eyes and did not speak. She could almost imagine walking along the river near his house, before all of this. She could imagine the feel of his arm across her shoulder as they sat and watched the sun sink towards the waters. They had often sat until the street lamps in the park sputtered to life and then walked back to his house where they would embrace beside her car. There had been too many good-byes, too many solitary rides to her apartment. She had long known that she was falling in love, but she did not resist. She knew that he would heal and that he was in love with her.

Her thoughts were interrupted when he stopped and released her hand. "I was thinking of the river" he said.

"So was I."

"I was thinking of the many times when I could have told you something. There always seemed to be time tomorrow, or later in the evening. It seemed that I would always have time to say—"

At that moment a messenger interrupted them. "Sir, Lady," he began breathlessly. "There is news, one of the white tear." Mike and Mary almost ran to the little knot of men, dwarves, and elves that were gathered around a goblin. It struggled to its feet at their approach.

"Big Man, Lady," it bowed awkwardly. "We catch survivors of siege of Blackthorn Hearth. Dark Lord not know you win. Cracktooth say tell you that we be ready!"

Mike smiled down at the orcai. "You have done well. Eat and rest. We must march, but I will leave instructions that you be cared for. Return when you have the strength."

The goblin protested so forcefully that Mike relented and gave orders that a place be made on one of the supply wagons for the goblin to ride. He was pleased to hear a kind of grudging admiration in the voices of those repeating the story. The Army was forming, and the scouts had already departed. There was no time to speak with Mary before they left.

The Pair mounted their steeds and soon the Army was on the move.

CHAPTER THIRTY-TWO

Four days later the Army was poised for the attack. They had captured a few orcai scouts, but there had been very little activity. Mike and Mary, along with Alsharon and Elsharone, were looking at the orcai army guarding the fortifications. The walls were crude but looked strong. A stream trickled at the base of the wall and a drawbridge was lowered across it. The orcai were trained to raise it at the first sign of trouble. The Pair and the twins were too far away to see if any of the orcai near the gate were of the white tear; they would have to hope that Cracktooth had managed to get assigned near the gate.

They retreated to the army and explained what they had seen to DeauxEagles, King Arnyea, and King Kextar. Their plan was to attack with cavalry, attempting to reach the drawbridge before it was raised and to hold it. If they could fight through then they could close it against the orcai and advance on Aster, the palace of the southern King, where the Dark Lord waited. If this proved impossible they would slice through the horde, attempting to separate and confuse the orcai, and get them to break and run. DeauxEagles was confident that he could cast a spell to break the Dark Lord's influence if the orcai were hard pressed and confused.

The cavalry gathered and rode forward through the early morning mists. Great care had been taken to secure loose tack and to pad anything that might make a noise. Even the horses seemed to sense the need for stealth; very few blew or snorted. They had finally arrived at a small rise that screened them from the enemy. Hand signals passed right and left along the lines, and all was ready.

Mike glanced at Mary who was beside him as she had been for so long. She smiled to him and drew her sword. Mike returned her smile and drew the Sword of the Ancestors. The elven blade shone in the light, a counter to the grayish sky. Thousands of swords whispered from their sheaths, and Mike urged his mount forward. As soon as they were free of the underbrush the cavalry spurred their mounts to a full gallop and literally thundered down the slope of the hill.

The ground shook under the impacts of thousands of hooves, and the dwarves began a battle cry that was immediately picked up by the elves and men. The orcai, mercenaries, and renegades that composed the opposing army were caught totally unprepared. Their camp resembled an anthill disturbed by a child. Almost immediately, though, the battle plan became useless. The gates were already closing and the drawbridge rising. Mike adjusted his path towards the center of the slowly-forming orcai lines. He grew apprehensive as he recognized that they were forming a classic defense formation. His apprehension grew as he noted extra-long lances being brought from the center of the camp. These lances were the most modern defense against cavalry. They could be braced against the ground and raised enough for a charging horse to impale itself. He estimated that they would engage before the lances were in place.

He stood in the stirrups and signaled a change in the attack to concentrate the full force of the charge in the center of the line. Seconds later he and Mary crashed into the defenders and forced their way through several ranks before their progress was slowed. The warriors following pressed past them as they engaged the enemy.

The massed cavalry was too much for the orcai, and it quickly broke through the lines and wheeled around to attack again, breaking through before the enemy streaming from the camp surrounded them. Mike saw a gap in the orcai reinforcements and spurred his horse towards it. He could feel Mary beside him, and a glance showed that the Elf twins, Alexar, Peter, and James were close behind. They closed quickly on the stream in front of the wall.

Cracktooth had told Mike of a place just upstream of the gate where the stream had not been deepened and a horse could easily cross. The small band reached the ford, and a single arrow bounced off Mike's shoulder. He heard three bows answer and a scream of agony as their arrows reached their mark. Mike grinned at Mary and mouthed his thanks. They pushed across the stream and were met by a force of orcs with a red fist emblazoned on their chests. Mike and Mary fought their way through, but the others were stalled. They raced towards a sally port as more arrows dotted the ground around them.

The orcai archers soon learned that to expose themselves was to invite swift death. The enchantments on Mary's bow and her innate skill meant that she almost never missed. As the Pair reached the sally port, the gates opened slightly, revealing a melee of white tear and red fist orcai battling. They had to dismount and leave their horses behind so they could slip through the gates, which were forced closed after they entered. The Pair joined the fray inside. One of the white tear came close and shouted, "You must go, dark mage, the servant, make big trouble. There!"

The goblin was struck down as he pointed to a small gazebo on the top of a hill not far away. His killer did not survive him for long, and the Pair disengaged and sprinted toward the structure. As they approached they saw a man in black robes chanting and dropping items in a brazier. The sunlight dimmed even though there were no clouds in the sky. The mage held a staff topped by a dark crystal, which he pointed to the four points of the compass as he spoke.

CHAPTER THIRTY-THREE

Abstidian, servant to the Dark Lord, worked at his greatest spell. He should have had months to prepare, but the sudden appearance of the Army of the Light had changed that. Instead of a gradual strengthening, it would have to be cast full force. He compressed many days of activity into a few minutes, spurred on by the clamor of battle in the distance. He did not hear the Pair approaching until their armored boots clanged against the flagstones of the gazebo.

He turned to face the noise, leaving the spell almost complete. Recognition came quickly as he faced the man and woman. A barrier spell had stopped them. "The buffoon and tramp from the tavern. I am rarely fooled, but you did escape me. A shame really. All of this unpleasantness could have been avoided. I do not know what that fool of a gnome, DeauxEagles is it now, told you? Most likely a story too fantastic to believe and too alluring to ignore. Sadly it has been all for naught. Look." Abstidian gestured and a picture appeared in the air. "See the immense army that waits for you. What have you? A few traitorous goblins."

His words fell smoothly from his lips, and Mary recognized the spell he sought to ensnare them with. She spoke the counter and then banished the barrier spell. It took much more effort than it should have, but the dark mage's surprised expression encouraged her.

"Ah," he recovered his composure quickly. "You have much talent. Perhaps I can use you, if the master's anger can be abated." He quickly cast another spell, which Mary again countered. He was wary enough to immobilize the big warrior so he could concentrate on the woman. "See how hard it is to use your magic. Here, dark magic is supreme, as it shall soon be in all of Heavenshire." He was unable to score against the woman, but she could not press the attack either. He transformed his staff into a lance and pierced the man's armor. He could not draw blood; the protection enchantment was still too strong. "You cannot protect yourself and the man both. You are not that strong."

As Mary heard the words, she knew Abstidian had made a fatal mistake—he had underestimated Mike. When the dark mage turned away for an instant, she attacked with what strength she could muster. The result was not as strong as she had hoped, but it made him concentrate on her. She saw Mike's mouth move as he spoke the word that would release him. When Abstidian turned to her, his back was to Mike.

Abstidian took a chance, casting one more step of the great enchantment, and was nearly singed as Mary took advantage of his distraction. The grayness increased slightly and a look of triumph crossed his face. It remained only for an instant. The staff was wrenched from his hands and a steel-gloved fist crashed into his face, knocking him to the ground. He screamed as Mike reversed the staff and smashed the crystal against the stones.

An almost tangible darkness escaped as the crystal shattered. It was like a foul odor in the mind as it passed outwards. Some of it flowed into the grayness, some into the ground itself, but most into the man now lying on the ground. Mike slowly approached Mary and smiled the slightly crooked smile he often used. He was just about to speak when she screamed; he whirled just in time to deflect Abstidian's sword with an armored arm. The stroke sliced through armor and into Mike's flesh. The man was covered in the darkness from the crystal, and his eyes glowed red. He quickly recovered and aimed another blow at Mike's head. Mike ducked under the blow and grappled with the mage. He managed to get a hold on the sword arm, but the mage's strength was multiplied by his insanity. All Mike could manage was to hold the sword away from him.

The mage beat on Mike's armored gut and lifted his knee into his groin in a fruitless effort to break his grip. Mike could not release either hand to strike at the mage or he would be skewered. The big man was rapidly beginning to tire, but the mage showed no sign of weakening. Mike gathered his remaining strength to attempt to break free and draw his sword. As they separated, the mage just vanished. Mike drew the Sword of the Ancestors and spun around looking for his opponent. He saw Mary stagger slightly and stepped to her side.

Abstidian felt the knight twist to break free; he released the man as he swung his sword towards the knight's unprotected back. A maniacal grin started on his face because he knew this would be the deathblow. Suddenly he felt himself lifted, and he hurtled through the air at a fantastic speed. He could see his army beginning to surround the puny force arrayed against it, and he knew a moment of triumph. It was a fleeting moment; he began to descend at the same great speed, and the triumph turned to terror as he saw the ground rushing to meet him. His mind failed him, and he could think of no defensive spells to save his life. Just before impact his body slowed, as if he were being tossed from twice the height of a man. He hit the ground with the forward speed of a horse at full gallop, rolled, and tumbled until he crashed into a low stone wall.

The Dark Lord's mage lay in a tangled heap at the base of a wall separating a farmer's house from his fields. One leg lay at an unnatural angle and broken ribs stabbed his lungs as he tried to draw a breath. He felt almost no pain for the moment, but he knew that it would come soon. His face was turned towards the cottage, allowing him to see the window flower boxes that still held the last flowers of the fall. He could smell their scent on the wind, a fragrance that he knew. The door to the cottage opened, and a woman rushed out and towards him. She was familiar to him; he could never have forgotten her face. It was older now, but still filled with the innocence he remembered from her youth. Memories flooded his mind, and tears, not of pain—no, tears of regret flowed from his eyes.

The woman knelt beside him, and her hands fluttered as though she would touch him. Abstidian closed his eyes, yearning for and yet fearing the feel of her hand. Finally she laid her hand on his forehead and whispered, "Sir, can you yet hear me? My father is coming from across the field. We will help you. We will do what we can to ease your pain."

Abstidian forced his eyes open, forced himself to look on the face of the woman he had left so long ago. He thought to himself, *Such is God's vengeance that I must suffer the regret of a wasted life in the moment that I die.* He saw recognition begin in the woman's eyes, so he forced himself to speak. "Abigail, I am so sorry."

"Abstidian!" Abigail's hand clasped her mouth. "You have come back to me. My prayers are answered. Don't try to talk, Father is almost here. We will bind your wounds, I will care for you. You will be well again." As she dropped to her knees and tenderly cradled his head in her hands, he saw a flash of light. It was as though a veil had been pulled from his eyes, and he saw the flush of her face from the exertions of her run. He realized that the taint of darkness had been lifted from him. Her tears flowed even harder.

The sound of boots pounding and a man's voice calling to Abigail intruded on his consciousness. The farmer recognized him as well, but not with fond memories, for he knew of this man's deeds. Abigail argued fiercely with her father and convinced him to help. Abstidian lost consciousness as they set his broken leg. The next he knew, a soft darkness settled around him, not the darkness of the Dark Lord but a cool shade. A canvas tarp had been set up to protect him from the elements. Abigail's voice came to him. "Father has gone for a neighbor to help move you inside. We have stopped the bleeding, and I will prepare a draught against the pain.

Mary had regained her balance before Mike reached her. Her eyes were wide in wonder. "I just wanted him to go away." She shook her head as if to clear it. "Let's get away from here." They began walking away from the gazebo. After they were again on the green grass, Mike stopped and Mary turned to him. Under the gray skies the two armored figures faced each other. The hill was strangely silent as though the world held its breath.

Mike plunged his sword into the soil, stepped up to Mary, and drew her close to him. "Milady, we have come so far, and you have never faltered, never doubted me. Now I think I have led you to your doom. The army of evil waits just beyond that hill, and I have nothing left with which to fight, except one thing I have carried in my heart all these years—ever since I met you. The first time I saw you, I did not just see a woman, but a goddess, a vision of beauty that I had no words to describe. My ears were filled with fantastic music, and my heart nearly burst with a longing for your touch. My shame is that I have walled that feeling deep into my heart and denied its depth, even its existence. I have loved you hopelessly and completely from that minute. Only now, when all is lost, have I the courage to tell you, to show you, that I love you."

Mary was looking into the face of not only a knight, but of a lover, seeing eyes that she knew, eyes as familiar as the voice that issued from the helm. She reached up with a gloved hand and loosened the catch. Then with both hands she lifted the helm and his face was revealed. There was no trace of sadness in those eyes, and it seemed the most natural thing in the world to lift her face and let her lips meet his. Time seemed to stand still as they kissed, oblivious to all around them. After an unknown amount of time had passed, Mary leaned back slightly. "I love you, too. I would not change any of this if it meant I could not spend this time with you. My life has been fulfilled these past years. If we go to our doom, let it be together." They embraced, their armor glowing as though reflecting the unseen sun.

The darkness around them lightened as the purity of their love countered it.

"If I may interrupt, you will need your mounts to go anywhere." They turned as one and saw Alsharon standing there, holding their mounts. "As much as I enjoy hearing you say what has been obvious to everyone for three years, we have destiny to fulfill." He raised his free hand and a great cheer erupted from the plain behind him where the armies of Men, Dwarves, and Elves poured through the now-opened gate. "You cleared the way, but could you have not at least opened the gate?" he smiled to show the levity of his words. The army was forming with great precision, companies aligned to their best effect, no matter what race was next to it. It was truly the Army of the Light.

Mary bent down and retrieved Mike's helm. "Sir Michael, your helm." He took it and lightly kissed her lips once more.

"Thank you, My Lady, but yours is gone." He heard Alsharon cough and glanced at him. The elf was holding Mary's helm.

"I thought you would want this." Mary thanked him as she took it.

Mike turned to the massed army, still much smaller than what they faced. "The one true source of light has brought each of us to this place, to this time. We have all faced battles, the loss of friends and companions. In all of this the Light has strengthened us. It would be foolish to enter into this final battle and fail to acknowledge that fact. Dismount all, and uncover your heads." His voice somehow was audible to all those assembled. The clamor around them reached a crescendo and then stilled. There was only an occasional sound of a horse snorting or stamping. Into this silence, Mike, as Sir Michael, spoke. "To the Source of all things pleasing, of all things wonderful, of all that is good, of all that is light—the Creator of all things—we give glory and honor. We dedicate our very lives this day to Your victory. We ask that You welcome into Your rest all the souls that have fallen in this great cause, and those that will fall today. Amen."

Sir Michael shouted to the Army of the Light, "Set your armor and mind the Word." He turned to Mary; Lady and Knight set their helms on their heads with the word of magic.

King Arnyea rode near. The knight drew the Sword of the Ancestors from the soil and presented it. "As I promised long ago. I return to you that which you have given me." King Arnyea accepted the sword with a bow. Mike turned one more time to Mary. "My Lady."

She smiled and mounted her steed. "It is time, my love!"

"Indeed it is, my love!" Mike mounted and raised the Sword of Kings, commanding the army to "Mount!" Thousands of warriors mounted their steeds. "Present Arms!" Thousands of warriors drew their weapons. "Ahead, Parade March!" The sound of drums rolled across the plain at a slow, steady cadence. The massed army began to move as one, each step creating thunder of its own. As the army reached the hill, the kings spread out ahead of the masses and the Pair rode out in front of them. They crested the hill and viewed the army of darkness arrayed on the plain.

Sir Michael rode forward until the rear-most rank had a view of the valley. It was literally filled with more than a hundred thousand dark warriors. He raised his sword and called "Halt!" The order was relayed, and the Kings gathered around the Pair. "You know the battle plan. Our place is at the fore, as the prophecies foretell. You will control our ranks. You know that what happens on the plain is not the key. What happens in the palace of Aster is. When we break through you must be ready to follow. If we prevail you will know, as you will know if we fail."

The kings nodded their heads and King Kextar spoke. "Let there be no talk of failure. On to Victory!"

Sir Michael bowed his head and then turned his steed toward the enemy. "Let's see if we can sow some discord of our own." He rode down the hill a ways, just a bow shot from the enemy line, Mary at his side with her bow drawn to discourage any who might try for a lucky shot at that distance. As they rode they searched for any of the white tear in the ranks. He sat for a moment and then called in a loud voice, "Where is your General, the master of strategy? Oh, he was also the master of treachery. Well, here is his scepter." He raised the staff with the broken crystal. "Ha! His power is broken, and he has crawled away to die." Noticing movement to his left, the knight rode down the line a bit. "What did he promise you? Power, position, wealth? It is all gone. See, he would never relinquish his symbol of power." He broke the staff in two and threw it into the mud. There were many disturbances in the dark army, and it seemed about to turn on itself. He still could not see any of the white tear in the front ranks.

Suddenly an evil voice boomed from the far end of the valley. "Do you think that one setback can vanquish me? What is one mere man to *me*? Come forward, knight, taste my power."

Sir Michael stood in his stirrups and laughed. "We have ridden a long way already. I think a courteous host would come to me. Are you cowering in your palace, afraid to step into the sunlight?"

At this Mary hissed, "Not too thick, my love."

The ground shook at the inarticulate scream of rage that issued from the palace. The Knight turned to his Lady. "Too late." A huge fireball followed the scream, burning dark warriors from the walls. As one the Pair spoke the word to shield them, and they could hear the kings lend their support as well. The fireball struck an invisible barrier in front of the Pair and splashed sideways and upward, causing more casualties among the beast's army. Then a bolt of energy rose to the sky and turned the day into twilight. Mike and Mary had been inching their mounts backwards; they spun and raced up the hill to meet their charging cavalry. They again reversed course, and Sir Michael and Lady Marilyn led the charge toward the weak point they had identified in the ranks of the Dark Lord's army. A ragged volley of arrows sped towards them, but was poorly aimed and came nowhere near the charging warriors. The sky over the Army of the Light's cavalry darkened with arrows from their own archers, crashing into the enemy ranks seconds before the horsemen smashed into the lines. The cavalry penetrated into the lines and then retreated toward their own advancing ranks. Parts of the enemy line followed them into a devastating archery volley. This caused further confusion, and the Pair again led the cavalry into the opening and back out. Finally the enemy cavalry committed, and the forces of light engaged them in a wild melee between the two armies.

The light's cavalry seemed to break and retreat into their own lines. The enemy gleefully pursued, only to be impaled on long pikes braced against the ground and concealed by the front ranks. The Army of the Light's cavalry wheeled and counter-attacked, cutting through the remaining enemy cavalry like a scythe into the confusion they had created. The infantry of both armies continued their advance and came together in the center of the plain. The Army of the Light's cavalry could withdraw through its lines, and the cavalry of the Army of Darkness was wary about following after encountering the lances. The Light's cavalry could then regroup and attack through another place in the line.

The Pair rode side by side, cutting down any who dared stand and ignoring those running away from the battle. They gave no quarter to orcs or goblins, cutting through the massed army like a vicious two-bladed saw. A troll forced its way through to them and stared in confusion at the space where its arm had been cut cleanly off as its foul heart was pierced by an arrow. The ranks of men, dwarves, and elves continued a grinding, crushing advance against the larger Army of Darkness. Warriors on both sides fell, and the ranks closed around them. The kings kept in close contact to the front ranks and were often involved in running battles. When the enemy shifted strategy and attempted to close on the Pair, the Kings led the reserve cavalry on a counter thrust that forced the enemy to stand and fight. At long last the Pair reached the gate to the inner wall. It was held slightly open by the body of a troll; the Pair vaulted from their steeds and through the opening.

Inside the walls there was relative quiet; most of the noise of battle was shut out by the thick stone. Mary picked off an archer that tried to shoot Mike and gave up the bow for her sword. She cut down half a dozen goblins who were trying to close the gate as Mike advanced into the courtyard, leaving a trail of dead and dying. She saw the portcullis start to descend, and she stopped it with a word. She found the gatekeeper and used her magic to throw him from his position. Then she caught up with Mike, and they advanced to the palace and passed through the wide, front entrance.

The hall seemed to be filled with orcs and a few trolls, and the Pair went to work. They finally, through much bloodshed, reached the door to the King's hall. Mike shouted a word that caused the bolt inside the door to fly from its brackets. His shoulder pushed it open as he realized that the enchantment on his armor had all but faded. Mary was close behind as they entered. On the dais was a huge, scaly figure. It's head of great fangs and horns rested on a body with six legs and four arms.

As they entered it threw fireballs that the Pair let slip around them to blast the wall behind them. It struck with the weapons it held in its arms, and the Pair fought back, even forcing it from the dais. Steel rang against iron, shattering the impure metal. The beast grabbed Mary with a clawed foot and began to crush her. Mike sliced the tendon of the wrist engaging him and spun across the intervening distance, striking the leg with all his strength. His sword struck true and severed the foot. The battle paused for a moment, and the beast laughed. It stretched out the stump of the severed limb, the foul blood stopped flowing, and a new foot formed. In that moment Mike felt despair; he saw in his mind the thousands of dead and dying in the fight, and the beast that he could not seem to kill. Mary saw his despair and her heart flooded with love for him.

"I love you," she shouted as the beast grabbed him and pinned him to the wall. The newly formed foot struck her and threw her against the wall as well.

The beast's foul laughter continued. "Love? It will do you no good here. Can't you see that you've lost? You can stop the bloodshed, Knight. Serve me or die!" It began to squeeze, crushing the mortar and stone of the wall. Somehow Mike freed his arm and swung his sword at the wrist holding him. The blow was intercepted, the sword wrenched from his grip and dashed to the floor where it shattered. The foul laughter reached a new level. It seemed to have forgotten Mary, who was barely conscious. She could see the pain that wracked Mike's face as his ribs were crushed. Somehow she found her bow and her last two arrows. The beast swung its face near the trapped knight as it taunted him. She drew her bow and aimed an arrow at the glittering black eye she could see. The arrow flew true and pierced the eye. The beast writhed in pain and swung its head toward Mary.

She smiled as she whispered, "Watch this!" Her last arrow sped true to its mark and pierced the other eye. The beast's tail whipped around, struck her in the back, and flung her against the wall at Mike's feet.

CHAPTER THIRTY-FOUR

Outside the walls of the palace a great battle raged. All of the many creatures of Heavenshire fought for the darkness or the light. The sounds of battle filled the valley and rose high into the skies. Even there the battle raged as the great eagles fought the dragons that the Dark One had created. The dead and dying were strewn everywhere, and yet the battle continued. A strange sort of unity held as elf and dwarf stood side by side battling trolls and orcs. Men guarded elven archers who rained havoc on the massed army of evil. Into this scene of carnage and mayhem, a single man approached from the rear of the Army of the Light.

As the man approached the rearmost ranks of the armies, the fighting around him ceased. All who saw him just stopped and stared. The man was not dressed for battle; he wore no armor or weapons, just simple clothes and a worn travel cloak. Still as he walked through the battle, all fighting ceased; an eye of calm radiated outward from his presence. The Elf and Dwarf Kings, surrounded by a knot of trolls and orcs, were hard pressed to hold their own. Swords and clubs, axes and pikes lowered almost of their own accord, and the man walked directly through the fight to stand before the Kings. He acknowledged them with a half bow and turned towards the palace.

He advanced through the battle, a wave of silence following him as the myriad individual encounters were stilled. The sound in the valley reduced to silence as he reached the gate. He paused before the gates for a moment and turned around to look over the now quiet valley. He did not speak. He did not need to. He simply turned and entered the courtyard. The battle inside also died as he strode through the gate. Forward to the palace and on to the throne room, leaving silence behind. He neared the sound of the struggle from the throne room itself.

Great howls of pain filled the room, and the beast clenched its clawed hand. Mike had managed to draw the dagger from his belt, the same weapon he had carried from his first day in Heavenshire. As his last breath was driven from his lungs, he saw a man enter the throne room. Suddenly the darkness emanating from the beast was banished by soft, pure light. In that instant Mike understood who had entered. He flipped the dagger towards the man who reached out his hand and caught the weapon. The hood fell back, and Nesoch's face was revealed. The dagger in his hand shimmered and grew into the true Sword of Kings. The howls of pain from the beast turned into howls of rage. "No! It is not possible, you are dead! You died a traitor's death, and your body was cast from the wall of the city. It cannot be!"

Nesoch raised his Sword. "Yes, it can be. You know that in the ancient Book of Magic it is written that He whose innocent blood was shed will return to claim the throne of the Father and will reign over Heavenshire for a thousand years. Your time is done. Return to the abyss where you belong, along with your minions."

The beast howled and struck with a serpent's quickness, but the blow was too slow. Nesoch struck with the Sword of Kings deep into the beast's chest and pierced the black heart that beat there. The beast howled again and collapsed into a heap on the floor. Its body shrank as the light in the hall brightened

Alsharon and Elsharone had fought through the silent throng to the door of the hall of Kings when the final shriek of pain issued from the throne room. They witnessed the darkness draw in on the body and then explode outward in a million specks of dust. The knight's body slid down the wall onto Mary's and settled into a pile of broken armor and twisted limbs. The Kings entered the hall as Alsharon reached the Pair that now lay in a tangled heap. As he placed his hands on the bodies he knew that no life remained in them. Tears filled his eyes as he looked to Nesoch. "How can it be?" The other kings bowed their heads and their tears flowed like rain.

A voice from the doorway interrupted their grief. "What shall I tell the armies?"

Nesoch raised his head. "Tell them nothing yet. The hands of the King hold healing." He approached the twisted bodies and bade Alsharon help him to lay them straight on the floor. Removing the breastplates from both sets of armor, he placed his hands over their still hearts. He bowed his head and spoke two words, but they were not words of magic—or maybe they were words of the strongest magic of all. "Live, Love," was all he said. Outside, the armies still faced each other in the valley, and everyone looked to the sky as light seemed to flow from a thousand sources and swirled down into the palace. Inside the hall of the King the light flowed into Nesoch's body until he was too brilliant to look upon. Then light flowed from his hands and into the bodies of the Pair. A great outwash of power spread from the room to cover the entire realm, washing the last traces of darkness from the sky and banishing the last of the shadows of darkness.

As one, the chests of the Pair heaved and they gasped. Through the rents in their armor, those in the room saw their blood flow back into their bodies and their flesh mend. The light faded and each of the Pair opened their eyes as they groaned. Nesoch spoke gently to them. "You are badly injured. Do not try to move too quickly."

Mary groaned and looked around. "It's over?" Elsharone helped her to sit and gave her some water. Mike had not yet moved; Alsharon cradled his head in the crook of his arm and gave him water also. Mary spoke again, this time to Nesoch. "I think I know you, but I cannot ever remember seeing you before. I remember being very cold, and I heard your voice calling to me. Before that all I remember is…" her voice trailed off as she twisted to look at the center of the room, where the beast had lain. "Where?" Her eyes returned to Mike and she gasped. Then she looked at her own armor and ran the fingers of her right hand over a rent in it.

Mike finally spoke. "Did we win?" he gasped. The absurdity of that question was too much for Alexar, who was still standing in the entranceway. The dwarf began to laugh, and the laughter spread even to Nesoch.

After a few moments, the dwarf said, "I knew ye tae be a daft 'un. Y'd not be seein' the light iffn ye had lost. Of course we won, and all o' Heavenshire!"

Mike closed his eyes for a moment and then said, "That's good." Then he awakened more fully and struggled upright. "Mary?"

"Here, my Love. We can rest for a while. Our task is finished, isn't it?" This last was directed to Nesoch.

"Yes your task is done. Now everyone listen to my words." His voice was soft but it was heard inside and outside of the palace and in every corner of Heavenshire.

CHAPTER THIRTY-FIVE

"The great Evil is banished. The curse that has troubled Heavenshire for a hundred generations is lifted. Very soon the age of magic will draw to a close and a new age will begin. The Creator is, was, and always has been. It was His pleasure to create Heavenshire and to send his servants to tend to it. The elves, gnomes, and fairies prepared the world for His greatest creation—Man. Once there was only Man and the magical creatures in Heavenshire. They took possession of the land and began to subdue it. Elves, Fairies, and Gnomes gave way before them as the Maker decreed.

"All was well until the Dark One came to Heavenshire. He was filled with pride and sought to supplant the Creator even though he had been created as a servant to Him. This prideful one beguiled some of the men who inhabited Heavenshire into coming to the Dark Mountain. The Creator had decreed that no Man was to set foot on the Dark Mountain, but the Dark One promised riches and power to those who would meet him on the plateau. Some who heard the message ignored the temptation completely and were not cursed. Some came to the mountain but did not set foot upon it; they received a lesser curse because although they listened to the Dark One, they did not disobey the decree. They were commanded to dig into the mountains and spend most of their lives in their depths, only occasionally coming into the light. Their legs became bowed and short, and their bodies did not grow tall. They are the dwarves.

"Those who climbed the mountain received the full curse. They were driven deep onto the bowels of the earth away from the light. The Creator caused the deep to open up and provide them with dwelling places and dim light to appear for them. Their skin took on the pallor of death, and their feet and hands became swollen and misshapen as did their faces. They are the orcai, the outcast.

"Now the curse is lifted. See how the skin of the orcai has lost its pallor? See how the dwarves stand taller? In time they will once again be seen as men. For the next thousand years, Men, Dwarves, and Orcai will become only Men. They will once again be given the choice to obey the Creator of Heavenshire or be cast into oblivion. I shall stay with you for a while and show you the Creator's will. Then I will leave to return at the end of the age to judge your choices. Though I am gone away, I will still rule supreme in Heavenshire."

As the last of the words faded away, every warrior on the field of battle able to stand fell to their knees and bowed their heads. Silence reigned where chaos had long held for several minutes. Nesoch spoke again. "Arise, return to your homes and families, tend to your wounded, and prepare for winter. I will travel throughout Heavenshire in the spring and will make known my Father's will for the Men of Heavenshire."

CHAPTER THIRTY-SIX

Spring returned to Heavenshire, and the ravages of war were slowly erased from the land. The Elves and other magical creatures gathered around the Jewel Castle. It was a time of reunion for the Pair as they once again saw their teachers and friends. Arnyea and Ilsidora greeted them warmly; the titles of King and Queen were no longer used among the elves. "It is at it was in the beginning," Arnyea told them. "As it will be in the end." Alsharon and Elsharone took great pleasure in showing Mike and Mary the wonders of the palace and the surrounding land.

Too soon the appointed day arrived; the Pair, Arnyea, Ilsidora, Alsharon, Elsharone, and DeauxEagles gathered in the main hall of the palace. The Book of Magic was in the center of the hall on a diamond pedestal. The seven took their places before the Book, and as many elves, gnomes, and fairies as could, crowded into the room. When everything was in place, Alothen descended the grand staircase and approached the Book.

The former Guardian of the Tome pronounced an incantation and opened the Book. As he stepped back, DeauxEagles stepped forward and read a paragraph in the Ancient tongue. In turn, each of the four elves read from the book. Mary then stepped to the place in front of the book and read yet another portion. Mike stepped forward, read the final line, and closed the book. For several long seconds there was silence, then, faintly, music began to fill the air—music so beautiful that it nearly stole the breath from those who heard it. A soft glow began over the Book and grew until it encompassed it and the pedestal. Still the glow grew and those surrounding it stepped back.

The glow brightened to an almost unbearable brightness and then faded, leaving in its place a stone arch like a garden entrance. The other side of the entrance was not visible. Alothen stepped forward and turned to address those assembled. "Creatures of magic, behold the gateway to the presence of the Creator. We alone can pass this way, and that only once. The time of magic is coming to an end. One by one we will pass through this gate, and when the last of us has entered, the gate will close. When the gate closes, the time of magic will end. Enter at your leisure, but do not tarry too long. I bid you farewell and will greet you on the other side."

He bowed to the assemblage and spoke directly to the Pair. "To you, I bid farewell. The thanks of an entire world go with you. You will walk a different path, but I believe I will greet you again some day." Mary stepped forward and embraced him for a long moment. When she stepped back, Mike clasped forearms and heard the former King of the Elves whisper, "You have been given a great gift, a second chance. Use it wisely."

Alothen bowed to each of the elves and to DeauxEagles. Then he walked through the arch and was gone. Arnyea and Ilsidora bade the Pair farewell and followed. The twins remained, along with DeauxEagles, for they had one task left to perform. The group made their way from the hall to allow those waiting for the gate more room.

Outside they were met by the fairies—Ariel, Alexis, Alicia, Arica, and Arrissa. Mike warmly embraced them, much to their delight, and endured a kiss on his cheeks from each. It was difficult to follow their conversation as it flowed from one to the others, each one picking up where another had ended. In the end, DeauxEagles roared into the chaos and silenced the quintet. "Of course you may attend. You had a part in the most important events ever to occur in Heavenshire. I doubt that even Sir Michael is brave enough to forbid that." This caused an even greater flurry of giggles and more than one kiss to Mike's rapidly reddening cheeks.

Spring had turned into summer when DeauxEagles ushered Mike and Mary through a portal that took them to an almost forgotten shed on a farmer's land. They were met by the quintet of fairies, Alexar, Niatia, King Kextar, and the Elf twins. Niatia ran to greet Mary. The girl had grown so that she was even taller than Alexar. King Kextar commented that all of the children were growing taller than their parents now that the curse was lifted. The friends shared a few moments of laughter until Alsharon pointed to the road.

A couple approached. At first glance they appeared to be beggars because they walked on bare feet. A more careful appraisal revealed that their clothing was of high quality and that the smaller of the two, a woman, was carrying a child strapped to her back. A wide-brimmed hat shadowed the man's deeply tanned face; when he stopped and grinned, Mary broke away from the group and ran to embrace him.

"Cracktooth! I wanted you to be here. It would have

been terrible to leave without saying goodbye." Mary was smiling broadly. "Is this your wife and child?"

The orc could hardly be called that anymore. His arms and legs were no longer spindly and crooked, and his teeth seemed to fit his mouth, although they were still somewhat oversized and warped. He spoke and his voice held only a hint of its former raspiness. "This is Ogala, my wife, and yes, this is my son. He was born soon after the final battle, and his name is Michael. Come, you must see the miracle."

Ogala had removed the baby from the carrier; he was waving arms and feet in the air. Cracktooth held out his hand and the baby caught hold of it with soft, pink fingers. The foot that waved in the air was as soft and normal as any human baby. "See, he has no sign of the curse. All of the people are grateful to the warrior woman and the big man who fought the Dark Lord and helped free us from the curse. I bring gifts from the people. To the dwarves, I bring the Heart of the Mountain. It is a diamond of great size and purity that we found deep in the earth." He took a bundle from his pack and handed it to Niatia, who presented it to the King.

"To Lady Marilyn and Sir Michael we give the Eyes of the Soul. These are a flawless sapphire and ruby that fit together to form a heart. We hope they will be the symbol of your lives for ever more." Mary accepted the package and unwrapped the gemstones. She handed the sapphire to Mike as she examined the ruby. The stones were not large, but they were beautifully cut; when Mike placed the sapphire against the ruby, they fit together so well it seemed that they were one stone.

"This is too precious. It should remain in Heavenshire,"

Mary protested. Mike was almost too overcome with emotion to speak, but he nodded his head in agreement.

"Nonsense," exclaimed DeauxEagles. "Were we to put the whole of Heavenshire into your pocket, it would scarce be thanks enough. Please accept this gift from the people."

Mary's eyes were wet with tears. All she could do was hug Cracktooth and Ogala. Mike reached out his hand and grasped the orc. "Thank you, my friend. We shall always remember who brought this gift. We will strive to fulfill your hope. I am humbled by the honor you do me. A name is a powerful legacy, and I know you will teach your son well. I have no gift to leave with you except my friendship."

DeauxEagles coughed and then spoke. "I sincerely regret, but we must make haste. The sun is rapidly dropping, and this must be done now." Everyone said their final goodbyes, and DeauxEagles waved his staff. Mike's red convertible appeared in the fading sunlight, slowing to a halt as it approached the couple. The Pair quickly took their seats, and Mike turned to look over his shoulder, waving a last time.

CHAPTER THIRTY-SEVEN

All that he saw was a road rapidly retreating. He snapped his head back around and fought to keep the speeding car under control. He pulled off the side of the road and looked at Mary. She was once again in her leather coat; Mike noted that he was in his jeans and boots.

They left the car and stood at the side of the road almost expecting to see the farmer's shack. Instead there was the abandoned manufacturing plant and gray December skies. Mary spoke first. "Did you...did that really happen?"

"I don't know, we were in another world, weren't we?" he asked. It was then that he looked down at the seat and saw two bundles wrapped in parchment, tied with twine. "Look, open those."

They each quickly unwrapped one; Mary found an exquisitely carved figurine of a woman casting a ball of light. She looked at Mike's hand and gasped at the beautiful jewel cradled there. She looked back to his face and was stopped by his expression. He spoke softly. "It is all true. Of all we have seen, of all we have done, even more precious than these gifts is this. I know I love you, Mary, and I want to spend the rest of my life with you."

There was no hesitation as Mary cried, "Yes, in this world or any other!" They fell into each other's arms and shared the first of a million kisses in their home world.

The sun shone brightly in the mid-spring sky. It was early in the afternoon on a Saturday, but the small church was filled nearly to capacity. A red convertible, parked in front of the main entrance, was festooned with balloons, ribbons, and tin cans. Inside the church, the groom waited more or less patiently for the music to begin. He resisted the urge to tug at the collar of his tuxedo and forced his hand to remain at his side. He thought to himself, *You have stood before Kings, Queens, and the Lord of an entire world. What is it about a simple wedding that make you weak in the knees? You've even stood here before.*

The music began with four familiar chords, and Mike turned with the rest of those gathered. Mary stepped through doors at the back of the church, and time stopped for Mike. She was even more beautiful than the day in Blackthorn Hearth when she had stunned Bardwind. Her black hair, neatly coifed and piled on her head, was held in place with silver netting with tiny tear-shaped pearl beads at each intersection of the wires. It gave the impression that her hair shimmered with the morning dew. Tear-shaped pearl earrings completed the vista; only one other person in the church knew that the pearls symbolized the teardrops the orcai had cried for the dwarf children. The bride wore a vintage wedding dress that her grandmother had worn on her wedding day. The dress had been restored and altered just for Mary. The ruby half of the Eyes of the Soul hung from a silver chain against her chest and seemed to glow with an inner light. The two youngest of Mike's nieces held the train, but were unnoticed by most of the crowd.

Just before time began its pace again, Mike saw the faces

of the Elves of Heavenshire looking down on the event and smiling. When they had faded, the image of Bardwind's smiling face remained for a fleeting moment before it too faded from view. Then he could hear the intake of breath of those around him as they looked at Mary, a sound echoed by the crowd. She took the slow, measured treads down the aisle towards him.

The rest of the ceremony was a blur to Mike. He knew he spoke at the appropriate times and then kissed his bride. There were no memories to haunt him, no sadness, no regrets. They received the congratulations and mingled with the guests before slipping off for the final pictures. They returned to cut the cake, make and receive toasts, and all of the other festivities. As the guests gathered to send them off, Mike called for quiet. He stood with Mary in front of their family and friends and slipped a small box from his inner pocket. He withdrew its contents and held up the sapphire half of the Eyes of the Soul. He gently snapped it into place in the setting designed for it. "Just as we two are now joined, this symbol of our love is joined together. May it never again be separated!" They turned and dashed through the shower of birdseed to the waiting 'Vette.

EPILOGUE

The old farmer paused a moment to look at his flock. He was still amazed at the run of twins he had enjoyed. It had started with the lamb that the King's own son had helped birth. That lamb had birthed twins when it was old enough, and those had birthed twins in their time. In a short span of years, a good-sized flock had grown. It was well timed also. The demand for wool had greatly increased after the war as men began to rebuild their shattered lands and as their new friends began to leave the underground and sought to find their way on the surface.

The farmer knew his daughter would soon seek him out with his lunch. She had long ago returned home to tend to her mother, staying to care for him after her death. Now she helped her father on the farm and tended to one of the casualties of the war. The farmer's face darkened for a moment, but his love for his daughter quickly overshadowed the anger.

A shadow fell across his feet and he looked up, expecting to see Abigail. Instead it was a man with a hooded cloak. He was looking at the flock, and the farmer could see that he was smiling. The stranger spoke and the farmer scrambled to kneel at his feet. "A fine flock. I told you that it would be so. No! Do not kneel before me. Stand and greet me, my old friend." Nesoch pulled back his hood and embraced the farmer. "You tend your flock well, friend. Now, as it so happens, I come seeking a lost sheep." The farmer turned quickly to the field, as Nesoch continued. "Not there. I seek the lost lamb that your daughter tends."

They turned and walked together to the farmhouse where Nesoch paused at the door. Abigail met them, bowed deeply to Nesoch, and stepped aside so that the Chosen One could enter. He walked to a small room at the back of the house that held only a bed and a chair where Abigail sat for many hours each day. The man in the bed was deathly thin and barely turned his head as they entered. Recognition flared in the sick man's eyes.

The ailing man spoke. "Do you come for your revenge now? Are you going to torment a dying man, or are you the reason I cannot find comfort in death?"

Abigail began to admonish the man, but Nesoch silenced her with a glance. "Abstidian, you heard my words to all of Heavenshire. The curse was lifted for all, even for you. You have a second chance to live, a chance to find your true destiny. I have come to give you a simple message. I forgive you."

Abstidian swung his legs around and sat up on the side of the bed. "I don't understand. I had you murdered. I laughed as you were beaten to death. I plunged the sword into your side. My actions caused the deaths of thousands in that war."

Nesoch placed his hands on the man's shoulders. "I have a message for you from He Who created you. It is this: you do not have to punish yourself. You are forgiven. He holds you no more or less responsible than anyone else. For *any* to be forgiven, *everyone* has to be forgiven. Your prison is of your own making, although your warden is fairer than most." Nesoch winked at Abigail. "You are free to create a new relationship. Walk this land again, see the changes. No one will know your past, not even the former outcasts. Rise Abstidian. Live again." The Chosen One then released him and turned to walk away.

Abstidian found that he had the strength to stand. "I don't understand. How will I live, what will I do?"

Abigail placed her hand in the crook of his elbow and stood near. "You have many talents that are needed now. We will find a way. Together."

The former wine taster of the king, once first servant of the Dark Lord, looked into her eyes and saw the love shining there. Finally he understood.

ENDNOTES

1 "Romeo and Juliet." William Shakespeare, London England, 1596

2 "Common Sense." Thomas Payne Boston Mass. 1776